In the Flesh

❧

She stood directly under the showerhead and felt the water cascade from her shoulders, and she felt the meandering rivulets that found their way down her body. That was when she felt his touch. The feeling was eerie and erotic at the same time, and she groaned.

She felt the caress move up, lightly, gently. Up her belly, up between her breasts, to her collarbone, to her chin.

It tilted her head up, and she heard a whisper. Only this time, she actually heard it. With her ears. Like a real voice. "Open your eyes."

She did, and there he was.

She gasped with the shock of seeing him standing before her. For a split second, she felt exposed, vulnerable. And then he smiled, and she melted.

His eyes, his face, his hair were all just as she remembered them from the one glimpse she'd had. But he was tall, taller than she'd thought, and she had to tilt her head to look at him.

He was every bit as beautiful as she'd thought him the last time.

He ran his hand down her arm and took her hand in his. He brought it to his chest, and she touched him. He felt almost, but not exactly, like a real, live man. She would have imagined she could put her hand right through him, that he'd be a mirage, an apparition. But the opposite was true. He felt, if anything, harder than a living being. He was firm, solid, and very, very real. . . .

Also by Olivia Quincy

My Lady's Pleasure

SPIRIT OF SEDUCTION

OLIVIA QUINCY

A SIGNET ECLIPSE BOOK

SIGNET ECLIPSE
Published by New American Library, a division of
Penguin Group (USA) Inc., 375 Hudson Street,
New York, New York 10014, USA
Penguin Group (Canada), 90 Eglinton Avenue East, Suite 700, Toronto,
Ontario M4P 2Y3, Canada (a division of Pearson Penguin Canada Inc.)
Penguin Books Ltd., 80 Strand, London WC2R 0RL, England
Penguin Ireland, 25 St. Stephen's Green, Dublin 2,
Ireland (a division of Penguin Books Ltd.)
Penguin Group (Australia), 250 Camberwell Road, Camberwell, Victoria 3124,
Australia (a division of Pearson Australia Group Pty. Ltd.)
Penguin Books India Pvt. Ltd., 11 Community Centre, Panchsheel Park,
New Delhi - 110 017, India
Penguin Group (NZ), 67 Apollo Drive, Rosedale, Auckland 0632,
New Zealand (a division of Pearson New Zealand Ltd.)
Penguin Books (South Africa) (Pty.) Ltd., 24 Sturdee Avenue,
Rosebank, Johannesburg 2196, South Africa
Penguin Books Ltd., Registered Offices:
80 Strand, London WC2R 0RL, England

First published by Signet Eclipse, an imprint of New American Library,
a division of Penguin Group (USA) Inc.

Library of Congress Cataloging-in-Publication Data

Quincy, Olivia.
    Spirit of seduction/Olivia Quincy.
      p.   cm.
    ISBN 978-0-451-23333-2 (pbk.)
    1. Businesswomen—Fiction.   2. Home ownership—Fiction.   3. Dwellings—Maintenance and
repair—Fiction.   4. Haunted houses—Fiction.   5. Murder—Investigation—Fiction.   6. Family
secrets—Fiction.   7. Cape Cod (Mass.)—Fiction.   8. Paranormal romance stories.   I. Title.
    PS3617.U538S68 2011
    813'.6—dc22   2011005309

Set in Adobe Garamond
Designed by Alissa Amell

147204767

SPIRIT OF SEDUCTION

CHAPTER ONE

❧

"Congratulations," the lawyer said to Zoe Bell as he handed her a set of keys. "You're the new owner of Chapin House."

She wasn't prepared for the flush of excitement that welled up in her when she heard those words. In her thirty-two years, she'd had her share of thrills. She'd started a company and sold it for tens of millions. She'd been on a business magazine cover. She'd even dated a B-list celebrity. But she had never yet owned real estate, and the idea of it made her heart beat faster and her throat tighten.

And it wasn't just any real estate. It was Chapin House, a big, rambling, picturesque building with a storied history and a mesmerizing view of Cape Cod Bay. Because her family had spent summers in the town of Danmouth when she was a girl, she knew the house intimately. All her life, it was this very house that had been her mental image of the perfect house, the house that defined houseness. And now it was hers.

Keys in hand, she walked down Danmouth's main street—called, of course, Main Street—with her boyfriend, Sam Stafford, and saw it all with new eyes. She knew every building, every storefront, every street sign, and even most of the people. But she was no longer just a visitor. She was one of them, and she felt the change.

"It's actually mine," she said to Sam, squeezing his hand. He returned the pressure and smiled. "I can't quite believe it," she said for about the fifteenth time.

"You'll believe it the first time the pipes burst and you can't get a plumber out there for a day and a half," Sam said with a grin.

Zoe wished he could have said something more in a congratulatory vein, but she was used to his wryness. She kissed him on the cheek. "Something tells me you'll manage to swallow your cynicism long enough to enjoy it."

"I figured out a long time ago that cynicism is perfectly compatible with enjoying other people's luxuries," he said, and Zoe laughed.

Just as they were walking past the Danmouth general store, its proprietor, Bill Hibbard, walked out the front door carrying a piece of wood with the number 4 painted on it.

"Hi, Mr. Hibbard," Zoe called as she waved to him. No matter how many years had gone by, she still thought of him as the little old man who sold her licorice whips for a nickel.

"Hello, Zoe," he said. "Congratulations on the house!"

Was word already out? It hadn't been even five minutes.

"Thank you," she said. "Real estate news travels fast, I see."

"All news travels fast around here," he answered. "But it's not quite official yet."

"No, I suppose it isn't." Zoe and Sam stopped and watched Mr. Hibbard walk to the far end of the big open porch with the rocking chairs and newspaper racks. There, on the wall, were four hooks. The rightmost three had numbers hanging from them: 8-1-3. There was a sign above the hooks that read: DANMOUTH POPULATION.

As they watched, Mr. Hibbard took down the 3 and replaced it with the 4 he had brought out.

"Now it's official." He grinned at the couple.

"Now it's official," Zoe echoed, and she and Sam went on their way.

"You've got to be kidding," Sam said.

"He's kept that tally since before I was born, and his father kept it before him. He doesn't have a computer, or even a television, but he prides himself on keeping that sign absolutely up-to-date. If someone dies or someone's born, if someone moves in or moves out, he adjusts it accordingly."

Sam rolled his eyes. "We're not in Kansas anymore," he said.

Sam and Zoe both lived in Manhattan, and Sam's first exposure to Cape Cod had come when Zoe, flush with the payout from selling her online seed and garden business to Amazon, had started looking for a summer house in Danmouth. He didn't find it easy to cope with the slower pace, the inhabitants' New England flintiness, or the complete unavailability of decent Chinese food.

They reached the end of the street, having traversed the entire town in three blocks, and got in Zoe's brand-new Toyota. She started the engine, rolled down all the windows, and opened the sunroof to let the June sun shine in. They headed north.

Chapin House was situated on eight acres of land that jutted out into the bay, about three miles out of town. When they turned off the paved road onto the gravel driveway, Zoe felt the pride not just of ownership, but of having fulfilled a long-held ambition. It really was hers.

They drove through the flat landscape of scrub pine, white oak, and wild blueberries for almost half a mile. That landscape, so particular to Cape Cod, always brought Zoe back to the summers of her childhood. She could feel the hot pavement on her bare feet, the sand in her swimsuit, and the salt in her hair. The sensation of pulling up in front of her own house, though, was new.

From the front, Chapin House looked ordinary, almost dilapidated. It was built in the early 1800s as a sea captain's house, and had an imposing two-story front. It had been added onto several times over its two hundred years, and the wings meandered away from the building's center in a way that made the house look even bigger than it was. The exterior was covered in cedar shingle that would have to be replaced in the next few years, and the white paint on the trim was peeling in spots.

They got out of the car and Sam started up the front steps. "Wait," said Zoe. "Let's go around the back."

It was the back of the house she knew best, having seen it from the beach and from boats every summer of her childhood. It was the back, with the long wooden deck and the rock stairway to the beach, that she wanted to claim as her own.

They walked around the house to the right. As they turned the corner, they entered a private world of sea and sand and sun. The house itself shielded them from the outside world to the south, and all they could see was what nature had wrought.

They climbed the wooden staircase on the side of the house up to the deck—two of the steps squeaked—and they both stood at the rail, looking out over the water, saying nothing. Not even Sam could be snarky about what was out that back door.

But he managed to be snarky about what wasn't there—no houses, no people, not even a boat. "We're *really* not in Kansas anymore," he said. "There's not much in the way of civilization out here."

It was Zoe's turn to roll her eyes. Why, why, why couldn't he *ever* say anything just plain nice?

"When did you get so attached to Kansas?" she asked him, her annoyance creeping into her tone.

Sam realized his remark had been graceless, and tried to make the line of discussion sound more reasonable. "Don't you think you're going to miss Manhattan?" he asked, more gently.

"If I miss Manhattan I can go to Manhattan," she said archly, crossing her arms in front of her and sticking her chin out just a little. "It'll still be there." And then her temper got the better of her, and she added pointedly, "And if *you* miss Manhattan, you're welcome to do the same."

It was a mild enough rebuke, and he probably deserved it, but she realized the instant it came out of her mouth that she had escalated the situation. Now they were at the point where they were headed for a full-blown fight unless one of them made a move to stand down.

For a moment, they looked at each other. He had his hands in his pockets, and she still had her arms folded across her chest. Neither of them moved.

And then Sam did. He took his hands out of his pockets, reached for Zoe's arms, and uncrossed them. He took her hands in his.

"I might miss Manhattan at some point," he said. "But I don't now. In fact, there's no place in the world I'd rather be."

He put his arms around her waist and softly kissed her left temple. She found him arousing and enticing, and their physical life together was exciting, varied, and vigorous. Tenderness, though, was something he rarely showed. Her annoyance melted away with that one kiss.

"I don't think I've congratulated you yet on your new house," he whispered in her ear, and that made everything better.

She rested her head on his shoulder and closed her eyes. She felt the cool breeze in her hair and Sam's warm hand on her cheek. He ran his fingertips along her hairline, behind her ear, and down the line of her jaw. She lifted her head just a bit, eyes still closed, and he traced a line down the soft skin of her neck to her collarbone.

He ran his thumb in the little hollow behind her left collarbone, and reached over with his middle finger to find the same spot behind her right. Then he drew his fingers together and ran them down her sternum, to the base of the vee in her V-neck T-shirt.

He slipped his hand under the shirt, and under the black silk La Perla bra. Expensive underthings had become a habit with her since she sold the business, and moments like these made every penny worth it.

"How can your hand be so warm when it's so cool outside?" she asked.

"That's raw animal energy," he said. "You'll find that all my extremities are warm."

"Will I, now?" she asked, and turned her back to him so she could nestle up against him, her hands behind her and hooking into his waistband. He put his hands under her shirt at the waist, and then ran them up the sides of her rib cage to the base of her bra. It hooked in front, and he deftly unhooked it. When he took her breasts in his hands, Zoe thought, as she always did, that there couldn't be a better fit. His hands were made to cup her breasts.

Her breathing began to quicken, and she moved her hands down to where she knew she'd find the outline of his erect penis. She ran each of her thumbs down the sides of the bulge, and he responded with a soft groan. She moved her hands to his hips and pushed her ass against him, gently moving left to right and back.

He groaned again, and his grip on her breasts tightened. He instinctively caught her motion, and his back-and-forth matched her side-to-side. He took each of her nipples between thumb and forefinger and squeezed lightly. She felt as though his hands on her breasts had a direct line to the wetness that was beginning to build deep inside her.

"It doesn't seem so cold anymore," she said to him, a little huskily.

"Funny, that," he whispered, and then ran his tongue along the channel behind her ear.

Zoe bent her head to the side, exposing her long neck, and Sam's tongue followed its graceful line down to her shoulder. There he kissed her and nuzzled into the base of her neck. Zoe felt his warm breath and the little prickly hairs that were asserting themselves even though he had shaved that morning.

She leaned her head against his and breathed in. She loved smelling him. He didn't always smell the same, but there was a distinctive musk, almost a funk, that was always there. If he'd just showered, it was there under the soapy smell. If he'd just exercised, it was there under the sweaty smell. She loved that musk.

She turned around and put her face against his chest. She was still for a few moments, and the clarity of her mind surprised her. Usually, once aroused, she could think of nothing else. This time, she hadn't lost her connection to where she was or what was happening around her.

Even as she felt the hardness of Sam's erection pressing against her, and she knew she would heed its call, she was suffused with the idea that she was making love to him in this, her newfound place in the world.

Mixed with his musk was the smell of the sea. The sound of his breath mingled with the sound of the waves. In all her life, she had never felt so complete, so grounded, so . . . so *arrived*.

She looked up at him. "Let's not go inside quite yet," she said.

Sam grinned. "I'm not sure how long I can hold out," he said, and rubbed against her in a way that made his point.

"No, I mean let's make love here, on the deck. I want to feel you inside, outside."

He raised his eyebrows. "I think I can make that happen for you," he said, and kissed her.

She always melted when he kissed her. His tongue on hers felt exactly right. It was soft and gentle, never hard and insistent. It swooped around her own, and she felt as though it drew her in, almost cast a spell. She felt her arousal building and spreading.

Sam then put his hands under her buttocks and lifted her bodily off the deck. She wrapped her legs around his waist and her arms around his neck and closed her eyes. She loved that he could lift her, effortlessly, right off the ground. She wasn't small—she was slim, but tall—and it took some strength. Sam did it as easily as he lifted the groceries.

He walked across the deck to a porch swing, a long bench supported by a frame that was built into the deck. There was a worn green cushion on the seat, and he laid Zoe down on it.

She reached her hand out to pull him down to her, but he used her hand to give her a gentle pull that started the swing in motion. Although it creaked a little, it seemed to swing smoothly and easily. Sam took a step back to make room for a bigger arc, and pushed the swing in earnest.

It went high, almost to the point where it was parallel with the ground, and Zoe couldn't quite separate the whoosh of the motion from the rush of her anticipation.

Sam let the motion die to a gentle back-and-forth, and he reached down to unbutton her jeans. He unzipped them, exposing panties that matched the bra. He knelt down beside the swing, slipped his hand underneath the panties, and cupped the mound of her pubis. With his middle finger, he found the opening within her labia and wet his finger at the fountain that was already gushing.

He moved his hand up so that finger was on her clitoris, and he rubbed it back and forth, back and forth, with the same rhythm of the gently rocking swing. She sighed a particular high-pitched, breathy sigh that came only when something was just right. Sam recognized it and smiled.

He felt her clitoris turn almost rigid, and he stopped. He lifted her shirt over her head, and the unhooked bra came with it. He slipped her feet out of the clogs she was wearing, slid her jeans and panties off, and she lay on the cushion, naked to the world.

He ran his hands up the tops of her legs. "Are you cold?" he asked.

It hadn't even occurred to her that it was a little chilly outside. She just shook her head.

He moved his hand back to where it had been and started the same motion again. He watched as her eyes closed and the muscles in her legs tensed. He heard that sigh. He loved that sigh.

She knew that, in a moment, she would be past the point where she could stop him, so she put a hand over his and stilled his motion.

She propped herself up on an elbow and said, "It's you that I want," and sat up. He was wearing khakis with a button fly, and she opened it by undoing the top button at the waistband and then giving an expert tug.

Underneath, his penis strained against the plain white boxers, and she released it. She took it in her hands, and then laid it against her cheek. She loved its heft, its girth, its solidity. She flicked her tongue up its underside, and he moaned and put his hands on her shoulders to steady himself.

His arousal always fueled hers, and she stood up and sat him down on the swing. She knelt and took off his worn white canvas shoes, which he wore without socks. She undressed the rest of him hurriedly— she was beginning to feel an urgency—and then straddled his lap on the swing.

There was a slat missing at the base of the back of the swing, and it left the perfect space for her knees as she fitted her body to his. She put her arms around his neck and felt his warm hands on her ass as he pulled her in close.

Then she felt his cock rubbing against her, first dry and then wet from her own dew. She smelled the smell of her mixed with the smell of him, still mixed with the outdoor smell of the water, and she knew she couldn't wait any longer to have him inside her.

She maneuvered herself over the tip of his rock-hard cock, moved so that the tip was inside, and then sat down in one swift motion, taking him all in. He groaned long and low.

She moved out and in, out and in, and her motion set the swing in motion. She felt the texture of him as his thrusts matched her movements, and she felt the wave building each time she had all of him inside her and her clitoris brushed the base of his penis.

To slow herself down, she made herself unclench the muscles that were tightening of their own accord. One of the great pleasures of Sam was their ability to lock on to each other's timing, to know exactly when it was right to let go. She let herself feel the hardness of him, the motion of the swing, the two together blocking out the rest of the world and captivating all of her.

Another thrust, and then another, and it was right. What she had let build smoothly and rhythmically she finally unleashed. She felt Sam's cock, already full, harden that last little bit. She felt the whoosh of the last layer of arousal before her climax, and then they were there, together.

It was long, and it was all-encompassing. She felt it not just at her core, but in her legs and arms—her toes, even. It was warmth and pleasure together, suffusing her. It was joy.

As she gradually relaxed, she felt Sam relaxing with her. She knew by his moans that his orgasm had been as full and as deep as her own, and that made the satisfaction so much the greater. Their sex together had always been good, but the experience they'd had with each other's bodies over the two years they'd been together made it even better. This was great sex, and she marveled that they had it so good, so often.

They sat on the swing, still gently rocking, for a few moments while the energy dissipated.

"Now I think we can go in the house," Zoe said.

"Good. All of a sudden, it's beginning to feel chilly again," Sam said.

"Funny, that," she said to him as she climbed off.

She ran across the porch to retrieve her bag, now feeling that her nakedness exposed her. She was rummaging for the keys when Sam said, "It's open." He was standing at the back door, which led into the kitchen, holding it for her. Its new owner crossed its threshold for the first time, stark naked.

She'd been through every room of the house several times while she went through the process of buying it, but she wanted to go through every one again now that she'd actually bought it. "Shall we start at the bottom or start at the top?" she asked Sam.

"Let's start at the thermostat," he said. It was in the kitchen, and they turned it up to seventy degrees. Zoe had arranged for all the utilities to be turned on, but she breathed a little easier when she heard the oil burner in the basement kick in.

"Well, all right, then," said Sam, rubbing his hands together. "Let's start at the bottom. That's traditional, isn't it?"

Zoe grinned, and they headed down to the basement. It was a large house, and it had a commensurately large basement, with several small rooms off one larger one. The large one had the furnace, oil tank, and water heater, and there was a big, heavy desk and some odds and ends in one of the smaller rooms. Other than that, it was empty.

From the basement, they went back to the first floor and walked through it room by room. All the rooms were small, and they were swept, but not really clean. Throughout most of the house, the original wood floors were exposed, in various states of disrepair. In the oldest part of the house, the floors were so bad that they'd been covered by a berber carpet, now worn and stained.

Zoe talked about what she wanted to change, plans she had for each room, which details she wanted to restore. Sam listened and nodded, but didn't say much. He was acutely aware that this was her house. Not his.

When they had met two years previous, Zoe had been struggling and Sam had been at the top of his game. He was a painter, and his first solo show, at a big-name SoHo gallery, had just gone up. She'd come to the opening and, though she couldn't make much of the paintings, she found the painter to be charming, irreverent, and better-looking than any man had a right to be.

Sam wasn't tall—he was just under six feet—but he had an athletic lankiness that made him seem taller. He was muscular, but not in a built-up way. He was slim and loose-jointed, and he moved with ease and grace. His hair was dark blond and straight, and his eyes were light brown and clear. His nose had just a hint of a Roman profile, and Zoe thought his looks aristocratic.

She was beautiful in her own right. Her hair was fine and thick, so dark brown that it was often taken for black. When she gathered it into a ponytail it filled her whole hand. It cascaded in the liquid, shiny way that was seldom seen outside commercials for hair-care products. Her skin was olive and her eyes a dark green that was almost brown. Her eyelashes were as lush as her hair, and they gave her a doe-eyed, ingenuous look.

She was slim but full hipped and breasted. Sam—and all the boyfriends she'd had before him—delighted in the difference between her narrow waist and the curves above and below.

When she'd walked into his show, she'd attracted his attention immediately. He made it a point to meet her, and he wasn't disappointed. She was vivacious and dynamic. She sparkled. Before she left the opening, he'd asked her to dinner the next night, and she'd accepted. From that evening on, they'd seen each other almost every day.

When they met, Zoe was two years into a business venture, and it was rocky. She sold seeds over the Internet.

"The kind you grow plants with?" Sam had asked.

"The kind you grow plants with," she'd answered. "I picked seeds because they're cheap to ship." While this was true, it was also true that she loved plants, and had always had a knack for them.

Her hook was that she would design an entire garden, given a customer's location, garden size, and plant preferences. Then she'd send all the seeds required, along with a diagram of the garden and instructions on how to plant the seeds and care for them.

The business was doing very well, and her problem was that she couldn't keep up with demand. She had been in the process of automating her Web site so that customers could design their own gardens, but the beta site was buggy and she was having trouble working with the programmer she'd hired.

"Hire a new programmer," was the advice Sam had given her, and she took it.

Within weeks, everything turned around. The site was beautiful, fast, and easy to navigate. Customers found all the information they needed to put together their gardens, and all Zoe had to do was mail out the seeds and instructions.

Then came the *Good Morning America* spot that changed everything. Her site had caught the eye of one of the producers, and next thing she knew she was on television, touting the virtues of her garden design business. The customers came in droves, and they brought their friends. Zoe's business increased by an order of magnitude, and then another. She hired people. She expanded. She prospered. And then Amazon came calling.

Meanwhile, Sam had met with setbacks. His show wasn't well received by the critics, and he sold only three paintings. He'd had dreams of not having to bartend anymore, but that was not to be. The failure of his show demoralized him, and that made painting, and trying to sell paintings, that much harder.

As he walked through the house with Zoe, listening to her plans, he never lost sight of the fact that she was a business tycoon and he was a failed painter. It wasn't easy.

The second story of the house was a warren of bedrooms and nooks and closets, and Zoe took him into the room she'd earmarked as the master bedroom. Although the windows in it were small, it had a beautiful view of the bay.

"We can knock out this wall and combine it with the room next door," Zoe said. "And we'll put windows next to the French doors so all we see is ocean." She put her arm around his waist and leaned her head on his shoulder as they looked out the window.

Sam tried to smile. He knew she was trying to make this his place as well as hers.

She took him into the last room on the corridor, which was small but brightly lit. It not only had windows on two sides, but there was a skylight directly overhead. Zoe took Sam's arm as they walked into the room. "I thought this could be your studio," she said, and smiled up at him.

She'd planned to offer him this room since she first made a bid on the house, and she thought he'd be thrilled. And he wanted to be thrilled. He wanted to appreciate both the space itself and her generosity in offering it to him, but he found that the difference in their situations was draining the pleasure from him.

When the house was something she was going to buy, the prospect of it was wonderful—a luxurious retreat on Cape Cod, his to use! Now that the house was something she owned, it simply put his own failure in stark relief.

He held her to him so she couldn't see his face. "Thank you," he whispered in her ear.

They stood like that for a few moments, and then he loosened his hold. "Should I run into town and see if I can't get us some groceries?" he said. They'd made no dinner plans, and she was no cook.

"That would be lovely," she said. "You know where the fish market is, don't you?"

He did. And everything else could come from the general store. They went downstairs, and he took the keys from Zoe's bag. "Back soon," he called, and went out the front door.

Zoe understood that the balance of power in their relationship had shifted, and she knew he felt it keenly. As she walked through the house in his absence, she thought about how she might make it easier for him, how she could welcome him into what she intended to be their home.

She had met him at a time that was difficult for her, and she had felt safer during that rocky period in the lee of his budding success. She felt that she, whom success was eluding, was hitching her wagon to him, for whom success was all but imminent. The confidence she'd gotten from his support and his approval, when he was operating from a position of strength, had helped her pull her business through.

Now that she was in a position of strength, she wanted to give back. She wanted to bolster his confidence, to give him time and space to work, to help him get back on his feet as a painter.

But lately there was an edge to him. His sarcasm sometimes crossed the line to meanness; his confidence sometimes seemed like bluster. There was a prickliness that kept her at arm's length. She put it down to his difficulties, and cut him a lot of slack, but she had to admit that he was easier to love when things were going his way.

She'd hoped that this house, this setting, and time away from New York would restore Sam to himself, and to her.

She stood in the kitchen, thinking of all this while she watched the light fade as the sun set on the far left of her horizon. In the still evening light she heard the creak of the stairs that led to the deck, and she went out to help Sam with the groceries, surprised that she hadn't heard the car.

She went out the door and over to the side of the house, but no one was there.

She was a little taken aback, because she'd thought she'd heard the steps clearly, but there were a lot of creaky noises in an old house.

But as she was walking back toward the door to the kitchen, she heard them again. Distinctly. She turned and felt her heart begin to race. Again, there was nothing. She strode back inside, quickly, decisively. As she went back into the house, a cold breeze followed her.

She stopped and shivered involuntarily, and then laughed out loud, deliberately, to shake off the creepy feeling. "Zoe Bell, don't tell me you believe in ghosts," she said in an admonitory tone, to no one but herself.

CHAPTER TWO

When Sam did get back with groceries, Zoe heard the car and turned on the outside light so Sam could see the front steps. It was that light that told their only neighbor, Curtis Nickerson, that the new owner of Chapin House had taken possession.

Nickerson lived in a little house, no more than a cottage, on the east side of Chapin Point, about a quarter mile from the main house. The house had originally been a boathouse, and had been converted to a caretaker's cottage more than a hundred years previous. Nickersons had seen to Chapin House and its property since the early 1800s, and one of the Chapins, more than a century ago, had seen fit to carve out a quarter acre of land, with the cottage on it, and bequeath it to the Nickerson of the time, with the stipulation that it stay in the family, passed down the male line.

Since then, the property, as required, had been passed down from eldest son to eldest son, and with it the responsibility of keeping Chapin

House running smoothly. Its current owner, Curtis, had lived there since the bone-chilling wind that came off the bay in the winter had induced his father to decamp for Boca Raton.

Nickerson, a lean, laconic man in his late forties, lived there alone, but his girlfriend, Greta Silva, was a frequent guest. She was there when Nickerson saw the Chapin House light go on.

"She's come," Curtis said.

"You knew she would," said Greta.

Nickerson sighed as he gazed out the window. "I never thought I'd see the house go out of the family."

Greta snorted. "There was no love lost between you and old Clara Chapin," she said, referring to the house's last occupant, an ornery old woman who had been dead several years. "And as far as I can tell, you've always resented the Nickerson thralldom to the big house."

"That's true," Nickerson admitted. "And I can't say I've been too fond of many Chapins over the years, but that can make the thralldom easier to bear." Here he grinned at her. "It makes it easier to be confident in Nickerson superiority. Still, it's hard to see change when it's been the same for so many years."

Greta got up and stood behind Curtis. She put her arms around his waist and laid her cheek on his back. "Change is underrated," she said.

Greta's parents had moved from their native Portugal to New Bedford, just off Cape Cod, before Greta was born. They'd come to fish, but found more success running a restaurant. Greta had been brought up to the business, but didn't take to it. Instead, she'd gone to the Rhode Island School of Design and become a graphic artist. Change, to her, meant opportunity, and she couldn't understand Nickerson's longing to have things stay as they were.

"Maybe she'll do everything to that old house that you tried to get Clara to do," Greta suggested. "We know she has the money."

"Oh, she'll probably just tear it down and build a McMansion."

"Come on, now!" Clara said. "You know this girl. You know she loves the house. Don't be such a pill."

"Oh, but I have to be a pill," he said, turning so he faced her and smiling slyly. "It's the very fabric of my identity. Ask anyone in town."

Greta rolled her eyes. "If you didn't play the curmudgeon so convincingly, you might have more friends."

"I have all the friends I need," he said, "and I have you." He held her face in his two hands and looked at her frankly and affectionately. The warmth of his smile, had they seen it, would have surprised just about everyone who knew him. He was thought of as taciturn, stubborn, and cranky, and Greta was one of only a handful of people who knew him to be warm, loyal, and intensely private.

She ran her hands up his chest, feeling the outline of his musculature through the worn flannel of his shirt. She loved his body. It was all ropes and muscles and sinews, authentically roughened by a lifetime of physical work. There was nothing soft, nothing easy about it.

Her hands reached his shoulders, and then worked their way down his arms, feeling the outline of his biceps. The feel of him, his strength and solidity, always aroused her.

She unbuttoned his shirt, pulled it out of the waistband of his jeans, and slipped it off him. She again ran her hands up his chest, feeling the same shapes, the same hardness, but with the tactile addition of his taut skin and wiry hair.

He was much taller than she was, and her mouth was just at the height of his nipples. She put her mouth around the left one and circled her tongue around and around it, slowly, until she felt it harden and she heard his breathing speed up. Then she did the same for the other side.

She reached both her hands down, knowing what she'd find. Despite being close to fifty, Curtis Nickerson was as virile as a teenager. "Ready to go at the drop of your drawers," Greta always said.

She found what she was looking for, in the condition she expected. She felt his erection through his jeans and then moved her right hand between his legs and cradled his balls, manipulating them so they rubbed against each other.

He gave a low moan and took both her hands to stop her. He pulled her close to him and reached behind her head to release her thick, wavy hair from the elastic she used to pull it back. He ran his hands through it almost roughly, knowing she loved his fingers on her scalp.

He gathered her hair in one of his hands and pulled it so her face tilted up toward him. He kissed her. He was a hard man, but he kissed softly and gently, and he tasted of a particular sweetness that made Greta hunger for more.

She reached for his waistband and released him. He stepped out of his jeans, erect almost to vertical, and pulled her sweater over her head. Her breasts were small and firm, and she never wore a brassiere, opting instead for camisoles that Nickerson thought far sexier.

This one was midnight blue, with a little bit of lace at the neckline. He reached underneath the bottom of it, but she shivered away from him.

"Your hands are cold!" she said, and held out her hands to keep him at arm's length.

"I don't know a better way to warm them," he said, and reached out for the belt loop of her gray wool pants to pull him back toward her.

She caught his hands in hers and tried to stop him, but he was much the stronger of the two and he broke out of her grip almost instantly.

She backed away, hands out in front of her. "So you're just going to manhandle me against my will?" she said, trying to sound serious but unable to completely repress a smile.

He advanced toward her. "That was my plan." He was better at playing serious, and managed to sound almost sinister.

She tried to play along, but lasted only about ten seconds before she burst out laughing. There was something inherently funny about a grown man wearing nothing but socks and a hard-on.

He laughed with her, and the two of them lay down on the rug in front of what used to be an open fireplace and what was now a woodstove. ("Less romantic, but warmer," Curtis had said of the stove when Greta said she missed the open fires.)

The rug was a genuine bearskin, but it was small. When Greta had first seen it, she'd asked Curtis if it had been a baby.

"A baby!" he'd scoffed. "It's a perfectly respectable black bear. My grandfather shot it in New Hampshire."

"I thought bears were bigger," she'd said, looking at the rug critically.

"That's only because you're used to seeing them in movies, and it's always a grizzly or a polar bear."

Over the years, she'd warmed to the rug, particularly since she talked Curtis into putting a bear-shaped pad underneath. Since then, they'd spent many intimate hours lying naked on the rug, talking, listening to music, and making love.

Curtis held his hands out first to the stove, and then to Greta for inspection.

"Warm enough?" he asked.

"Warm enough," she confirmed.

"Good," he said, and unzipped her pants. He eased them down, and she obligingly lifted her ass so he could slip them off, and her panties with them. He tossed the clothes aside and turned her facedown on the rug.

He knelt beside her and admired her body in much the same way she had admired his. She was small and compact, not so much thin as taut. He spread her legs wide enough so that he could kneel between them, and he ran his hands up and down the backs of her thighs.

She'd never exercised a day in her life, but she was a dynamo of activity and was in constant motion. Her body was firm and functional, the female analogue of his own, but with a softness his lacked.

He put his hand between her legs and nudged them apart. He felt the fine down on her thighs against the backs of his fingers as he moved his hand closer and closer to where her legs met. He could feel the moist heat coming out of her, and she moved ever so slightly side to side in anticipation of his touch.

When it came, she groaned aloud. He cupped her pubis in his hand and thrust his middle finger deep inside her, keeping his index finger against her clitoris. Then he moved it in and out, and in and out again, changing the pressure from strong to soft, strong to soft.

The soft, low sounds that came out of her aroused him almost as though she were touching him, and he felt his cock stiffen and throb. All his life, he'd felt his sexual desires urgently and acutely, and those feelings had barely abated with age. He was driven to make love to women. It was an absolute necessity for him, as fundamental as air or food.

He took his finger out from inside her, and took her ass in his two hands. He loved its shape, its firmness, the definitive ridge where buttock rose from thigh. He put his thumbs at the base of those twin ridges, and covered her two ass cheeks with his hard, calloused hands.

They were strong hands, and they gripped hard. Sometimes he was afraid he'd hurt Greta, but she had always responded to his strength in a way that made it clear there was no hurt involved.

Now she raised her hips up off the rug and pushed her ass into his hands. He held her harder, kneading her muscles with his hands. She pushed back, and he could see red marks on her buttocks where his fingers had dug deep.

Then he stood up, and he pulled her hips up so her feet and hands were on the floor, her ass high in the air. He pulled it against him and rubbed his cock in its crevice.

Although he was much taller than she, her height was in her legs, and in this position her cunt came almost to the level of Curtis's erect cock. If she balanced on her toes, it was just right.

He rotated her so she could brace herself against the couch, and she gripped its frame with both her hands. It was only in that position that she could push back against his force.

He pushed the two halves of her ass apart and thrust himself inside in one swift move. Once in, he held her still for a moment, savoring the sensation of her wet warmth on the length of him. Then he drew out slowly.

The first couple of thrusts spread her dewy wetness to the outside of her cunt, and the next couple went in smoothly and easily. And then they started getting harder. He pulled out slowly, and when the tip of his penis was just at her lip, he pushed in with the force of a man who could truly muster some force. Then out slowly, and in again, hard.

Greta's moans got louder, and her grip on the sofa tightened. The effort of keeping her balance involuntarily tensed all her muscles, including the ones that tightened around Curtis's erection. The harder he pushed, the tighter she got.

And he pushed harder. He didn't make any noise—he seldom did when they made love—but the raw power of his body pulsing against Greta's was a measure of his arousal. He held her hips in his hands and pulled them toward him each time he pushed his cock deep into her, and he felt his deepest, most urgent needs being satisfied.

His prelude to his orgasm built. With every thrust, his erection strengthened, until it felt like it encompassed his entire body. He slowed, just a little, to give his sensations time to get momentum. He only half heard Greta's rhythmic groans, but it was enough to tell him she was in sync with him.

And then it broke over him. It felt like rain, starting with just a sprinkling tingle, and then building as the storm rolled in. It took over his whole body, drenching him in the sensation that had been building from his inside out.

Even then, he was silent. His breath, shallow and fast, was the only audible clue to his turmoil of pleasure. Greta, though, could have been heard by the neighbors, had there been any. She let out a long, high sound that was a cross between a sigh and a cry.

They stayed there, Greta with her hands on the couch, Curtis holding her hips up against his own, for several moments, and then they collapsed, together, on the bearskin rug.

He held her in his arms while their hearts slowed back to normal, and then he kissed the top of her head and smiled at her. "Now comes the hard part," he said.

She nodded a little ruefully. As much as they enjoyed making love in front of the woodstove, it meant getting up and sprinting into the bedroom, which was inevitably cold, afterward. The longer they luxuriated in front of the warm stove, the harder it would be.

"Ready?" he asked.

"Ready."

He stood up and held out a hand to help her up. They ran across the living room into the bedroom, and dove under the covers. The first few moments under the down comforter were chilly, but their bodies warmed it up quickly. In the next few moments they were both asleep, still entwined.

When Greta woke the next morning, Curtis had already been up almost an hour. The coffee was made, the newspaper fetched, and bacon and eggs were ready to go.

She got out of bed, pulled her robe around her, and joined him in the kitchen. They breakfasted in companionable silence, reading the paper and enjoying the morning sunshine that streamed in through the kitchen window.

They looked up when they heard laughter. Because the house was so isolated, voices were an unusual occurrence. Curtis got up and went into the living room, which had the best view of the beach. He saw a young couple. Although he couldn't quite make out their faces, he thought they must be Zoe and a young man.

He went back into the kitchen. "It's Zoe Bell. I suppose I'd best get it over with." He took a light canvas coat off a hook by the door and was about to go out to the beach to meet them when Greta stopped him.

"Curtis," she said gently, as she took his arm and looked into his face. "You might like her, you know. And even if you don't, you'll be happier if you can have a good, neighborly relationship."

He looked down at the floor, knowing that she was talking sense, but unwilling to give up the cranky supposition that the worst New York City had to offer just landed in his backyard.

"And the work might be welcome, if she wants you to take care of the place," Greta went on, trying to make him see his own interest in all this. He worked as everything from a handyman to a general contractor, and business hadn't been as good as it could have been.

He looked up and gave a small half smile. He knew he needed this counterbalance to his standoffish distrust of outsiders. "You're right. We both know you're right," he said, and kissed her forehead. "I promise not to bite her head off."

With that, he headed out the door, determined to make friends, if friends could be made.

When Zoe saw him coming down the beach toward them, she quickened her step and extended her hand. "Mr. Nickerson," she said, shaking his warmly, "I'm glad to see you."

"Call me Curtis," he said. "Congratulations on the house." He managed to work some enthusiasm into his tone.

"Thanks," said Zoe, and put her hand on Sam's arm. "This is my boyfriend, Sam Stafford. I don't think you two have met."

"We haven't," said Sam, "but I certainly know your name." The two men shook hands.

"Zoe's known me since she was a little girl," said Nickerson, and then added, in a serious tone, "I suppose she's told you about the time I found her poaching in the clam beds."

"I was *six*!" Zoe protested. "How was I supposed to know you can't clam on Thursdays?"

Curtis actually smiled. "It's hard for me not to think of you as a little girl."

"I haven't been here much as an adult, but I guess that's all going to change now," she said, and looked over at Chapin House.

"Will you be here full-time?" asked Curtis, gesturing to both of them.

"Zoe's planning to be here for most of the summer, but I'll be going back and forth, since I still have a job in New York," Sam told him.

"What do you do?"

Sam always had a little trouble with this one. "I'm a painter," he said, "but I tend bar to support my painting habit."

Nickerson nodded politely, not quite sure where to go with that. He had an eye for art, and thought painting a fine pursuit, but he also believed a man should do real work.

Zoe, seeing the slight discomfort, headed the conversation down a different path. "I'm planning to do some work on the house," she said. "And I know you know it better than anyone. I don't know if you can take on any new projects just now, but if you've got the time and you want to talk about it, I'd like to get to it sooner rather than later."

Curtis was about to answer when all three of them heard the whine of a powerboat coming around the point. It was a small, open fishing boat with a center console and a young, bearded man at the wheel. As he sailed by full throttle, he looked at Nickerson, raised his hand, and flipped up his middle finger.

Nickerson did nothing in response. He watched as the boat drove off, and then turned back to Zoe and Sam.

Zoe wanted to know what that was all about—she didn't recognize the boat's driver—but she thought it might be intrusive to ask. Curtis, though, saw the curiosity and said simply, "Shellfish poacher."

Zoe's eyebrows went up. "He certainly looks old enough to know that you can't clam on Thursdays."

Curtis smiled despite himself. "It's more serious with him than it was with you. He's a commercial clammer, and he's been getting into the town clam beds at night. Since those beds are reserved for residents, he's stealing from everybody who lives here."

Zoe understood that this was a serious infraction, but it sounded small-time to Sam's ears. "Hell, next he'll be taking flowers out of window boxes," he said.

Curtis, who had no interest in explaining why poaching was such a loathsome crime, simply turned away from Sam and said to Zoe, "I can stop by anytime tomorrow."

"Tomorrow afternoon would be perfect," Zoe said. "Say around four o'clock?"

"Four o'clock it is," said Curtis, then nodded to both of them and headed back to his cottage.

"Poaching is serious, you know," she said to Sam when Nickerson was out of earshot.

"Apparently," said Sam. "He cut me dead."

"He does that a lot. You just have to let it go." She looked thoughtful. She had cringed inwardly when Sam had made the remark about the flowers.

They turned back toward Chapin House. "Shall we go into town and find ourselves some lunch?" Zoe asked with deliberate brightness.

"Is there a place to look?"

Zoe pursed her lips in mock exasperation. "There are at least two. One is a little pizza joint, and the other is the Danmouth Bakeshop. It's the best bakery in a three-town radius."

"A three-town radius?" Sam's eyes opened in exaggerated surprise. "Do you suppose there'll be a line?"

"Just so you know, at the height of the season, there's always a line." Zoe staunchly defended her town. "You're lucky to be here before the crush."

"Well, then, what are we waiting for?" The prospect of a decent lunch, even if it was just a sandwich, dispelled Sam's disgruntlement, and they headed back to the house in a happier state.

When the fact of a decent lunch—chicken salad on a crusty rye roll—replaced the prospect of one, Sam was downright cheerful. The weather had warmed, the sun was out, and Danmouth looked almost charming.

Sam took Zoe's hand as they strolled down Main Street. "Is there any art around here? Any museums, any galleries?"

Zoe laughed. I'm afraid you'll have to go to Boston for anything you'd consider art. There are lots of painters here, but most of them are of the weekend, watercolor-landscape variety." Watercolor landscapes were Sam's particular pet peeve. His own work was relentlessly abstract, with nothing that could be identified as a person, place, or thing.

"That empty storefront next to the bakery would be a perfect gallery," he said. "The light's just right." He was beginning to entertain the idea that life up here, with Zoe, might be a fine change of pace, and was thinking about ways to carve out a place for himself.

Zoe wasn't sure that Cape Cod was ready for Sam. Although she would never admit it to him, she herself had never been able to appreciate his art. She fervently wanted him to succeed, but she suspected that she wasn't alone in having difficulty picturing one of his canvases hanging in the living room above the sofa. Her faith in her own artistic judgment wasn't such that she was willing to say his work was bad. She could say only that she didn't much care for it.

Still, she admired him for creating something. He worked very hard at his art, and she had always been impressed by his drive and commitment. She'd never felt that kind of compulsion. Sure, she'd worked hard at her business, but she couldn't say it was a labor of love. It had been a good idea, and she'd kept her nose to the grindstone to make it a success. Now that it had been sold, and made her financially independent, she had no wish to do that kind of work again. She wished she had some of Sam's drive, some idea of what she was meant to do.

She squeezed his hand. "It is a nice space," she said, but didn't commit herself further.

"I could show my own work," he went on, "but we could show other stuff as well. There must be some summer people here with money to spend."

"There are," said Zoe, drawing out the two words as she tried to think of what to add to them. "But I'm not sure there are too many people capable of really understanding what you do. I think they're a watercolor-landscape kind of crowd."

She hadn't meant to rain on his parade, but once the words were out of her mouth she thought they weren't particularly loving or supportive. She had the money to make the gallery happen—it wouldn't cost a lot. But as much as she wanted him to succeed, she wanted him to do it under his own steam.

Sam made a noise halfway between a *hmmm* and a grunt. He understood that Zoe wasn't behind the idea, and he let it drop. He hadn't consciously made the suggestion that she should lend financial support to his career, but he realized that was how it sounded.

It was a little odd to both of them that such a short exchange could cast a pall over them for the remainder of a beautiful day, but those few words had somehow gone to the heart of what was going on between them. That evening, when they went to bed, neither of them had the energy to try to change the mood, and they lay awake, silent, for some time.

Eventually, Zoe felt her eyelids get heavy. She was on the verge of sleep when she was startled awake by a loud bang. She sat bolt upright, and Sam, who had been asleep, opened his eyes wide.

A break-in? An intruder? The house was so isolated that it was easy to entertain sinister thoughts. It was only when she felt the cold wind that she realized that the French door that led out to the balcony had flown open.

"It's just the door," she said to Sam. "I'll get it."

She climbed out of bed to shut it, and then settled back into the warmth of the covers. She had just closed her eyes when she felt a spot of warmth on her left cheek. And then another on her left temple. It was someone's breath; she felt sure of it. She sat up again, looking around a room that was obviously empty but for her and Sam.

"What is it?" asked Sam.

"I swear I felt something breathe on me."

"It was just the breeze," he said.

"No. It wasn't the breeze." She knew how strange it sounded as it came out of her mouth: "It was warm. I'm telling you, it was breath."

Sam made a show of leaning over and looking under the bed. "No monsters," he said, "so it must have been your imagination."

She looked at him, and the alarm in her face made him regret his flippancy. "You were jerked awake by a loud noise," he said, trying in earnest to soothe her. "Nobody thinks clearly when something like that happens. Try to get to sleep."

She lay back down, but she knew what she'd felt. It was breath.

CHAPTER THREE

T he next morning the alarm went off at six o'clock. Sam had to be
back in New York for a lunch shift, and that meant being on the
road by six thirty. He'd ridden his motorcycle all the way from the city,
and they were both happy to see the day dawn clear and calm. A four-
hour motorcycle ride in the rain would have been grim.

When he was gone, Zoe took her cup of coffee and went back to
bed. She was disquieted by how their couple of days in the new house
had gone. She'd hoped for a renewal of sorts, that a change of scenery
would let him rediscover their connection to each other. Instead, the
house, and the fact that it was hers and not his, seemed to exacerbate
his insecurities. She still had hope for them, but sadness had started to
make inroads into the love she felt for him.

The warmth of the bed trumped the kick of the caffeine, and Zoe
was lulled into a doze. When she woke up again, the sleep had made

Sam's departure seem far in the past, and she felt ready to start the day all over again.

Waking up to a day with no responsibilities, no to-do list, no work pressures was new to Zoe. She'd worked—hard—all her adult life, and the few months since she'd sold her company had been filled with the house hunt. Today, though, there was nothing on the agenda but her meeting with Curtis Nickerson at four o'clock.

She spent the day wandering around the house and the property, making lists. She went into town, visited the library, and checked out a couple of books on home renovation. She sat on the porch leafing through them in the hopes of getting some sense of builders' vocabulary before she talked with Nickerson.

She found, though, that the smell and sound and sight of the sea distracted her from her reading. It had always been that way, since she was a girl. Hundreds of times, she'd taken a chair and a book to the water's edge, only to find herself staring out over the water, looking at nothing in particular.

She was half sitting, half lying on the swing, and she closed her eyes and turned her face up to the sun, basking in the heat the way she'd seen the ocean sunfish do on the water's surface on a bright, warm day.

She was daydreaming about wide-plank pine floors and claw-foot bathtubs when she was startled back to the here and now by a shadow passing over her face. She opened her eyes, but all she could make out in the dazzling sun was the outline of a head, looking over her, and the shadow of a face.

She sat up, alarmed, and used her hand to shield her eyes from the sun. She squinted and looked around, but there was no one there.

She was unsettled. She'd been sure there had been a head, with a light-colored halo of blond where the sun shone through the hair. Was it possible it had just been a cloud? She looked at the sky, which was uninterrupted blue from horizon to horizon.

As her eyes adjusted to the light, and it became clear that she was alone, she shook her head to dispel the idea of a visitor. Then she leaned down to pick up her book, which had fallen to the deck, and she heard a voice.

I'm glad you're here, it said. Only it wasn't really a *voice,* and she didn't exactly *hear* it.

You belong in this house, it went on.

Zoe couldn't help looking around, even though she knew the deck was empty, because the voice had to be coming from somewhere. Except that it sounded as though it came from inside her head.

My God, she thought. Could she have actually bought a haunted house? She didn't believe in ghosts. She didn't believe in haunting. But she heard the voice as distinctly as if whoever it was had been sitting beside her on the swing.

And then the swing moved, just as though someone *were* sitting beside her. A slight warmth radiated from the space where the someone would have been.

It's my house, but I'm giving it to you in trust. Be good to it. Be true to it.

She nodded dumbly, not sure whether she should speak to this voice, or whether it could read her thoughts without her voicing them—it was already inside her head, after all. But she understood what the voice was saying: that the house was now in her care. And she had bought it in order to be true to its history, true to its character.

But who was this? He seemed young, he seemed male, and he seemed supremely confident. Zoe was a little surprised to find herself responding to him as though he were real. All she had to go on was the voice, but it was a voice that got her attention.

She looked at the spot next to her on the swing, as though willing him to materialize, but he didn't. She felt the warmth, and the movement of the swing, but she saw nothing.

But she heard something. Footsteps. Behind her.

She turned around, not knowing what to expect, but certainly not expecting Curtis Nickerson.

"I'm sorry if I startled you," he said. "I knocked at the door, but there was no answer, and I thought I'd check 'round back."

She stood up, trying to refocus her attention. "I'm glad you did. I'm afraid I lost track of time."

"That's okay. It happens to me all the time, especially down by the water."

The two of them looked out at the waves for a moment, and in the silence she heard the voice again. *Watch out for him,* it said. *He's not your friend.*

The tone had gone from welcoming to sinister, and it took Zoe a moment to absorb what had been said, what had been meant, and what she ought to do about it. All the while not giving away to Nickerson that she was hearing voices.

She covered her confusion by getting down to the matter at hand. "Should we go through the house? You can probably tell me a lot of things about it, and what needs to be done, and I can tell you what I'm thinking as far as changes."

Nickerson nodded, and they headed inside.

As they went in, Zoe took one look back at the swing, but it was still.

They went through every room in the house, and talked in exhaustive detail about refinishing floors, insulating walls, repainting trim, eradicating termites, fixing leaks, and generally reversing the house's decrepitude. At first, she had trouble concentrating on what he said, busy as she was trying to figure out why he wasn't her friend. After a while, though, she became absorbed in the discussion, and the ghostly warning faded from her mind.

It took them a full two hours to get through the house, and they'd been so focused on the work that she needed to do that she hadn't even gotten to the work she wanted to do.

They finished where they'd started, in the kitchen, so Zoe began to tell him how she'd like to remodel. She hadn't gotten past replacing the cabinets, though, before she started to sense his disapproval. Was it because she wanted to tear out the hundred-year-old countertops? Or maybe it was the granite-topped island she wanted?

When she got to the appliances, and asked him about the feasibility of putting a pot-filling faucet over the range, his eyebrows contracted and he practically scowled.

"Why would you want a faucet over the range?" he asked, in a tone that suggested that no reasonable person could ever need such a thing.

"To fill pots at the stove," she said, in a tone that suggested that it was perfectly obvious why such a thing would be useful.

"The sink is three steps away."

"A pot full of water is heavy and easy to spill."

During their house tour, Zoe had felt as though they were getting along well, even bonding. She knew Nickerson both personally and by reputation, and it was important to her to have a good relationship with him, although she knew it might be difficult. She didn't like the feeling that a little thing like a faucet was enough to send the meeting off the rails.

It occurred to her that he wasn't acting like her friend, but she didn't think something as simple as a disagreement over remodeling would merit the kind of warning she'd gotten from what she had already started to think of as her ghost.

"Look," she said to him, "I don't really care a lot about the damn faucet. I care that I turn this house into a place that's comfortable, and functional, and efficient. I want to do it in a way that's true to the spirit of the house. I'd like a few bigger rooms, and a few modern conveniences, but I'm sure we can find a way to do all that without turning the place into a monstrosity."

Nickerson looked at her and raised his eyebrows in a contemplative way. "Maybe we can," he said.

They just looked at each other for several seconds, neither of them willing to make the next move.

Nickerson blinked first. "Years ago, Clara Chapin had plans drawn up for some changes along those lines. You want to see them?"

"Clara Chapin actually wanted to *change* this house?" Zoe was incredulous. She'd thought old Mrs. Chapin was as rooted in the past as the two-hundred-year-old beech tree that grew in the front yard.

"Yup," Nickerson said simply.

Zoe considered for a moment before she said, "Yes, I think I would like to see them." She saw it as a chance both to see what the old woman had wanted to do, and to try to get the discussion with Nickerson on a better footing.

"I've got them over at the cottage. I could bring them over."

"Can't we just go look at them there? It would save you a trip."

"Sure," said Nickerson, "if you don't mind the walk."

The sun was beginning to go down, and the quarter-mile walk was beautiful. Nickerson opened the front door—Zoe noticed that it was unlocked—and they walked into a small entrance foyer. Curtis hung his jacket on a hook and patted the head of a large sea-green ceramic sculpture of a ship's figurehead. It was almost vertical, so it looked as if the ship were sinking under the floorboards, and the prow was the last thing to go down.

"I like the figurehead," Zoe said. "It's a very unusual color."

"My ex-wife made it almost thirty years ago. Everyone who comes in touches the head for luck."

Zoe touched the head, trying to imagine what kind of woman would marry Curtis Nickerson.

"She's called Angie, after the *Angela B.*, a three-master with a prow like this that went down in Cape Cod Bay some fifty years ago."

"She's quite beautiful." Zoe looked at the sculpture from all angles, and was surprised at the intricacy of the details.

"I've always liked her." Nickerson paused as his guest looked Angie over, and then suggested that she go in the living room and have a seat while he went up to the attic to find the plans.

"Would you like a drink?" he asked.

Zoe thought a drink was exactly what she'd like. "Yes, please."

"Are you a whiskey drinker?"

"If there's whiskey on offer, I'm a whiskey drinker," she said. For the most part, she limited her drinking to wine and beer, partly because that was what she liked drinking, and partly because she didn't have a good head for alcohol, but she didn't want Nickerson to think she was some city-slicker sissy.

He went to the cabinet in the corner and took out two glasses and a bottle of what looked like a decent single-malt. Zoe didn't know her whiskey very well, but she was under the impression that anything that started with "Glen" was good.

Curtis poured two fingers for each of them and handed her a glass. "*L'chaim,*" he said, clinked her glass, and took a swallow.

"*L'chaim,*" she echoed, a little surprised at his choice of toasts, and took a sip.

She wasn't used to whiskey, and the burning as it went down almost made her cough. She managed to swallow, though, and she hoped Nickerson hadn't noticed.

He had, of course, but he didn't say anything. He put his glass down on the table and left to find the plans.

Zoe was alone for longer than she'd expected—fifteen minutes, at least—and when Nickerson came back with a roll of drawings, her whiskey was half gone. She'd been warming to it, and drinking it faster than she intended. She already felt a little light-headed, but she made an effort to focus as Nickerson cleared a space on the coffee table and rolled the plans out.

He noticed that her glass needed filling, and he poured both of them quite a bit more of the Glen-whatever.

It took her a moment to map her image of the house to the drawings on the table, but once she was oriented she could follow Nickerson's explanation of what Clara Chapin had planned to do.

"Basically, she wanted more light," he said. "It always bothered her that a house so exposed to the sun should have any dark corners at all."

He pointed out windows she'd wanted to widen, walls she'd wanted to knock out, and skylights she'd wanted to put in. They spent quite some time looking at the plans in detail, sipping the Scotch as they went. Nickerson refilled her glass once more and his own twice as the evening stretched into the night.

They were sitting side by side on the sofa, both leaning forward to look at the drawings spread out in front of them. As she listened to Nickerson's explanation of the plans, she slowly became conscious of his presence next to her. She wasn't sure she liked the man, yet she found herself drawn to him. Maybe it was his physicality, his ropy outdoorsman's body. Maybe it was his clear mastery of the subject at hand. Maybe it was the contrast between him and Sam. Or maybe it was just the whiskey.

She shook her head briskly to try to clear it. She wanted Curtis to take care of her house and act as her contractor, and she didn't want to think about him in any other light.

"You don't agree?" Nickerson asked. He'd seen her shake her head.

Zoe didn't even know what he'd been talking about, but what could she say? *No, I was just trying to shake the image of the two of us making love on that bearskin rug*? That would go over big.

Instead, she improvised. "I'm just not sure. It's not quite what I envisioned."

"The skylight in the bedroom?"

Whew. At least now she knew where she was. "I'd actually thought about knocking that wall out." She pointed to the wall of what she had planned as the master bedroom. "And maybe putting in a glass cupola."

Nickerson took a deep drink of his whiskey. "A glass cupola?" he asked incredulously.

She took a drink to match his. "A glass cupola," she said with more confidence than she felt. And then, more plaintively, "What's wrong with a glass cupola?"

"What do you need a glass cupola for?"

"For light, and it'll look good. And so you can put a weather vane on top." She knew she was rambling. "A whale, or maybe a rooster. Or I saw one that was a fish with a tail like a map of Cape Cod."

"A fish with a tail like a map of Cape Cod," Nickerson said, his hostility giving way to amusement. "Maybe you want a saltwater taffy machine, or one of those 'I heart Cape Cod' bumper stickers." He gave a little snicker.

The snicker put Zoe over the edge. "Is it so very terrible to want a weather vane? Even one with a fish with a Cape Cod tail?" She could hear her words slurring, and she made a drunken effort to speak clearly and indignantly. "You're not the last word in what's good or bad in . . ." She couldn't find the word. "In . . . decorating!" She said it almost triumphantly.

He burst out laughing. He could hold his liquor better than Zoe, but he'd also had much more than she had and was far from sober. "It's not decorating," he said. "It's just good sense. You don't want to do big-city pretentious shit or wash-ashore tourist crap. You just want a nice house."

Zoe put her glass down on the coffee table harder than she'd intended, so it banged as though she'd slammed it. "I'm not a pretentious shit or a tourist," she said as she stood up, intending to leave in a huff. "I *do* just want a nice house, but I don't need *you* to tell me what a nice house is."

She turned her back to him and tried to stomp around the coffee table so she could get to the door, but her leg caught the edge. She just managed to avoid falling forward onto the floor, but the effort cost her her balance and she fell back onto the couch. It was Mission-style oak with black leather cushions, and she banged her head hard on the wooden back.

She let out a strangled cry of pain and put her hands to her head.

"Ouch," said Nickerson, and grimaced at the idea of the hit she'd taken. "Let me get you some ice or you're going to have a lump the size of a grapefruit."

He went into the kitchen and came back with a big plastic bag filled with ice cubes. He handed it to her and she tried to hold it to the back of her head, but it was unwieldy and the angle was awkward.

"Give it to me," he said. She did, and he had her lie down on the couch, propped up by pillows, and put the ice pack under her head. He sat on the edge of the couch, real concern in his face.

"Do you want some aspirin?" he asked.

"No," said Zoe. "It doesn't really hurt now. It's just throbbing."

"You know," he said, "I always thought you were the best of that bunch of kids who ran wild here every summer."

This was totally unexpected, and it threw her. She sat up a little bit and looked at him quizzically.

"You were the brave one. You were always the first to run into the water, or to get into the boat. You weren't afraid of the dark, or the emptiness, or the sea."

Zoe was staggered to find out that he knew this about her. When she bought the house, she wasn't even sure he remembered her name. "But you barely knew us." The *us* was her, her brothers, and the children of the other summer families.

"I was watching," he said. "All of us were. We still do. There's real danger out there, and we always mind the children."

Zoe found that she was very touched by this. Her ghost had been wrong. Nickerson was her friend, and had been all along.

Even had she been sober, she would have been moved by this, but her drunkenness amplified all her emotions. She reached out for Nickerson's hand, and he took hers and patted it.

"You were the best of the bunch," he repeated.

Through the fog of the alcohol, she felt a wave of tenderness. She sat up and looked him in the eye. And then she closed her eyes and leaned in to kiss him.

She was stopped, inches from his lips, by a gentle hand. Her eyes flew open, and she saw the expression, almost of pity, on his face.

"You're a very attractive woman," he said to her, "but I could never take advantage of a lady in such a state."

The wave of mortification made her face flush. She'd misread him, and she wanted to crawl under a rock.

She got up from the couch, unsteady but determined to get out of his house and back to hers as soon as she could.

"Let me take you home," Curtis said. "You're not in any condition to make that walk alone."

"I can manage it," Zoe said, feeling the room spin a bit, but keeping her feet.

Curtis stood up and took her elbow. "Come on," he said. "We'll go together."

"No!" Zoe almost shouted. And she added, more softly, "I couldn't bear it." Then, adding to her mortification, she burst into tears.

"Zoe, Zoe, don't cry." He was at a loss. He patted her back in a fatherly way. "I wish you could understand how flattered I feel."

This helped just enough for Zoe to get her sobbing under control, and she fled the house.

She took the path back to Chapin House almost at a run, glad that Nickerson let her go alone. Once or twice she almost fell, but managed to make it home without mishap.

But Nickerson hadn't let her go alone; he'd followed her at a distance to make sure she came to no harm. It was only when he had seen her safely inside that he turned around and went home.

CHAPTER FOUR

⁓✦⁓

Zoe lay awake, willing the walls and ceiling to be still. She tried to stop the scene of her aborted kiss from playing over and over in her mind, but she couldn't banish it. She couldn't remember the last time she'd felt so ashamed.

It was over an hour before she finally sensed that her eyelids were drooping and her thoughts wandering away from the events of the evening. She was on the very verge of sleep when, suddenly, she jerked upright. Someone—something?—had gotten into bed with her. She'd felt the mattress move. She'd heard the bed frame creak. And she thought she made out a shadow on the side of the bed.

Her heart was beating in her throat and her breath was coming fast. All of sudden, she felt stone-cold sober. She made a concentrated effort to slow her body down. She inhaled deeply and exhaled. And again. If her ghost was back, she didn't think she needed to fear him, but the middle of the night in the bedroom seemed scarier than the bright afternoon on the porch.

He did something, didn't he?

"Curtis Nickerson?" She said it aloud before she realized she was talking to a spirit she couldn't see. But the spirit answered.

Curtis Nickerson. He must have done something or you wouldn't be so upset.

It was partly a desire to defend Nickerson, and partly a need to get it off her chest that made Zoe tell the story. She never would have told a real person, but an empty room was okay. She felt a little silly talking to someone, something, she couldn't see, but she had a sense that her secrets would be safe with someone who wasn't real, someone who might not even exist.

When she finished, there was no response for a few moments, and Zoe thought she was alone again. But then the voice was back.

Are you sure you misread the situation? Maybe it wasn't you. Maybe he changed his mind. Or he could have led you on inadvertently. You're an attractive woman and any man would want you.

That hadn't occurred to her, and Zoe replayed the scene in her mind as best she could. She remembered how he had looked at her, how he'd told her she'd always been his favorite. And it all made sense. It seemed completely plausible.

And his compliment wasn't lost on her. Beneath her distress there was the soft satisfaction of knowing she was admired.

She felt the barest whisper of a caress on her hand, and it gave her goose bumps.

You shouldn't feel bad.

The bed creaked again, and she knew the presence had left.

But it had left her with a different way of looking at what had happened that night. The more she thought about it, the surer she was that she hadn't been wrong. He had led her on. He had wanted her. He must have changed his mind. It was even possible that he did it deliberately, wanting her to make a move so he could rebuff her—and she fell for it! As much as she hated the idea that she might have been duped, she liked it better than the alternative—that she'd misread signals from a man practically old enough to be her father. She was by no means sure which was the truth, but the alternate explanation helped ratchet her shame down a notch or two.

She longed for the clarity of morning and sobriety, but she couldn't stop the wheels that were turning in her mind. After half an hour of lying awake, she reached for the bottle in the nightstand drawer.

Zoe had prescription sleeping medication for her occasional bouts of insomnia, but she didn't like to take it, because Sam had told her that she seemed to sleep restlessly and had even walked in her sleep a few times when she'd used it. Still, she figured a pill was the only way she was going to get to sleep, so she opened the nightstand drawer and took one.

Ten minutes later, she was out.

~❦~

Seven hours later, she was up, but fuzzy and groggy and distinctly hungover. Her memories of all that had happened the night before had a dreamlike quality, as though last night had happened years ago instead of hours ago.

She wanted to be able to put the events behind her, and she thought it might be easier if she got out of the house. The bakeshop made pretty good coffee, and she thought it was just what she needed, so she headed into town.

Zoe sat in the window of the bakery, a mug of coffee warming her hands and the local newspaper on the counter in front of her. She wasn't reading, though. She wasn't even thinking, really. She was just looking out the window, hoping the coffee would bring her back to herself.

"Excuse me," said a woman's voice behind her.

Zoe turned around.

"You must be Zoe," said the woman whose voice it was. "I'm Lorraine Nickerson." She held out her hand.

Zoe took it and shook it. She didn't recognize the woman, who looked to be in her late forties. She had dark, wavy hair, cropped close. Her eyes were brown and bright, and her smile was cheerful and welcoming.

"You won't remember me," Lorraine went on. "I knew you briefly when you were very young. I was Curtis Nickerson's wife for about fifteen minutes when you were just a toddler, and I left town when we split up. I just moved back a few years ago."

Great. Just when she was trying to get away from all things connected to Curtis Nickerson, his ex-wife popped up at the coffee shop. But this woman seemed bright and engaging, and it would probably be a relief to talk to someone new.

Zoe's memory of the adults who had populated her childhood summers was hazy at best, and she couldn't place Lorraine at all. She was nevertheless happy to see a friendly face. "I'm glad to know you now," she said, and gestured to the empty seat next to her.

Lorraine sat down. "How are you liking the old Chapin place?" she asked.

"It's beautiful," she said automatically, and then reflected for a moment. Was it possible that someone with a history in Danmouth could tell her something about the ghost? "But it's complicated."

Lorraine's eyebrows went up. "Complicated?"

Zoe thought perhaps she shouldn't have broached the subject. Could she really tell a total stranger that her house was haunted? Lorraine saw her hesitation.

"Tell you what," she said to Zoe. "Why don't you come around the corner with me? I make better coffee than this, and I'll show you my studio."

There was something about her—her openness, her smile—that invited confidence, and Zoe accepted the invitation. She paid for her coffee, and the two of them walked the block to Lorraine's house.

It was probably the smallest house in Danmouth. Its footprint was no bigger than fifteen feet by twenty, and it was two stories tall. She had fireproofed the back of the bottom story and installed a kiln, and used the front as a combination workspace/showroom. There was an apartment on the upper level, and that was where she lived.

While Lorraine made coffee, Zoe walked around the tiny showroom, looking at the mugs, bowls, and vases. When she wandered into the space where Lorraine kept her wheel and her clay, she thought she might like to try this someday.

Lorraine saw her looking. "Tempted?" she asked with a laugh.

"Yes, actually." Zoe picked up a piece of clay and began shaping it. "The idea of making something out of what is essentially dirt is very appealing."

Lorraine laughed. "I know what you mean. There's something primal about clay. If you ever want to learn how, I'd be happy to show you."

"Thanks," said Zoe. She put the clay down and went back to the showroom.

She thought Lorraine's work was quite good. While the shapes were conventional, the colors were unusual. "I love that deep orange," she told Lorraine, pointing to a bowl on a high shelf. "I don't think I've ever seen a color quite like that on pottery."

"I've always liked experimenting with glazes," Lorraine said. "Although I've had some spectacular failures, I count that as one of my successes." She handed Zoe a cup of coffee and the two sat down at a small round table.

Zoe was tempted to tell her that she admired the glaze on Angie, the statue in Curtis's foyer, but she wanted to avoid any mention of the man. Instead, she just nodded.

"Now," said Lorraine, "tell me about your house."

Zoe found herself telling a complete stranger much more than she thought she would have. She felt like she couldn't just launch into the story of the ghost, so she talked instead about all the work the house needed, and that it was a bigger job than she'd thought. She couldn't help but touch on Nickerson's disapproval, but she tried to skim over it so she wouldn't have to talk about him. Lorraine, though, picked up on it.

"Curtis doesn't want you to do a bloody thing to that house, does he?" Her laugh was musical and pleasant, and there was no ex-wifely ill will in it.

Zoe smiled. "No, that's not quite it. He thinks it would be okay to knock out some walls and make the rooms bigger. I don't know what he's got against granite countertops, though."

"He's got nothing against granite countertops. It's change that he has something against. He's a bit of a stick-in-the-mud."

Zoe nodded, but she wasn't sure that was it. There was more than just resistance to change in Nickerson's disapproval.

They talked awhile longer about the structural problems with the house, and then Zoe finally broached the question that had been on her mind.

"Have you ever heard . . ." she began, and then paused. She felt silly even using the word. "Have you heard that Chapin House"—she looked down at her coffee—"is haunted?"

She felt like a little girl asking for a ghost story. Haunted!

But Lorraine took her up on it immediately. "Oh, sure," she said. "Everyone says it's haunted."

Everyone? If everyone said it was haunted, Zoe wondered why no one had told her before she bought it.

"Does everyone say who haunts it?" she asked.

"I think they say it's old Clara's son. Have you had an encounter?" Lorraine asked this in a mock conspiratorial tone that implied that she didn't believe in hauntings or in ghosts, so Zoe played down her experiences.

"Oh, just the usual creakings and groanings," she said lightly. "I figured there must be stories."

"Oh, there are stories. If you want to hear them, you should ask Tom, Dick, and Harry. They'll enlighten you, I'm sure."

"Tom, Dick, and Harry?"

"You haven't met them?" Lorraine was surprised.

Zoe shook her head.

"They're the three old guys who sit on the rocking chairs outside the general store."

Zoe knew them by sight, and had exchanged one or two good mornings with them. "I didn't know those were their names."

"They're not. Not really. One is Tom, and one is Dick, but the third one is Bartholomew. But who's going to call them 'Tom, Dick, and Bartholomew'? It's gotten to the point where the poor guy actually answers to Harry."

"And they know about the house?"

"They're the keepers of all the local lore—and perpetuators of all the local lies, so you have to take everything they say with a grain of salt."

Zoe laughed. "I'll go there with my shaker." And then it occurred to her she'd talked about nothing but herself and her problems.

"What brought you back to Danmouth after such a long absence?" she asked.

"I finally realized that I never should have left in the first place. This place has a hold on me. I lived in Atlanta for years, and I had a real job, but what I really wanted was to have a pottery studio, right here." She gestured around the room.

"Congratulations," said Zoe. "I know the satisfaction of starting your own business."

Lorraine made a *hmmph*ing sound. "I don't know that I'm at the 'satisfaction' stage yet. Right now there's anxiety and poverty, but I hope to graduate to satisfaction soon. Tourist season always helps."

Zoe lifted her coffee cup in a toast. "Here's to a lucrative tourist season," she said.

Lorraine clinked mugs. "From your lips to God's ears," she said, and drank the last of her coffee.

Zoe thanked Lorraine and stood up to take her leave.

"Stop by anytime. I'm always glad for an excuse to take a break."

"I'll do that," Zoe said, and the two women said their good-byes.

Zoe found herself feeling much better as she headed back past the bakery and toward the general store. She'd planned to go there for groceries, but now she also wanted to have a chat with Tom, Dick, and Harry, if they were there.

Two of them were. Zoe smiled as she approached them. "I know I ought to know this," she said, "but is it Tom, Dick, or Harry who's missing?"

"Tom," said one of them.

"Dick," said the other.

"It's been so long that we really don't remember," said the first one.

This was obviously part of their shtick, and Zoe laughed, but she detected a note of none-of-your-business, and thought she might have been overly familiar.

"My name's Zoe Bell," she said more formally. "I just moved into Chapin House."

"We know who you are," said Tom, or Dick, or Harry.

"I've heard you know who everybody is."

"Everyone in a ten-foot radius, at least."

This wasn't going the way Zoe had imagined. Generally, when she exercised her charm, she was met with warmth, particularly from men. These two, though, seemed determined to be crusty. She decided there was nothing for it but to take the bull by the horns.

"It's outside the ten-foot radius, but I was hoping you could tell me about the ghost in my house." She sat down on the step, hoping to give the impression that she was settling in to be told a story.

One of the two men betrayed just the faintest hint of surprise in the form of a raised left eyebrow.

"There's a ghost in your house?" the other asked placidly.

"I don't know," said Zoe, matching his tone. "Seems like it."

"How so?" asked he of the raised eyebrow.

"Oh, the usual," Zoe said. "Cold breezes, footsteps, whispers. You know."

"That would be Robert," said Raised Eyebrow definitively. His friend nodded in agreement. "That would be Robert."

They didn't go on.

"Clara's son?" Zoe asked, hoping to prompt them into saying more.

"Clara's son," they both said, almost in unison.

Zoe swallowed her irritation. She wasn't going to beg these guys to tell her the story. If they wanted to tell her, they would. She stood up. "Gentlemen," she said, and nodded at them, and then went into the store for groceries.

She nodded at them again as she went out, but didn't say a word. As badly as she wanted the rest of the story, she wasn't going to prostrate herself to a couple of old gossipmongers.

When she got home, she was surprised to see Sam's motorcycle in the driveway. As she pulled up, he came out the front door.

"Hi, baby," he said.

"Hey!" she said. "I didn't expect you until Tuesday." It was only Thursday, and he'd not even been gone two days, but Zoe was very glad to see him. Although she'd been disappointed about how their time together had gone when he'd been there before, she took his coming unexpectedly as a sign that perhaps he'd been disappointed too, and wanted to get on more solid footing.

Besides, having him there would help her banish the thoughts of Nickerson.

"I got coverage at the bar, so I've got a couple of days."

"That's great!" she said with real enthusiasm, and kissed him.

As they approached the front door, she saw that there was a note on it, a folded piece of paper with *Zoe* written on it. She couldn't imagine that it was from anyone but Nickerson, and she didn't want Sam to read it, in case he alluded to the events of the previous evening. She took it down, skimmed it quickly, and was relieved to find that there was nothing incriminating.

Zoe, I know you wanted to finish talking about the work on the house. Unless I hear otherwise, I'll stop by tomorrow around noon.

That was all it said. She hoped it meant that Nickerson wanted to put their evening behind them, and that what had passed between them was what it had seemed, a misunderstanding, and not the power play the ghost—Robert?—had told her it was.

She handed the note to Sam and started to put the groceries away. He read it and tossed it on the table. Work on the house was not what was on his mind, and while Zoe was reaching up to put away a can of tomatoes, he put his hands on her hips and kissed her softly on the back of the neck.

Her reaction was immediate, and completely outside her control. Her muscles contracted, her blood warmed, and her skin started to tingle. She leaned back into him and let out a small, soft sigh. As always, her body danced to his touch.

He moved his hands around her waist, and then down to the front of her thighs. He buried his face in her neck and kissed her harder, more insistently. She leaned her head back on his shoulder and covered his hands with her own, intertwining their fingers. She felt the hard pressure of his already erect penis against the top of her ass, and then the harder pressure of his teeth against the side of her neck.

Sam knew that Zoe hated for him to leave marks, and so he pressed just hard enough to make an impression but not leave a bruise. She groaned softly, and gave herself up completely to the sensation.

Sam ran his hands roughly up her body, and took one breast in each. He first cupped them, and then tightened his grip and held them firmly. He took each nipple between his thumb and forefinger and squeezed gently.

Zoe felt the sensation radiate through her, and the fountain inside her began to flow. Sam pushed her up against the counter, and she put her hands on it to steady herself. She pushed her ass backward and moved it back and forth against Sam's cock.

He answered with pressure of his own, and that was when she discovered the smooth ceramic drawer pull at exactly the right height to rub against her. With Sam's hands on her breasts, his cock up against her ass, and the hard ceramic globe against her clitoris, Zoe felt like she hit the trifecta of pleasure.

Sam was used to gauging Zoe's arousal, and pacing himself to her, but he didn't know about the drawer pull. He kept his rhythm and his pressure at a level that she could barely stand, but she couldn't pull away, couldn't make him stop.

She felt consumed by the sensations. They were centered in her pussy, but encompassed every nerve. It was as though her whole body were at the edge of a precipice.

She pressed her ass harder against Sam, and broke the connection with the drawer pull so she could try to recover herself. But he again responded by pushing her back against it.

When she again came in contact with the smooth, hard surface—why did it have to be *right there?*—she knew there was no going back.

There were a couple of small waves as the ecstasy built, and she knew what was coming. She attuned her body to it, waiting for it to overtake her.

That was what it did. Her orgasm began small and concentrated, and then worked its way through her body, spreading and growing.

She let out a high-pitched moan, a sound Sam knew well and which was his first indication of what was really going on. He was taken by surprise, but he knew exactly what to do. He squeezed her nipples, hard, and gave her orgasm a second life. It was as though he had strengthened the signal, boosted it so her pleasure stayed loud and long.

She moaned again, and pushed up against the drawer pull to keep the pressure against her clitoris. She gave herself so completely to the sensation that her knees almost buckled.

Sam held her firm, though, and gradually those sensations subsided, leaving her feeling cleansed.

He moved his hands back down to her hips and held her against him—he was more aroused than ever. "Where did that come from?" he asked softly, his mouth next to her ear.

Zoe moved to one side so he could see the drawer pull, and he laughed.

"Your secret weapon," he said.

"Something like that." She turned around to face him and put her hands in the waistband of his jeans.

"Do you think you've got another one in you?" he asked, running one fingertip around the outside of her breast.

It was the touch of that fingertip that made her think that maybe she did. She would have guessed that she'd be completely depleted, but that finger made her feel faint stirrings deep down.

"I might," she told him. "I just might." She took his hand. "C'mon." She knew she'd have to fan the embers of her orgasm quickly or they'd die away completely.

She led him up the stairs to the bedroom almost at a run. They pulled off their clothes unceremoniously and fell back on the bed. The feeling of skin on skin revived Zoe's arousal, and brought Sam's almost to the breaking point.

She pushed him back on the bed and straddled him. In a moment, she had him inside her, and the fullness, the completeness, the rightness of it made her tingle.

She leaned forward so her breasts just about touched Sam's chest, and she slowly raised her hips so almost the whole length of him slid out, and then lowered them again to bring him inside. As wet as she was, the friction of him coming in and out electrified her.

He took her hips in his hands, first following her motion, and then trying to take control of it to speed it up.

"Not yet," she said as she took his hands in her own and pinned them by his sides. "Not yet."

She continued her slow up-and-down, feeling him get harder inside her.

And then she felt the warm caress on the back of her neck, and she froze.

It felt like a hand moving from the base of her neck down her spine.

But Sam's hands were pinned under hers, and they were alone in the room.

"What's the matter?" Sam asked.

Zoe couldn't very well tell him she felt a hand on her back. She shivered.

"Are you cold?"

"No," she said. "I just felt something weird. It's gone now." She knew full well what it was, and now she even had a name to put to it. It was Robert, Clara's son.

But she obviously couldn't tell Sam about him, and she figured the best way to distract him from it was to pick up where she had left off. She started her rhythm again, and Sam was quite ready to resume.

She felt his erection come back to life inside her, but most of her energy was focused on the spot on her back where she'd felt that touch. She wasn't afraid of it—it had been warm, almost loving—and she could almost say she wanted to feel it again.

And there it was. This time she was ready for it, and she didn't break stride. Instead, she tried to make sense of it. It did feel like a hand, but a soft whisper of a hand. It was like a cross between a touch and a breeze. It was warm, it was gentle, and it made the hairs on the back of her neck stand on end.

It aroused her inordinately.

Suddenly, she felt her body heat up and all her liquids begin to flow. The center of this new wave of pleasure was the warm spot just at the top of her spine. It felt as though someone—something—were breathing into her, filling her with light and heat.

Without her being entirely aware of it, her body sped up. She was fucking Sam, but it felt as though some other presence were fucking her. It was an otherworldly sensation that took control of her. Through it, she heard Sam's quick, low moans, and knew he was on the cusp.

And then they were over it—together, but separate. Zoe felt her boyfriend come inside her, and she came too, but not with him. She came with the touch on her back. She came with the breath on her neck. She came with the idea of the other presence. And it was wonderful.

She sat straddled atop Sam, eyes closed for a few moments, and then she climbed off. She lay down next to him and he turned on his side so she could spoon up behind him. She pulled the comforter over both of them, and tried to think about what had just happened.

She was exhausted; she was confused; she was warm; she was comfortable. In moments, she was fast asleep.

By the time she woke up it was late afternoon, and she was alone in the bed. She could hear Sam moving around downstairs, and she smelled onions being sautéed. She hoped that meant Sam was making Bolognese sauce, a dish she loved.

She didn't get up right away. Instead, she lay under the covers trying to reconstruct the events of the last couple of hours. The nap had made everything seem remote, and she tried to recover the immediacy.

Had anyone asked her a month ago, she would have said that she didn't believe in ghosts. She would have laughed while she said it, as though the whole idea of it were ridiculous. Yet here she was, in her own house, absolutely convinced that she shared it with one of those spirits she didn't believe in.

Worse, though, than believing in a ghost was feeling something for a ghost. Absurdly, she was beginning to sense this ghost as *someone*. It was just this morning that she'd learned that other people believed there was a ghost, and that he was the spirit of old Clara's son, and already she thought of him almost as though he were flesh and blood.

She willed herself to get out of bed and return to the real flesh-and-blood world and her real flesh-and-blood boyfriend. She put on her bathrobe and sheepskin slippers, and straightened the covers on the bed.

She looked in the mirror to fix her hair, and that was when she saw him.

He was over her left shoulder, small, as though he were far away. He was a man, about thirty-five. Blond. He was wearing a fisherman's turtleneck sweater, and he smiled broadly as she caught his eye in the mirror.

Her heart almost stopped. She thought he was the most beautiful man she'd ever seen. He had an open, engaging face and deep blue eyes that were wide-set and turned slightly down at the outside corners. His nose was broad, but not large, and his smile was wide and bright. She looked at him for several seconds, taking him in, and then she turned around.

She was alone in the room. She turned back to the mirror, and all she saw was her own reflection.

But she was absolutely sure of what she'd seen. It had been the ghost, her ghost. He had smiled at her in a way that only men with intimate knowledge of her smiled. It was he who had touched her, had breathed into her, had filled her.

She sat down on the edge of the bed, trying to process her certainty.

But she knew she had to go downstairs and rejoin Sam, so she shook her head as though to dispel the ghostly presence and stood up.

As she was walking out of the room, though, she heard a voice.

Only a truly beautiful woman is beautiful in a bathrobe.

She felt herself blush, and the blush deepened at the thought that she was blushing to an empty room. It was a straightforward enough compliment, but she felt a telltale little flutter that meant it hit its mark.

I don't think he's good enough for you, the voice went on. *An exceptional woman needs an exceptional man.*

She sat back down on the bed.

"You don't understand," she said.

I do, he said, and she felt a warmth brush her cheek. *I assure you, I do.*

Then she heard Sam shout from downstairs, "Is it too early to open the wine?"

She smiled. Every time he cooked, he asked her the same question, no matter what time it was. Her heart went out to him, and she stood up to go downstairs. She wasn't sure whether Robert was still there, and she looked around the room even though she knew she wouldn't see him.

"He's better than you think," she said softly, but Robert's words had tapped into something about Sam that she had refused to acknowledge to herself: There was a part of her that did feel that she might do better.

On paper, the difference between them was readily apparent. She was a rich, successful entrepreneur and he was a poor, unsuccessful painter/bartender. But it wasn't the paper difference that nagged at her. After all the time she'd spent with Sam, she still wasn't completely convinced he was solid at the core.

But this she wouldn't admit to Robert. She could barely admit it to herself.

So she went downstairs to tell Sam that it most certainly wasn't too early to open the wine.

CHAPTER FIVE

Z oe had some trouble following Sam's conversation during dinner. He was all enthusiasm, full of news of a man he'd met at the bar who expressed interest in his paintings. Sam guessed he was loaded. He was wearing a two-thousand-dollar suit and drinking really good wine, so he must have an appreciation for the fine things life had to offer, including art.

Zoe smiled. She nodded. She even asked one or two relevant questions. But her mind was on the ghost, her ghost. Robert. She thought about what he'd said, but she also thought about him. She knew who he was, but she had no idea what he was. What kind of man, what kind of spirit?

Whatever he was, he felt real. He had spoken to her. He had made love to her, after a fashion. He had admired her; he had complimented her. He had told her Sam wasn't up to the mark, her mark.

He was courting her.

"Are you listening?" Sam broke into her reverie.

She couldn't say she was. For all she knew, he'd just told her that little green men had invaded Danmouth.

"I'm sorry. I'm a little distracted by all the house stuff." She smiled ingratiatingly. "Do you mind starting again?"

He just rolled his eyes and began to clear the dishes.

Zoe got up, took the plates out of his hands, and kissed him on the cheek.

"I'm sorry," she said again, but she meant it this time. She hated when people didn't listen to her, and she felt bad for having done it to Sam.

"You made dinner. Let me clean up."

When she was finished, she poured two glasses of cognac and joined Sam on the deck, where he'd been leaning on the rail, watching the water. It was dark, but the moon was full, and they could see the beach and the bay clearly.

"Do you think he's really going to buy?" Zoe asked, returning to what she remembered of Sam's new potential client in an effort to undo her earlier discourtesy.

"I don't know," he answered, in a tone that said he forgave her.

For the next hour, they talked about Sam. His art, his job, his potential. Zoe focused. He was good enough, she told herself. He was smart; he treated her well; he was interesting. And he certainly was attractive. He was more than good enough.

That he was talking about his work with enthusiasm and optimism helped. This Sam—the Sam who was full of ideas, who was dedicated to his work, who had dreams of making his mark in the art world—was the Sam she had fallen in love with. This was Sam at his best.

They sat on the deck, talking, until Zoe started yawning, and then they went upstairs to bed. Sam made overtures, but between her tiredness and her confusion, she felt like she couldn't oblige. She rebuffed him as gently as she could. He didn't seem crushed—he was snoring gently inside five minutes.

And Zoe, who had been dead tired until the moment her head hit the pillow, was suddenly wide awake.

She closed her eyes and willed herself to be sleepy again. She fluffed her pillow and adjusted the covers. She turned onto her left side, and then onto her right. But sleep was not to be had.

After half an hour, she realized it was hopeless, and she got up to get her reliable little pill out of the vial in the medicine cabinet. It worked like a charm.

She woke up to Sam, a concerned look on his face, gently stroking her hair to wake her up.

She tried to shake off her sleep, but it was heavy and persistent.

"What time is it?" she mumbled.

"A little after ten."

That was late. That was very late. She was usually up by seven at the latest.

She made the effort to sit up, and Sam handed her the cup of coffee he'd brought for her.

"Drink," he said.

She sipped. It was good. It was strong. Who could live without coffee?

"Do you remember anything from last night?" Sam asked.

She looked at him sharply. "What?"

"I'll take that as a no."

"What happened last night?" There was alarm in her voice.

"You sleepwalked."

She was actually relieved. Although she didn't like the idea, she knew she sometimes did it when she took the medication.

She sighed. "Where did I go?"

"Out back."

"Out back? I went outside?"

"You did. I woke up, and you weren't in bed or in the bathroom, so I went downstairs to find you. The back door was open, so I went out on the deck. You'd gone down the stone stairs and you were walking out toward the water."

Zoe held her hand to her forehead, willing herself to remember something about this. She drew a blank. "I have absolutely no memory of it."

"At first, I thought you might have just gone outside because you couldn't sleep, but there was something about the way you were moving. So I went down to meet you, and you had that glazed look."

The idea of this was very disconcerting to Zoe. That she did something that she apparently had no conscious control over, and no memory of, was disturbing.

"I hope I didn't give you any trouble," she said wryly.

Sam smiled. "No, I just led you back to bed."

"What time was it?" she asked, but then held out her hand to stop him from answering. "No, don't tell me. It was about three thirty."

When she had sleepwalked in the past, it had always been at about that time. There must be something about the way the medication worked its way through her body.

"Close," Sam said. "It was closer to four o'clock, but that means you probably got up around three thirty."

"That's the first time I've ever gone outside," she said.

"Well, it was a lot harder in New York. You would have had to get down the elevator and past the doorman."

"I'm going to have to change medications. I hate to do it when it works so well, but I'm not comfortable with the idea that I do strange things in the middle of the night."

Sam leaned over and kissed her forehead. "I've got some pancakes almost ready to go. Have a little more coffee and then come downstairs."

She nodded and nestled down into the pillow, cupping the warm coffee mug in her hands. She took a sip and listened to him bustling around the kitchen.

And then she heard it, clear as day: *You're wasting your time with him.* It was as though Robert had a direct line to her brain. Nothing was spoken aloud, but she understood him as clearly as if it had been.

The experience of yesterday came flooding back. She felt her skin flush, remembering the sensation of what she thought of as his touch. She pictured the face she'd seen in the mirror, the face that went with the voice. It was only two days ago that she'd "heard" it for the first time, but already she was getting used to it.

But how did he know so much? How did he know about Nickerson? And how could he know to probe her deepest, darkest concerns about Sam?

She wanted to ask him, but she couldn't get used to the idea of talking, out loud, to a ghost. She'd done it when she told the story of the aborted kiss with Nickerson, but she'd been drunk and it had been the middle of the night. Now, sober, in daylight, it felt very strange to talk to nobody.

Was it possible he could understand her if she just *thought* her response? Did she even want to respond?

She focused and thought her response, trying to project it to Robert. *How do you know all this?* She closed her eyes as though to send the thought vibe through the ether.

No response.

Apparently, the protocol for ghost-human communication required that the human actually speak aloud.

"How do you know all this?" she said in a whisper.

I know everything, Robert said. *It's one of the privileges of being dead.*

For a moment, Zoe's questions gave way to curiosity about the science of the paranormal. "Everything?" she whispered. "Like the date of the Battle of Hastings and how antimatter works?"

The ghost laughed, which felt like a tiny vibration deep in Zoe's head. *No, not everything like that. I know everything about people. I can see their true nature.*

Zoe raised her eyebrows. "How do you know?"

Robert scoffed. *How do I know?*

"How do you know it's their true nature? Why can't you be fooled like anybody else?"

I just know. I see it clearly whenever I see someone new. When you're alive, you just have your five senses to rely on, but when you're dead, you have this other sense. People sense.

"I'll look forward to that," Zoe said dryly. And then, more seriously, "What do you see in Sam?"

He's false.

She wasn't sure she wanted to hear this.

But Robert went on. *He's false because, deep down, he knows he lacks true artistic talent, but he wants so desperately to be an artist that he's built his whole identity around it. He's spent his whole life developing that identity, and he's hanging on to it with everything he's got.*

Zoe was silent. Over the last several months, as Sam's prospects had dwindled, she'd been afraid of just that. When he had been doing well, she had been willing to accept the world's opinion of his work, even though she didn't understand it herself. Once the world seemed to change its mind, though, she started to wonder whether she believed in his talent. And she even wondered whether he believed in it himself. If he didn't, then Robert was right.

Worse, she harbored a vague suspicion that Sam might see her newfound wealth as his ticket out of his life. The comment he'd made about the gallery space in town came back to her. It wasn't that she doubted his feelings about her, but the idea that those feelings might be colored by her money made her very uncomfortable.

She wished she could see Robert. She wanted to look into his eyes.

You, though, you're the exact opposite. You're modest and circumspect. You worked hard and accomplished something remarkable. Your talents are very real.

Then she felt pressure on the bed next to her. She looked, and she didn't see any indentation, but she knew with certainty that he was sitting on the edge of the bed. She felt warmth on her cheek, a gentle stroke of something that wasn't quite a hand.

Her heart gave a leap, and she felt the tingling of her nerves and the tightening of her muscles that came from the excited rush of her body's response to a man she wanted. It was strange to her that the fact that there was no man in the room didn't seem to matter.

"Pancakes are up," Sam shouted from downstairs.

Zoe didn't move.

Go downstairs, Robert told her. *Wherever you go, I won't be far away.*

Zoe went downstairs feeling self-conscious and vaguely disloyal. The table was set, there was a fresh pot of coffee on, and Sam was just flipping pancakes off the griddle. He stacked three on a plate and set it in front of Zoe. Butter and maple syrup were on the table, and she found she was hungry. And if she was eating, she would get a reprieve from talking.

Sam set his own plate down and sat across from her, clearly enjoying the relish with which she was eating.

"I love cooking for you," he said.

Zoe swallowed before answering, "Because I love eating?"

Sam nodded, and smiled the smile that always drew her in. There was nothing false about it, and it had nothing to do with his art, or his talent, or his prospects. It was a lot easier to believe that he wasn't good enough for her when he wasn't actually in the room.

When she'd finished the pancakes, she leaned back in the chair, enjoying her second cup of coffee and the sense of satiated hunger. Then she looked at the clock and stood up. "I need to get in the shower, since Nickerson's coming over at noon to talk about replacing windows and floors."

Zoe was very apprehensive about the meeting. It would have been awkward enough facing him alone, but Sam's presence complicated it.

She considered canceling, but thought better of it when she reasoned that it might be the best way to get past what had happened between them.

And if Robert had been right, and it was a power play, it might even be better to have Sam there. In any case, she thought that the longer she put off meeting Nickerson, the harder it might be.

Nickerson arrived promptly at noon. If he was surprised to find Sam there, he didn't let on. The two men shook hands and nodded to each other, and Zoe and Curtis got down to business.

But the business, Zoe found, didn't go smoothly. It had two strikes against it, given that she was profoundly uncomfortable and expected that he was as well. She thought the best way to put both of them at their ease would be by talking about the house, but that just proved to be a source of friction. It was as though they were both making the effort to prove that there was no affection between them.

She wanted to change out all the windows in the house for top-of-the-line, energy-efficient replacements, but Curtis made it clear he thought that was extravagant. "Most of the windows are just fine, and some are only a few years old," he said. "It's wasteful to replace them all."

"But I want them all to match," Zoe said. She had thought he'd be in favor of new windows, and was irritated to find that he objected.

"They'll look almost identical. Do they really need to match precisely?" Nickerson asked.

She'd thought it was a rhetorical question—it was obvious why the windows should all match—and wasn't going to answer, when the voice in her head said, *Tell him.*

For a moment, she was confused. Since Robert had been silent thus far, she thought he'd decided to stay away. Besides, she didn't expect a ghost to interest himself in home renovation. Apparently, he did. *Tell him*, Robert said again. *He's trying to assert his power and you can't let him.*

Zoe looked at Nickerson, who seemed to be expecting an answer.

She told him. "I think the house will look better if all the windows match."

"The last time all the windows matched was probably the day it was built," Nickerson said, and there was an edge to his voice that verged on contempt. Zoe didn't like it.

It's your house. You call the shots. Zoe, still unused to having a participant in the conversation audible only to herself, took a moment to figure out that this was Robert speaking, and not Sam.

"I don't think matching windows is such an outrageous thing to want," was what she said to Nickerson.

She wished Robert wouldn't interfere just then—this was hard enough to deal with when it was just Sam and Curtis—but she couldn't very well ask him aloud.

The conversation, first about the windows and then about the floors, went on in this vein for quite some time, with Zoe getting more and more distracted and increasingly irritated. Curtis found fault with everything she wanted to do, Robert kept interrupting, and Sam looked on as if this were a spectator sport.

She snapped.

"Okay!" she said to no one in particular. "I've had it!"

And then, to Nickerson, sharply, "I understand that you have your preferences, and I'm sorry they're not closer to mine. . . ." She trailed off. She'd intended to tell him he could turn around and walk right back home and she'd hire someone else to do the job, but their eyes met just as she was about to, and she knew she shouldn't. She couldn't.

It came to her that this meeting might be very difficult for him, that Sam's presence might put him on the defensive, that it would be difficult for him to negotiate the situation.

"Look," she started again, in a more conciliatory tone, "I'm sorry we don't see eye to eye, but I hope you know that I want to be true to the house. I'm not trying to turn it into something it's not." She wasn't quite sure where to go from there. She didn't think she had anything to apologize for, but she also didn't want to do irreparable harm to her relationship with Nickerson.

"Can we talk about this another day?" she finally said. "I had a bad night's sleep, and I'm not at the top of my game."

It wasn't what she said, but the way she said it, that made Nickerson soften.

"We all have days like that," he said. "I'll stop by tomorrow."

And then he left without another word.

"What's wrong?" asked Sam, when Curtis had gone. "You're not yourself."

Her irritation rose again in her throat. "I'm not myself? Why? Because I want my windows to match?"

Now that Nickerson was no longer standing in front of her, her anger not mitigated by his presence, she gave vent. She ranted about Nickerson thwarting her at every turn, about his being deliberately obstructionist, about his saying it was black just because she said it was white. She knew her anger was out of proportion to the offense, but she couldn't very well tell Sam it was fueled by her confusion about what had happened between them two nights before.

She ended up by lashing out at Sam as well. "And you might have jumped in to help me," she said with some vehemence.

"Whoa!" he said. "This is between you and him. I've got nothing to do with it."

You're right. He should have helped you, said Robert, but Zoe was in no mood.

"Shut up!" she yelled, and covered her ears.

Sam looked at her, astonished that she would say that to him.

"No, not you," she said, flustered. She took a couple of deep breaths to try to calm down. "I just need to shut the world out for a bit while I get my bearings. I'm going for a walk."

She turned away from Sam and walked out the door and stood on the deck, looking at the sea. She started to feel calmer after just a few minutes, but then that voice came back. . . .

You can see what I mean, it said. *Curtis Nickerson thinks you don't belong here. He wants you gone.*

Zoe didn't answer. She didn't want to have this conversation.

She was beginning to realize that, as intriguing as she found the idea that she had her very own ghost, she didn't want her very own ghost all the time. If she were going to preserve her sanity, she needed to be able to shut him out sometimes, to give her space to navigate the real world. She walked down the steps to the beach and headed west along the shoreline.

Now she was glad she couldn't talk to him just by thinking. If she didn't say anything, there could be no conversation.

And it worked. After a very little while, she felt that he was gone. She walked, and she breathed, and she gathered her thoughts. How had things gotten so complicated so quickly? Was Nickerson the man

Robert said he was, or was he what Zoe had thought him all her life—crusty but good-hearted?

She tried to make sense of it all, but she was tired and confused, and she didn't think it was the kind of problem that could be reasoned out. After a while, she tried to simply clear her thoughts, to calm the buzz in her mind, to enjoy the beach and the sea.

She'd been gone nearly two hours when she walked back up the stone steps to the back porch of Chapin House.

Sam came out the back door, walked to the top of the steps, and watched as she made her way up toward him.

She stood on the step beneath him, her head level with his abdomen. "I'm sorry," she said, and put her arms around his waist and rested her cheek against his flat, firm belly.

He put his hands on her shoulders and rubbed a little. "Are you okay?" he asked.

"I'm okay," she said. "Just a little discombobulated."

"Seemed like it."

She nodded.

He stroked her hair, and then led her inside. "Come upstairs with me."

He took her into the bedroom, and she saw that he had made the bed and picked up all their clothes. The pillows were fluffed against the headboard, and there were two glasses with mismatched candle stumps in them.

"Where'd you find the candles?" Zoe asked. They didn't look familiar.

"I scouted around until I found them. There's still some junk in that room in the basement."

Zoe nodded. She'd been a little put out when she first saw that room, because the house was supposed to be cleared out when she bought it, but that one room had a few scraps of things, and one large desk that looked like it was too big to get out the door. She had no idea how it had gotten in there in the first place.

Sam lit the candles with kitchen matches, which he'd apparently brought up for the purpose, and then turned to Zoe. She was wearing a light, sheer angora sweater, and he lifted it over her head. Underneath was a simple satin cream-colored bra, and he reached around her to unhook it. He unbuttoned the fly on her chinos and pulled them down so she could step out of them. When she was absolutely naked, he flipped back the comforter and bade her to lie down. She did.

He was wearing cargo shorts and a T-shirt, and she made a move to divest him of them, but he stopped her.

"Just lie down. I'm in charge here."

She smiled, and felt what remained of the day's tension dissipate as the cool sheets warmed to her body.

He went into the bathroom and she heard the water running. He came out with two warm, wet washcloths, and draped one over each of her feet. He rubbed first the right, and then the left, and Zoe relished the feel of the rough terry cloth on her arches and between her toes. After her walk, Sam's gentle touch on her feet was heavenly.

He tossed the washcloths onto the bathroom floor, and turned his attention back to Zoe's feet. He took one in each hand and squeezed. She loved having her feet massaged, and she sighed with every exhalation. He pressed his thumbs into her arches and made small circling motions. He cupped her heels in his hands and rubbed the spot where her ankle narrowed just above them.

Then he leaned down and took her big toe in his mouth. It felt so warm and soft that Zoe moaned involuntarily. All the cares of the day dissipated, and there was only Sam's tongue. Her eyes were closed and there were no other thoughts.

He moved down her row of toes, darting his tongue between them and running it over them, all the while holding each of her feet firmly in one of his hands.

When he finished one foot, he moved on to the other, never releasing the pressure of his hands.

He reached the little toe of the second foot, and then kissed her arch before taking leave of her feet and moving up her legs. He reached his hands around the back of her calves and gently kneaded the firm muscles. Then he spread her legs, knelt between them, and stroked the tops of her thighs with the backs of his hands, with a touch as light as it was possible for a touch to be.

Zoe felt goose bumps on the entire length of her legs, and she found it strangely arousing. She wasn't sure whether it was the touch itself or the promise of other touches to come that started to open her inner floodgates. She felt her body wanting him almost of its own accord.

She reached for him to pull him down to her, but he stopped her. "I told you, I'm in charge here. You just lie there and do as you're told."

She smiled at his seriousness, and obeyed.

He moved his hands from the tops of her thighs to the soft skin between her legs, still barely touching her. It was as though an electric charge moved from his hand to her skin, and then straight through her to every nerve ending.

Sam worked his way slowly up her inner thigh, but stopped before he reached the junction between her legs and worked his way slowly back down almost to her knee. Barely touching, barely stroking. Zoe was barely breathing, anticipating the moment when his touch would become real.

Back up her thigh, and a little closer this time, and then back down again. Her body arched up, but Sam pushed her down again. "Lie still," he said.

And she tried, but her body was becoming more and more charged, every muscle tingling.

His hands were moving upward again.

"Do you want me to touch you?" he whispered.

"Yes . . . yes."

"Can you lie still if I do?"

Zoe moaned. She said she could, but she wasn't sure it was true.

And he did touch her. He circled in, starting wide, tracing an arc around either side of her pubis with his index finger. Then he did the same around her vulva. Then he cupped her entire cunt in his hand and exerted a quick, pulsating pressure.

This was too much for Zoe. Her hips strained toward him as she let out a soft, high-pitched moan.

He took his hand away. "I told you to lie still."

She made a sound that was somewhere between desperation and arousal. "I will, I will," she said, with some urgency.

He put his hand back, and the pulses began again. Zoe willed herself to stay still. The heel of Sam's hand was up against her clitoris, and the vibration had her very warm and very wet.

The pulses sped up, and then slowed, and sped up again. Just when she thought she was too close to climax to stop herself, Sam would change the rhythm and prolong her ecstasy.

The next time he slowed, he also reduced the pressure. And then he slowed some more, and softened his touch so Zoe could barely feel the pulses. She willed her hips to stay on the bed and not reach up to him.

He stopped pulsing altogether and held her in his hand. She opened her eyes, a little surprised. She had been so close!

"Close your eyes," Sam said. "And lie still," he added.

She did.

She felt him change position between her legs, and the next thing she felt was his tongue flitting back and forth over her clitoris. She moved just a little, involuntarily, and Sam stopped abruptly.

"I told you not to move."

"I didn't move! It was just a tic. I didn't move!" She lay as still as she could. "Look, I'm perfectly still."

Her eyes were closed tight, and she didn't see Sam's smile, but she knew it was there.

His tongue was back. Back to flitting back and forth. Slower, and then faster, just as he had done with his hand. And slower, and faster again.

He would sometimes move down and lick her labia, and push his tongue deep inside to taste the juices that were gushing from deep inside her. And then he'd go back to her clitoris, back to the back-and-forth.

Had she not had to focus on lying completely still, her orgasm would have come almost immediately, but the distraction and the discipline prolonged the buildup.

But there was a point beyond which it could be prolonged no longer, and somehow Sam knew exactly where it was. Just as she began to feel overtaken by the climax that was to come, he put his mouth over her whole cunt, hard. He kept up the back-and-forth motion, and Zoe felt his wetness mingle with hers, and she was there.

It was explosive. It was enormous. Its power left her breathless. It came in waves, and it felt like it would go on as long as Sam kept his mouth on her. It was as though she were plugged into him.

He did keep his mouth on her, until finally the sensations began to subside. It wasn't until her body relaxed and her eyes opened that he sat up and looked at her.

"That was astonishing," she said.

He smiled a little sheepishly, which was uncharacteristic. "I thought you needed to relax."

She laughed out loud. "Well, that certainly did it."

"Now all you need is a glass of wine and some dinner."

"Let me take you out," Zoe said. "I read that there's a new sushi place that's supposed to be good in Morton."

"There's good sushi on Cape Cod?" Sam asked. "Or is Morton in another state?"

"Morton's all of two towns over, and if there's one thing Cape Codders know, it's fish. It's not such a stretch that there would be good sushi here."

"Well, there's one way to find out."

Only as she was dressing to go out did Zoe think of Robert. Since she had ignored him on the beach, she hadn't heard his voice or felt his presence. She wasn't sorry, exactly, but she couldn't help wondering whether he knew what had gone on in the bedroom. *Top that*, was what she wanted to say to him.

Zoe took more pleasure in Sam's company that evening than she had in a long time. It seemed as though he was going out of his way to be charming and engaging, and she saw in him all the things that had made her choose him in the first place.

That night, though, as she lay sleepless and he snored softly beside her, all her doubts came flooding back. As much as she had enjoyed their day, she knew something crucial was missing. At dinner, he'd reached over and touched the back of her hand, and the tingling, the tightening wasn't quite what it used to be.

She tried to banish all unpleasant thoughts from her mind, and thought of the rhythmic motion of the waves on the sand in an effort to lull herself to sleep, but it didn't work. She tried to lie on one side, and then the other, but couldn't get comfortable. There was a buzz of energy running through her body and mind that told her sleep would not be in her future without chemical intervention.

After having sleepwalked the night before, she was reluctant to take a sleeping pill, and she lay awake for at least an hour without feeling the slightest hint of drowsiness. Finally she gave in and took the little tablet. It always worked.

She had no idea how many hours had elapsed between her drifting off to sleep and her being jolted awake by Sam's shakes.

"Zoe. Baby. Wake up," he was saying. "Somebody's at the door. Pounding on it."

She could hear the loud knocking. "What time is it?"

"About seven thirty."

"Who comes over at seven thirty?" she asked. It was hard to shake the grogginess.

"I don't know, but whoever it is *really* wants to come in."

Zoe got up and wrapped her robe around her. She went downstairs, with Sam right behind her.

When she opened the front door, she saw a man she didn't know. He looked to be in his early thirties, dark haired and fine featured. His good looks didn't register, though, because Zoe was looking at the badge he was holding out.

"Miss Bell?" he asked.

She nodded.

"I'm Detective Andrew DuBois." He pronounced it *Doo-bwah*. "I'm with the state police."

"Is something wrong?" Zoe asked, bewildered, looking from DuBois to Sam, who looked as mystified as she was. She had absolutely no idea why the police would want to talk to her.

"May I come in?" he asked.

"Of course." She opened the door and he came in. She led the way to the kitchen so she could make some much-needed coffee as they talked. She bade the detective take a seat at the table, and switched on the coffeemaker, which she'd set up the night before.

"What can I do for you?" she asked.

The detective looked at her, and then at Sam, and then back at her.

"Can I ask where you were last night between midnight and six a.m.?"

Zoe raised her eyebrows in surprise. "We were here. Asleep."

DuBois looked at Sam. "Both of you?"

"Yes," said Sam.

"Did either of you leave the house for any reason?"

"No," said Zoe. "We were asleep."

"Did you see or hear anything out of the ordinary?"

Zoe shook her head and looked at Sam. "Did you notice anything? I took a sleeping pill just before midnight. I would have slept through a world war."

"What's this about?" Sam asked.

"Curtis Nickerson was killed last night."

CHAPTER SIX

Zoe and Sam looked at each other, horrified.

She couldn't absorb it. Nickerson had been there just yesterday afternoon, arguing about windows and floors. And now he was dead?

How? Why?

"What happened?" asked Zoe.

"I'm sorry; I can't tell you much about an ongoing investigation," said DuBois sympathetically. "I'd like to be able to give you more of the details, but I'm sure you understand."

Zoe nodded dumbly. She didn't think she'd ever been as shocked, and she had no idea what to say or do.

"I'm going to have to ask you a few questions," said the detective, his look encompassing both Zoe and Sam.

Again Zoe nodded.

The coffeemaker beeped, and Sam poured a cup for himself and one for Zoe. "Would you like some?" he asked DuBois.

"Very much," he said. "Thanks."

When they all had coffee, DuBois took out a notebook and pen. "How long had you known Nickerson?"

Zoe explained that she had known him when she was a child and then again as an adult. She ended up explaining her family's relationship to Danmouth, and her buying Chapin House. He asked her about her dealings with Nickerson since she'd moved in, and whether those dealings had gone smoothly.

Zoe explained that they hadn't, and told DuBois about every conversation she'd had with him. The only thing she left out was the aborted kiss. She didn't like to omit a detail like that to a cop, but she certainly couldn't tell that story in front of Sam, if she told it at all. She thought she would have the option to tell DuBois the whole truth, if it seemed important, later—when they were alone.

Thinking about that evening, though, made her feel real sadness, and not just shock, at his death. As difficult as he'd been, she had to admit that she'd been drawn to him.

She put her head in her hands. "I can't believe he's dead."

"I'm sorry," said DuBois. "I know this is hard, but I'm going to have to go into a little more detail."

He asked for specifics about her conversations with Nickerson, and whether their arguments had been at all heated. He asked whether she had liked him, and she wasn't sure what to say.

"I did," she said finally. "He may have been difficult, but he was authentic."

Sam snorted, and DuBois turned his attention to him. "Did you like him?"

"I barely knew him, but he seemed pretty cantankerous."

DuBois asked Sam how long he'd known Nickerson, and Sam said he'd met him only twice—the first time for only a few minutes, and the second time for a couple of hours the day before. After one or two more questions, DuBois turned back to Zoe.

"That's all I have for now," he said, "but it's likely I'll have to come talk to you again in the course of the investigation. Do you plan to be in town?"

"I do, but Sam goes back and forth to New York."

DuBois nodded. "Where can I reach you there?" he asked, and Sam gave him his address, phone number, and e-mail.

The detective stood up. "Again, I'm sorry to be the bearer of such grim tidings," he said. "If you think of anything, or you have any questions you think I could answer, don't hesitate to call." He handed Zoe a business card and thanked her for the coffee.

❦

DuBois left them sitting, still stunned, in the kitchen, and crossed Zoe's name off his list. Next on that list was Lorraine Nickerson, Curtis's ex-wife, and DuBois headed into the village to find her.

❦

He found her at home, in the apartment above her studio.

She lived nominally alone, but Tim O'Donnell, a chemistry teacher at the neighboring town's high school, was there often. He wasn't exactly her boyfriend; in the many years since her divorce from Curtis, Lorraine hadn't let anyone get really close to her. But she liked having someone in her life, someone to share her bed, and Tim fit the bill. He wasn't any more interested in a serious relationship than she was, and enjoyed sex just as much. Their relationship worked for them.

He was there when Andrew DuBois went up the staircase on the side of the building and rang the bell to the little apartment. It was he, not Lorraine, who answered the door.

"Can I help you?" he asked, not knowing who DuBois was. The detective showed his badge, and asked whether Ms. Nickerson was at home.

"Come in," said Tim. "She's just in the bathroom. Can I make you some coffee?"

"No, thanks, I've had plenty." He was reaching for his notebook as the bathroom door opened and Lorraine came out.

"Hello, Andrew," she said. DuBois was the state detective called in for serious crimes in Danmouth, and he lived nearby. Many of the residents knew him by name. "To what do I owe the honor of this visit?" She sat down in one upholstered chair and gestured that he should sit in the other.

"I'm afraid it's no honor at all," he said soberly, and took a breath. "Curtis Nickerson was killed last night."

Lorraine gasped and sat back in the chair. "Curtis? Dead?" She looked at Tim, and then at DuBois, and then at nothing at all. "Who on earth would want to kill Curtis? He kept so much to himself."

"Someone clearly did want to kill him, and it's my job to find out who. We'll be talking to everyone who had any connection with him, and I'm afraid I'm going to have to start by asking you where you were last night."

"I was here," she said. "We both were." She paused. "How . . . how . . ." She couldn't finish the question.

"I'm sorry, but I can't tell you how he was killed," the detective said matter-of-factly. "It may help our investigation if we don't release the details of the crime."

He asked them his standard list of questions and took careful notes. When he was through, he told them he might well need to question them again, and took his leave.

After he left, Tim wasn't quite sure what to say to Lorraine. As much time as he'd spent with her, it wasn't the kind of time that gave him insight into what she might need under these circumstances. She'd been married to the man, and although it was more than two decades ago, she must feel this acutely.

He went over to the chair where she was still sitting, and knelt at her feet. "I'm so sorry," he said.

She looked at him, dazed. "So am I. I can't quite believe it."

He looked at her a little helplessly. "Is there anything I can do?"

"I don't know," she said. "I honestly don't know. I can't believe that someone killed Curtis. I can't believe he's dead. I can't get my mind around it." She put her face in her hands and made a sound that seemed almost, but not quite, like a sob.

Tim reached for her hands and pulled her up out of the chair so he could put his arms around her. She held him tight, and they rocked back and forth.

They stood there, clasped together, for minutes. He had no idea what he could do to comfort her. He was shocked himself, but he had barely known the man and felt no grief. He knew she had stopped loving Curtis long ago, and felt no jealousy for her emotion. But Lorraine was obviously deeply affected.

He loosened his grasp so he could step back and look in her eyes, but she didn't let him go. Her head was on his shoulder, her arms around his neck, and she held him as though her very life depended on it.

"What can I do for you, baby; what can I do?" he whispered in her ear. He could feel her shaking in his arms. It crossed his mind that this was probably the most intimate moment they'd ever shared.

"Just hold me. Just hold me." Her voice was hoarse.

He did.

She rocked; she shook; she gripped him tightly. She did not cry.

Finally, she loosened her hold. She moved her head so her cheek was against his.

"I need you to make love to me," she said in his ear. As she said it, she moved her hands to his upper arms and gripped them tightly.

He wouldn't have been more surprised if she'd told him she needed him to stand on his head or recite the Pledge of Allegiance. Although sex was the foundation of their relationship, he'd assumed it would be the last thing on her mind at that moment.

"Now?" he asked, a bit stupidly.

"Now." Her voice had taken on a kind of urgency, but it wasn't of the intimate variety. She sounded remote, distracted, almost fierce, and she didn't look at him.

He wasn't quite sure how to respond to this, and for a moment he said nothing. She went on. "I couldn't tell you why. It's this confusing boil of emotions. I can't sort it out. I loved him once, but that was a long time ago. You'd think this wouldn't be so difficult." She still gripped him.

She still shook, and he assumed she was crying, but when he separated himself from her enough that he could see her face, he found her dry eyed.

"Death is hard," he said, with some tenderness.

She made a noise that was almost a snort. "Hard? Death is impossible. Death is devastating; death is permanent. Death can't be undone. It's just so fucking irrevocable." Her words ran together, and she again pulled him to her. Her fingernails were digging into his shoulders, and it was as though she were talking to herself, and not to him.

She suddenly pulled away from him and put her hands on his chest. "I . . . hate . . . death," she said, and hit his chest with the flat of her hand with each word. "I . . . need . . . life." She hit him again, harder.

This was a Lorraine Tim had never seen. She'd kept him at arm's length emotionally, and he'd caught only the barest glimpses of what was below her surface. Now, though, she was completely overtaken by whatever it was she was feeling. He felt as though he had a stranger in his arms.

His next surprise was that he found it compelling. Suddenly, the slap of her hand on his chest was arousing. Maybe sex *was* the best answer to death.

He took her face in his hands and kissed her. She kissed him back with a vengeance. Her lips pressed hard against his, and her tongue explored the surface of his tongue, the edges of his teeth. She drank from him.

The bed was behind a screen in the corner of the room, and she backed him toward it. When they reached it, she pushed him down on the edge of it and pulled his T-shirt over his head with some force.

When they'd first met, Lorraine had gotten a little rough once or twice, but it had been clear that it wasn't really his thing, and tenderness and gentleness had been her hallmark ever since. Now her energy and assertiveness reinforced the sense that he was about to make love to someone he didn't know.

He went with it. She pushed him back on the bed and practically yanked his flannel pajama pants down and off, and he imagined she was someone he had just met, someone whose name he didn't even know, someone whose eye he'd met at a party whom he'd taken into a strange bedroom. Someone in black leather boots.

Although Lorraine was dressed like he had been, in loose men's pajamas, imagining the black boots wasn't a stretch. She looked so fierce standing there by the side of the bed that he could imagine the whip that went with the boots. She took off her own clothes with the same ceremony with which she had removed his. He looked at the familiar body, but it wasn't Lorraine's anymore. It was his stranger's.

She stood there, naked, looking down at him, also naked. There was a steeliness, almost a coldness in her eyes. Her muscles were tensed and her mouth was tight. "I'm going to fuck you," she said.

This gave his fantasy a new dimension, and he felt a surge of pleasure.

He had a momentary sense of disloyalty for imagining she was someone else, but her strange behavior made it seem almost as if she *were* someone else.

"Fuck me," he said. "Fuck me hard."

She could see by the girth of his erection that he meant what he said, but it seemed to hardly matter. She took his cock in her hands and stroked it firmly, moving the taut skin against the hard rod beneath. He closed his eyes. He was back in that strange bedroom, and his cock was being stroked by a girl he'd just met. Why was the touch of someone strange so different from the touch of someone familiar?

Tim moaned and Lorraine stroked harder. It was almost—but not quite—to the point of pain.

And then it was pain. A sharp pain as she pinched his right nipple. He gasped, but there seemed to be a connection, a taut wire between the pain in his nipple and the pleasure in his cock. He wasn't sure he liked it, but it aroused him almost against his will. He closed his eyes and saw the stranger, and the boots.

Tim had never before deliberately imagined himself making love to someone other than the flesh-and-blood woman he was actually making love to. But Lorraine was being very peculiar, and it felt like she also was imagining herself somewhere else, with someone else. He went back to his stranger, to the bedroom at the party, and his cock was about as hard as it got when Lorraine straddled him in a way that was almost impaling. One moment he was outside her, and the next he was in. All the way in. She was wet. Soaked. Gushing.

She lifted herself up slowly so only the tip of his cock was left in her, and then dropped down again, hard. And then again, and he felt the lips of her cunt caress the sides of him as she lifted up. When she dropped down, it was as if he were under a waterfall—the sudden pressure, the slippery wetness. It was glorious.

Tim reached behind him and held the posts of the bed's headboard with both hands. His eyes were squeezed shut, and he gave himself over to the feel of an anonymous cunt, hot and wet.

Lorraine leaned forward slightly and put her hands on his chest. She took a nipple between the thumb and forefinger of each hand. As she lifted her body slowly up his cock, she squeezed his nipples, first softly and then, finally, hard—as hard as she had before. He again gasped at the combined sensation of the stab of pain and the slow pleasure of her wet pussy pulling off him, but he didn't open his eyes.

She did it again, and then again.

And then she stopped. He was back in real life in an instant, and he could tell that she was trying to keep herself from reaching orgasm. He lay completely still so she could recover herself, putting his imaginary partner on hold. Her breathing was fast; her eyes were closed; her concentration was obvious. He felt a small spasm from deep inside her, and he thought she might have been too late, but a moment later she started rocking, just a little, front to back. Her eyes didn't open, but his did, and he could see that she was far, far away.

His erection hadn't subsided at all, and so he closed his eyes and picked up right where he had left off.

She put her hands on his shoulders and leaned down so her breasts grazed his chest, her nipples moving up slowly and down quickly with her rhythm.

Then she made a noise he had never heard before. It was almost like a low, pulsating hum, and it fed his fantasy because it was new to him. It was soft as she was drawing herself off him, and then peaked as she dropped herself down.

With each stroke, it got a little louder, and both the Tim who was in the room and the Tim who was at the party knew there would be no stopping this time.

The physical sensations he was experiencing, coupled with the novelty of his fantasy, were bringing him to climax right along with her. Her hum told him they were right in sync, and he let himself build to orgasm as she gradually got louder, and harder, and faster.

And then she worked him like a piston, up and down, up and down. He felt her force, and her tightness, and her urgency. It was all so unfamiliar, so erotic, so novel. He came in an uncontrollable rush. He felt as though he were spurting his very life into her, that it was being pulled out of him by an ecstasy that reached deep inside him.

Lorraine's hum turned to a cry as she came with him. Her motion slowed, and softened, as she seemed to prolong the waves of her orgasm by rubbing herself against him.

And then, at last, she was still. She lay down on top of him, his penis still inside her, and put her head on his shoulder. She stayed that way for quite some time, and, as her body relaxed, he could feel Lorraine, the Lorraine he knew, coming back.

She propped herself up so she could look at him, and he could see that she was really seeing him this time. She was back to herself.

"I'm sorry," was what she said.

"Sorry?" he exclaimed. "What on earth do you have to be sorry about?"

"I forced this on you."

He knew that she was apologizing for not being fully present with him, but since he had taken advantage of the opportunity to not be fully present with her—and enjoyed it immensely—he didn't want her to feel bad.

"Look at me," he said, and shifted his weight so he could look in her eyes. "I have never, in my entire life, been forced into sex. I did it because I wanted to, and I loved every minute of it." This was absolutely true.

"Yeah," she said, "but it was weird that I wanted it, wasn't it?"

"Who's to say?" he said. "There's no accounting for how we react in extraordinary situations."

"No, I suppose there isn't." Lorraine kissed his cheek and rolled out of bed. In a few moments, he heard the shower running. He got up and pulled on running shorts and a T-shirt, and took his running shoes out from under the bed.

"I'm going for a run," he called to Lorraine, who was still in the shower, and he went out the door and down the stairs.

He had meant what he said about enjoying the sex. He had meant what he said about there being no accounting for how people reacted in extraordinary situations too. And although he couldn't help feeling that it *was* weird that she had wanted it, he was still marveling at how exciting it had been. Perhaps he should open his mind to sex that was more than soft and sweet.

As he ran, he pondered the possibilities.

It was several hours later that Andrew DuBois pulled into the state police barracks at Allerton, about ten miles from Danmouth. Although he'd worked there for three years, he still felt like a stranger.

In a way, he was a stranger to the police force in general. He'd been halfway through the coursework for a doctorate in philosophy when he'd decided he wanted to be a cop—a decision motivated by watching the police sift the evidence from the scene of the death of his roommate, who had died in a drunken fall from a fifth-story window. The tools they used to reconstruct the scene of the fall, the way they were able to establish that it had been an accident, the techniques they used to question witnesses, had all fascinated Andrew.

He'd dropped out of school, taken the test, and made it onto the Boston police force, where things hadn't been entirely comfortable for him. Most of his colleagues came from blue-collar families, and they were slow to warm to an overeducated newcomer whose parents were both professors and whose name was French. They called him DewBoys.

He was good at his job, though, and although he was never popular on the force, he was accepted. His abilities were noticed by the state police, and he was recruited to join them, and advanced quickly. When he was promoted to detective, he was transferred to the Allerton barracks.

Cape Cod was an insular place, and he had expected difficulties establishing both personal and professional relationships, but he eased into the community life without difficulty. He suspected that his natural quietness was interpreted as the kind of New England stoicism prized in the region. Nevertheless, he didn't feel quite as though he were one of them. He couldn't quite shake his otherness.

He'd finished his preliminary round of interviews with all but one of Curtis Nickerson's closest connections. Ethan Grant, his nephew and presumptive heir, was unreachable. He was a lobsterman, and had gone out that morning at dawn. He'd be back by late afternoon, DuBois estimated, and he'd try him again then.

The most difficult interview had been with Greta Silva, Nickerson's longtime girlfriend. DuBois had navigated it carefully. The significant other was always high on the list of potential suspects, and the detective looked attentively for signs of genuine surprise when he told her that Curtis had been murdered.

He had thought he saw them, but her reaction had been so subdued that it was hard to tell. She didn't gasp, or cry, or ask him why. She simply put her head in her hands and sat, silent. When she finally looked up at him her face was ashy pale. "What do you need to know?" she had asked in a hoarse whisper.

He had asked his questions, and she had answered in a straightforward way, without elaboration. Like every last person he spoke with, Greta had been home, in bed, asleep, when Nickerson had been killed. DuBois wished fervently that victims would all have the good grace to get murdered during the day, when people's whereabouts could be accounted for.

When he got back to the department, he steeled himself for the task that lay ahead of him—reconstruction of the presumed murder weapon. Curtis Nickerson had been killed by Angie, the ceramic figurehead that had been in his foyer his entire adult life. His head had been bashed in by a blow from the heavy statue, and the broken shards had been scattered all over the floor.

Under normal circumstances, putting those shards back together was the kind of job he'd turn over to the crime-scene unit, but they had no particular expertise in ceramics. He, however, had grown up with a mother who threw pots, and he had thrown his fair share himself. He knew the statue would have to be reassembled with great precision if he were to get good prints off it, and he felt as though he knew clay better than anyone else he might entrust this job to. Besides, he liked that kind of thing.

DuBois had been lucky that the man who had discovered the murder, seventy-year-old Caleb Jermyn, who lived a mile down the beach and made a habit of early morning walks, had seen what was clearly Nickerson's dead body through the window and knew enough not to walk all over a crime scene. He'd peered in to see whether Nickerson was up and about—they often shared a cup of coffee at that hour—and immediately called the police when he saw what had happened.

When the Danmouth police arrived, it was obvious that a homicide had taken place, and they'd called the state police—standard protocol in a town too small to have its own homicide detective. DuBois had been on call, and had gotten to the scene within half an hour.

He hadn't immediately been able to get close to the body for fear of stepping on one of the shards. Although he couldn't be absolutely sure, it certainly looked like Nickerson had been hit on the head, and whatever the weapon had been had shattered all over the floor. How those shards were scattered, and what they formed when he put them together, might be critical pieces of information.

He had asked Jermyn about Nickerson while he waited for the crime-scene techs to come and examine the house and grounds. Once the body had been photographed, the shards could be picked up and bagged, and DuBois could begin the painstaking process of putting them back together.

He found the job very absorbing. It was a big 3-D jigsaw puzzle, and, although it was difficult to find two pieces that fit together, he made enough progress to keep him from getting frustrated. The more progress he made, the smaller the pool of potential pieces from which to choose, and the faster he worked.

He was surprised when, two hours later, it was half-done. Jermyn had told him what the statue looked like, and had even sketched its shape for him, so he had some idea what he was trying to reconstruct. The hardest part wasn't fitting the parts, but avoiding smudging any fingerprints.

DuBois took a break, and tried again to get hold of Nickerson's nephew, Ethan Grant. This time, Grant answered his cell phone.

"Mr. Grant?" said DuBois. "I'm Detective Andrew DuBois, of the state police."

There was a pause. "You're calling about my uncle's death, yes?"

DuBois was relieved that Ethan had already heard of the murder. He hadn't been looking forward to telling him. "Yes, I am," he said. "I'm going to need to talk with you about it."

"I'm headed in right now," said the lobsterman. "I'm about half an hour out. Do you want to meet me on the dock?"

DuBois agreed, and half an hour later he watched Grant's lobster boat, the *Esmerelda*, pull into the marina. Grant jumped off the boat and tied it up to the dock.

He was a big man, well over six feet, and broad in the shoulders. He was in his mid-thirties, but had spent enough time in the sun to make him look older. A decade of physical labor had hardened him; all his movements gave the appearance of effortless strength.

DuBois introduced himself and the two shook hands. "I'm sorry about your uncle."

"So am I. We weren't that close, but he was a good man. He was also a tough old bird. It's hard to imagine someone killing him."

The two sat down on a bench by the water, and DuBois went through his list of questions. Grant had been asleep, alone, until five a.m., when he woke up to get to work. He was at the marina by five thirty, and on the water a few minutes later. That was where he was until just now. He knew about his uncle's death because he'd found six messages from friends and relatives on his cell phone when he picked it up after pulling his pots. All were some version of "Call me; it's important."

It was his father he called back, and from whom he heard the news.

Ethan's mother, Nickerson's sister, had died when he was a child, and he had been raised by his father. When Grant senior made the decision to move to Boston ten years before, Ethan had taken over the house and started his lobster business.

His father hadn't been happy with the decision. "For this I sent you to Harvard?" he had said.

"I think it would be an exaggeration to say you sent me to Harvard," his son had told him. Ethan had mostly paid his own way, and his father's contribution had been small, as were his means.

"But don't you think you're throwing away your education?"

"My education has made me an educated man, and you never throw that away."

They'd had many iterations of that discussion over the years, but it wasn't really a source of friction. His father, though an accountant, was easygoing at heart, and didn't really hold it against his son that he wanted to work outdoors with his hands.

Ethan's choice had brought him nearer to his uncle—both literally and figuratively. He now lived about ten miles from him, and his decision to make his living from the sea brought him into alignment with his uncle's worldview. Still, Curtis wasn't an easy man to know well, and although Ethan saw him regularly, he didn't think of them as close.

He explained this relationship to DuBois, and the detective asked him whether he knew his uncle well enough to know whether he had any enemies.

Ethan gave a little laugh. "It depends on what you mean by 'enemies.' A lot of people disliked him, but almost everyone respected him." He paused for a moment, thinking. "The only real enemy I can think of is Steve Cromwell—do you know him?"

DuBois shook his head.

"He's a commercial clammer, and he's gotten into trouble for poaching in the town shellfish beds. He hates—hated—my uncle." He corrected himself on the tense. "Curtis caught him taking quahogs at night and turned him in. He got a heavy fine and almost lost his license. They've been feuding ever since. That's his boat right over there." He pointed across the marina to a battleship-gray clamming boat.

As DuBois wrote down Cromwell's particulars, it occurred to Ethan that he himself might be suspected of the crime.

"I must be on your short list of suspects," he said.

"We're not ruling anyone out, or in, at this point."

"I think I inherit his estate. He always gave me to understand he'd leave everything to me. I know there's some complication about the house, something about when the Chapins gave it to the Nickersons in the first place. But if the house does go to me, I've certainly got a motive."

"Yes, you do," agreed DuBois, and looked at Ethan, waiting for him to go on and tell him he didn't kill his uncle.

But he didn't. "I'm going to miss him," was what he said.

DuBois asked him a few last questions, and then thanked him and turned to walk down the pier.

"Detective," Ethan called after him.

He turned.

"Am I responsible for his effects? For clearing out his house?"

"I don't know," said DuBois. "We haven't seen the will yet, so we're not ready to sort that all out."

"When will you know?"

"Probably by tomorrow."

Ethan Grant nodded and went back to his boat to unload his catch, and Andrew DuBois walked down to take a look at Steve Cromwell's boat. He was just writing down the registration number when a voice behind said, "Can I help you?"

It was Cromwell himself, and DuBois introduced himself and explained his business. Cromwell, like almost everyone on Cape Cod, had already heard of Nickerson's death, and wasn't surprised that the police wanted to question him.

The interview was short. Cromwell was straightforward about his feud with Nickerson. "I made one mistake, a long time ago, and Nickerson could never let me forget. Every time he saw my boat, he got out his damn binoculars to see where I was going. I couldn't stand the guy. But I wouldn't have killed him over it."

Where had he been the night before? "In bed, with my wife."

Did he know of anyone who might have wanted to kill Nickerson? "Besides me, you mean? Not really. Lots of guys didn't like him, but he never really did anyone any harm—he just pissed people off."

DuBois closed his notebook, thanked Cromwell, and went back to the police barracks to finish reconstructing his statue. He'd managed to get the hang of gluing the shards together, and it took him only an hour to finish it.

When he was finished, there were only a couple of tiny shards missing. He had fit everything together carefully, and any fingerprints ought to come off intact. He wasn't looking forward to sorting through all the fingerprints. Old Caleb Jermyn had told him that everyone who came through the door touched the head, and he expected to find samples from everyone Nickerson knew, layered and overlapping.

He checked the extension for Jessie Pratt, the fingerprint tech, and called as he looked at his watch. It was almost five o'clock, so he wasn't sure he'd get her, but she picked up on the first ring.

"Hey, Jess, it's Andrew. I've got a ceramic statue that needs dusting. It's probably covered with prints—it's got a smooth glaze that should be easy to read. Any chance you can take a look at it before you go home tonight?"

"Sure thing," she said cheerfully. "I'll be right up."

She came up with her kit and started dusting methodically, starting at the head and working down. "There's nothing here," she said.

DuBois was looking over her shoulder and could see that she was right. She'd begun with the part of the statue that ought to have been wall-to-wall prints, and there was nothing. Not even a partial. Not even a grease spot! It was perfectly clean.

Jessie slowly went over every inch of the thing and, just at the head, found one little smudge. At first, she wasn't even sure it was a fingerprint, but she looked at it under magnification and could make out a blurry pattern of whorls and lines.

"We've got a partial, but it's not a good one," she said.

"Is it good enough to submit?" DuBois asked, hoping they could send it to IAFIS, the FBI's fingerprint identification database.

"Not sure," said Jessie. "We might need some help from Boston on this one." They had better equipment and better-trained personnel. "Should I call Veronica?"

Veronica McSweeney was the go-to cop for tough fingerprint IDs. She was smart, and thorough, and very good at her job. She was also a curvy redhead who read a lot and swore like a sailor. Andrew liked her and was always glad to have a reason to call her in.

"Call Veronica," he said.

CHAPTER SEVEN

❧

Zoe was having a very bad day.

The news about Nickerson had floored her, and it was very difficult for her to try to make sense of it in Sam's presence. She couldn't tell him about their whiskey-fueled evening, or about Robert's contention that Nickerson wasn't what he seemed. She didn't know whether she and Curtis had made a kind of connection that night, or whether she'd just been his pawn.

After DuBois left, it was clear to Sam that she was distraught, and he didn't understand why.

"You didn't even like the guy," he had said, in puzzlement rather than censure. "Why are you so upset?"

She improvised. "A man gets murdered a quarter mile from my house, and you wonder why I'm upset?"

"But are you upset about *him*, or are you upset about the threat to *you*?" Sam asked, quite reasonably.

The threat to herself hadn't even occurred to her. She'd been so preoccupied with the idea that Nickerson was dead that she hadn't thought of it. But it was a convenient misdirection.

"It's both, of course," she said. "It's both. I'm worried because we're so isolated here, but I *knew* the man. He was here *yesterday*. I can't help but be upset." There was a note of irritation in her voice, which had gotten progressively higher in the course of her declaration.

"Sam," she said, lowering her voice and trying to sound reasonable. "It's been a shock. I just need time for it to soak in, and I'm sure I'll be fine."

Sam took her in his arms and kissed her forehead. "Is there anything I can do?"

"No," she said. "I think I'm going to tackle the basement."

Sam knew what this meant. Whenever Zoe had to deal with something that made her sad, or angry, or confused, she cleaned. She cleaned with a vengeance, and woe betide the dust or grime or germ that got in her way.

She changed into a grungy pair of shorts and an old T-shirt, tied her hair back, and assembled her arsenal of buckets, brushes, sponges, and cleaning products.

"Do you want some help with that?" Sam asked, but they both knew it was a halfhearted offer.

What Zoe really wanted was time to herself. "No, thanks," she said. "You know I always clean alone." She managed a smile, and headed for the stairs. "You know where to find me," she said over her shoulder.

She started in the far corner, behind the furnace, and she hadn't been at it for ten minutes before she broke a sweat.

That was when she heard the voice. *You're better off without him.*

Robert was back. She had wondered when he'd reappear, and had even looked forward to it. It was almost like when she'd had a good first date and was waiting for him to call again. But her shock over Nickerson's death overshadowed all those feelings.

"Better off without Curtis? I don't think so." She spoke in a voice barely above a whisper, so Sam wouldn't hear.

That's only because you didn't know him well enough.

"I think you might have misjudged him. I think he was kind of prickly, but straight-up." Now that he was dead, it was hard for Zoe to think ill of the man.

Robert made a harrumphing sound that buzzed in her brain.

That's the great Nickerson hoax. They're all like that—the men, at least. They're all just bad-natured enough to make everyone believe they're solid at the core. Why can't anyone believe that a man who seems *bad-natured is bad-natured? That is, after all, the simplest explanation.*

"But he isn't bad-natured. He's just a little cranky. Was a little cranky."

Now, why do you think that? Robert asked.

"You can just tell." As she said it, she wondered: Why *did* she think that?

How? What has he said or done to make you think he's a good guy masquerading as a bad guy, and not just a straight-up bad guy?

She considered. "He watched out for us when we were children. He knew where we went and what we did. He paid attention."

So he's an observant bad guy.

"He cares about this house," she said.

Robert made the harrumphing noise again. *He's jealous of this house. He wants to stop you from doing what you want to do because it's your house and not his. Nickersons have been jealous of Chapins ever since there were Nickersons and Chapins, and since you own the house now, you're just a Chapin by another name.*

A Chapin by another name.

She'd grown up coming to Danmouth each summer, spending two weeks with her family in a modest cottage a few blocks from the water. She'd played with the same kids—locals and visitors—each season. All the kids were intrigued by Chapin House, the big, rambling house on a spit of land also bearing the Chapin name.

They were equally intrigued by the house's sole inhabitant, Clara Chapin, who seemed to Zoe to be old enough to be medieval. And she was, in truth, very old—already almost ninety when Zoe was ten. She was old; she was solitary; she lived alone in a rambling house verging on dilapidation. All the kids had thought she was a witch, and most of them had been afraid of the house.

Zoe hadn't been afraid, though, and as she got older she grew to love the house. The Chapins were a seafaring family who could trace their roots back, if not to the *Mayflower*, then to the early 1700s. They had built this house, as well as several businesses that still bore their name. The name, and the house, represented everything that her family didn't have: wealth, history, roots.

The Chapins, and their house, represented the old America that Zoe's family, second-generation Polish immigrants (Belovski, they'd been) with a bloodline as confusing as a Boston street map, was a stranger to. She was by no means ashamed of her working-class parents, but it was something grander that she wanted for herself.

When selling her business gave her the means to buy it, what she wanted was Chapin House.

Although an old house couldn't put the patina of age on her new money, it could still give her a connection to the tradition, the stability, the respectability.

And now Robert had said she was a Chapin by another name. It made her blush. She was almost ashamed to think that a pedigree had such resonance for her, but she knew that it did.

Could he be right that Nickerson had simply been jealous? That he had been determined to quarrel with her not because he cared about the house, but because it pleased him to thwart her?

She'd been bending down to dust off the water pipes, which looked like they'd accumulated a decade's worth of crud, and she wiped her forehead with the back of her hand.

Don't mourn him, said Robert, and she felt what seemed like his breath on the back of her neck. *There's an impassable divide between Chapins and Nickersons, and you're on this side of it.*

Zoe recognized this as a shameless appeal to something closely related to snobbery, and recognized also that it was working. From her childhood, "Chapin" had meant roots, and sophistication, and money, and standing in the world. And now the very name triggered a Pavlovian response in her, reminding her of all that she had been missing in her own family, and how badly she wanted it.

She wasn't proud of that response, and she tried to swallow it. "I don't think buying the house makes me a Chapin," she said. She lifted her head a little higher to feel the barely perceptible caress around her neck.

No, but I'm glad you're here.

As she heard this, that barely perceptible caress became an all-enveloping warmth. It was a feeling Zoe had never had, and it was strange—as though she were suddenly wrapped in a weightless, invisible fur. It was the faintest pressure, just enough to let her know something was there.

She stood still, and it swirled around her. She closed her eyes. It felt as though it were inside her clothes, and her skin tingled from the contact. Her breath quickened.

You're very lovely. Irresistibly lovely, he said, as the pressure increased almost imperceptibly. It was a kind of grip, and it held her where she stood—or at least she thought it did. When she tried to move her leg, though, she found she could move it freely, and the grip simply moved with it, swirling and tingling all the while.

It warmed, and her skin warmed with it. And then it cooled, and she cooled.

You deserve the best of men, said the voice in her head, in a whisper she could barely hear. And then the presence, the pressure, started to work its way inside her. She gasped as she first felt it circling the lips of her cunt.

Let it happen.

She took a step back and leaned against the cold wall of the basement. She would let it happen. She spread her legs just a little and let it happen.

It was a strange feeling, the pressure coming inside her. The closest thing she'd ever experienced was when she and Sam had spent the night in a hotel room with a huge Jacuzzi, and he had positioned her right over the jet. The water had washed over her pussy and deep inside her, and it had brought her to climax faster than she had thought possible.

This was a gentler feeling. It ebbed and flowed, sometimes rhythmically, sometimes randomly. She closed her eyes and let herself simply feel it.

It was hard to lose herself in it, because she was a little afraid that Sam would come down to check on her. She periodically opened her eyes and looked toward the passageway that led to the stairs.

He's not coming. Don't even think about it.

And the pressure became a little more emphatic.

It worked its way between her legs. It brushed the tops of the insides of her thighs, and swooshed into the crease where her legs met her pubis. And then it went behind her, up between the cheeks of her ass.

She gasped again, surprised.

She felt the pressure rimming her asshole, going around, dipping in, coming out, and going around again. All the while, the jet in her cunt continued, and the feeling was intensified by the pressure on her ass.

She stopped thinking about Sam. She stopped thinking about everything.

She was enveloped by this pressure, and the tongues of it in her pussy and her ass felt as though they were meeting in her middle, igniting her.

And then there was a third tongue, just barely licking at the top of her lower lip. Her mouth was open just slightly, and she felt it ease in, flicking between her teeth and lips, tantalizing her. It was soft, but it was dry. It was warm, but it was insubstantial. It was ghostly.

The three tongues worked together, and they worked magic. They would pulse together, and then separately. Zoe tightened the muscles around the ones inside her without knowing she was doing it. It felt so much as if it were real.

She never completely lost her awareness of who was doing this to her. She had that picture in her mind, the picture of the man she'd seen in the mirror, the handsome blond man with the fisherman's sweater.

She didn't just want *this*. She wanted *him*.

In her mind, this wasn't a disembodied presence. It was Robert Chapin. He was fucking her against the wall of the basement. He was fucking her under the very feet of her boyfriend. He was fucking her in a way that she couldn't resist.

He fucked her to an orgasm that made her toes curl. It took over her body and made every muscle stiffen. Her breath, her heart, her mind—all gave way to its power.

The presence and the pressure remained until all was again still within her. And then it withdrew.

I'll be back, Robert said. *Soon.*

Zoe sat down on the floor, recovering herself, and then considered.

It was Sam she was considering. Over the last few days, her doubts about him had become clearer to her. She thought, looking back, that they'd always been there, but she'd been unwilling to pull them out from the dark recesses of her mind and expose them to the light of day.

Now her changed circumstances—this house, this ghost—had made her confront them. And, once she had articulated those doubts to herself, she knew there was no help for it: She was going to have to split up with him.

But would she have to do it today? She knew that she could use his company and support as she tried to deal with the aftermath of Nickerson's death, but she also thought that, once she made up her mind to part with him, she should do it right away. Anything else would be unfair and false.

She sat there for a good fifteen minutes, steeling herself to the task. And then she went upstairs.

Sam was sitting at the kitchen table, his laptop open in front of him.

"Your wi-fi works pretty well," he said. "Is the basement sparkling clean? And, more important, do you feel better?"

She sat down across from him. "One little corner of the basement is sparkling clean, and it has come home to me that it is a very large basement," said Zoe. "As for feeling better, I really don't know." She looked at him, pointedly and sadly. "In a way, I feel worse."

As she'd sat in the basement, she tried to figure out how to do this, what she could say that would be least hurtful. She had seen that something crucial was missing, but if he pressed her to tell him just what that crucial element was, she wouldn't know what to say. She couldn't very well tell him she'd been convinced by a ghost that he wasn't good enough for her.

She needn't have worried. As soon as Sam saw her face, he suspected what was coming. "This isn't about Nickerson, is it?" he asked, looking hard into her eyes. She shook her head. "It's about you and me?" She nodded and felt unexpected tears welling up.

"You're breaking up with me, aren't you?"

She nodded again.

He closed his computer and asked, simply, "Why?"

There was nothing angry or hostile in his tone. It was gentle and sweet.

"It doesn't feel right," she said. "I find myself looking for something permanent, and I don't think we're it." A couple of tears made their way out, despite Zoe's best efforts to contain them. "I just don't think we're right for each other," she said.

Sam got up, walked around the table, and came over to kneel at her feet. "Why are you crying if this is what you want?" he asked gently.

Why couldn't he have gotten angry? Or at least been hurt? Why did he have to be so damn reasonable? And kneeling there, looking up at her with doe eyes? Was he doing this on purpose?

She couldn't hold it back any longer, and she started sobbing.

It wasn't just that she was saying good-bye to Sam. It was partly the shock of Nickerson's death, partly the confusion of making sense of her feelings about Robert, and partly a general sense of being completely at loose ends, unmoored from her familiar life.

It all came over her at once, and she was shaking, gasping, weeping. And, through it all, she was ashamed. She knew she and Sam had to part—it was her decision to break up with him—yet here she was, crying like a schoolgirl.

Sam took one of her hands in his and gently stroked it as she tried to get her emotions under control. His question had been perfectly legitimate. Why *was* she crying if this was what she wanted?

It took a few minutes for her to get her tears down to a trickle. When she could talk again, she answered him. "Because I like you. Because there were times when I thought we might have a future. And because it's sad. It's just sad."

He put one hand on the back of her neck and with the other patted her thigh softly. "I know," he said.

She put her head on his shoulder. "I'm sorry," she said.

He stroked her hair. "Me too."

But Zoe wasn't at all sure he was. She couldn't make out whether he was hurt and hiding it masterfully, or whether this was actually something he wanted, and her breaking up with him saved him the trouble of breaking up with her. It had never occurred to her, until that moment, that *he* might have had doubts about the relationship.

This threw her for a loop. She'd been prepared for protestations, for questions, even for anger, but not for this reasonable acceptance that was downright supportive. And then there was that perverse but inevitable sense that if *he* had wanted to split up with *her*, he was that much more desirable.

But if she took what he said at face value, it ought to make this easier. "I'm sorry," she said again, looking at him through tear-reddened eyes.

He stood up. "I guess I should go."

She nodded, but neither of them moved for a moment. And then Sam said, "I'll go pack my things," and went upstairs.

Zoe sat at the table with her head in her hands. She hadn't expected to feel this unhappy. Why had it seemed so clear when she was down in the basement, and so much less clear now that she'd actually done it? She went through her rationale again, trying to make herself as sure as she'd been a half hour earlier.

It worked, sort of. In the few minutes it took Sam to collect what belongings he had, she'd worked herself back to some semblance of certainty that she was doing the right thing.

When he came downstairs with his bag, though, that certainty was hard to hold on to. The thought that she'd never kiss him, never make love to him, maybe even never see him again was hard to bear, certainty or no certainty.

She stood up and walked with him to the door, neither of them saying a word.

He got to the door and she opened it for him. He went halfway out and turned around. She was holding the door open, leaning against the doorframe. The sunlight came from behind him, and she saw the man who had first attracted her at the gallery opening. She touched his cheek and kissed him softly.

She tasted the sweetness, the familiarity, and she wanted, desperately, to kiss him again. But she knew where that would lead, and she mustered all the discipline at her command. "Good-bye, Sam," she said.

He gave her a half smile, turned around, and left.

She closed the door before she had a chance to change her mind. When she heard his motorcycle start and growl away down the driveway, she knew she was alone.

She felt her eyes fill once more, but she was determined to shed no more tears over this. Without knowing precisely where she was going, she picked up her wallet and her car keys and left the house, locking the front door behind her. Alone was what she didn't want to be.

As she drove, she thought maybe she'd go to the bakeshop and have coffee, maybe talk to the locals about what had happened to Nickerson. She needed something to connect her to the world around her.

As she parked the car, though, she thought better of the bakeshop. Instead, she went around the corner to Lorraine's studio.

She wasn't at all sure she'd find Lorraine there. She must have heard that her ex-husband had been murdered, and no one could blame her if she needed a day or two to absorb the news before she opened up shop again.

But the OPEN sign was on the door, and Lorraine was inside alone, up to her elbows in clay.

She looked up when she heard the door open.

"Hey, Zoe," she said. "Nice to see you. Give me a moment to clean up."

She turned off her wheel and washed her hands. "You've heard, of course?" she said. Zoe nodded. "I'm so sorry. Even though it was a long time ago, it must be hard to lose someone you were married to."

Lorraine sighed. "It is. Surprisingly hard, I'd say. I wouldn't have thought I had any feelings for Curtis at all, but when I heard he was dead . . ." She trailed off. She shook her head briskly, to dispel those feelings, and then offered Zoe a cup of coffee, which her visitor gratefully accepted.

The two women sat at the little table in the back of the shop and talked about Curtis. They speculated as to who might have killed him, but neither woman had any idea. Lorraine told Zoe stories from her marriage, and Zoe talked about her regret that the last conversation she'd had with him had gone so badly, although she omitted the part about the evening with the whiskey.

"I wouldn't worry about that," Lorraine said. "Curtis had conversations like that all the time, and he took them in stride. He wouldn't have held it against you."

As she had in their one previous meeting, Zoe felt comfortable with Lorraine, as though she'd known her for years instead of days. And, as she had in their one previous meeting, Zoe ended up telling Lorraine much more than she'd intended. Lorraine's ready smile and warm candor made Zoe feel like she had a friend, and a friend was just what she needed.

When she walked into the shop, she certainly hadn't planned to talk about Sam, but talk of Curtis seemed to lead her there, and she told Lorraine the whole story of their relationship and its end. From there, it was just a hop, skip, and a jump to Robert. Although Zoe left out some of the more intimate details, as well as Robert's theory that Nickerson wasn't what he seemed, she confessed to being taken with a ghost.

"It sounds so silly when I tell you about it," she said, "but he feels so real." She sighed a little sigh. "And he's incredibly beautiful."

"You've seen him?" Lorraine asked, and sat back in her chair.

Zoe grinned. "I have."

"All of him?" Lorraine asked.

Zoe's grin widened. She nodded.

"Wow," said Lorraine. "That's wild."

And from there, most of the intimate details she'd omitted came out. It felt so good, so normal, to be talking to a girlfriend about a guy.

When Zoe had finished the story, Lorraine leaned over her coffee cup and smiled broadly. "Nothing like a good session of ghost sex to make you feel at home in your house, eh?"

Zoe nodded. "Weirdly, it does. But for all I know, he's a figment of my imagination."

"Then it's your imagination telling you something, that you've entered a new chapter of your life, that you're moving on from Sam. You should listen."

Zoe nodded. It seemed mercenary to be thinking about moving on while Sam's spot in her bed was still warm, but she had split up with him because moving on was exactly what she wanted—needed—to do.

"Now that you've cleared the decks, I assume you've got your antennae up for what Danmouth and environs have to offer in the way of menfolk."

Zoe gave a half smile. She couldn't decide whether Lorraine was refreshingly candid or disconcertingly crass. Candid, she decided. Any young, single, red-blooded woman would be aware of the young, single, red-blooded men she happened to meet. "It's only been about fifteen minutes," she said. "But give me a couple of days and I'll think about getting back on the horse."

"There's a horse named DuBois who might deserve your consideration," Lorraine said, raising her eyebrows. "If I were twenty years younger . . ."

Zoe laughed. She had, of course, noticed the detective's youth and good looks, but the circumstances of their meeting had all but ruled out thoughts along those lines. "Somehow, dating and murder investigations don't go together very well."

They went on to talk about a few other local possibilities. It was just girl talk, but it made Zoe feel grounded again. On the heels of a murder and a breakup, it was just what she needed.

Their talk was interrupted by customers, and while Lorraine helped them pick out a set of bowls, Zoe wandered around, looking again at the pieces in the studio, picking one up here and there. Seeing Lorraine's work, the product of her imagination and her wheel, made Zoe miss, for the first time, her days of running a business. Yes, she'd been stressed and overworked. Yes, she'd had daily frustrations with employees and suppliers and logistics. But she'd been doing work she felt good about. She'd been helping people plant gardens, grow things.

When she'd sold the business, she had looked forward to a life of leisure, but now had an inkling it wouldn't suit her. Although she certainly planned to enjoy her time off, she could foresee the time that she'd want to do something, to make something, to build something.

A few more customers came in, and it was apparent that Lorraine would be busy for a while, so Zoe said her thanks and headed for the door.

"Come back soon," Lorraine said. "There's always coffee on."

Zoe said she would, and meant it.

CHAPTER EIGHT

❧

The day after Nickerson's death, Andrew DuBois found that he had died intestate. The lawyer who had handled his very few legal affairs, a man named Chad Helmsworth, not only had no will on file, but told DuBois that Nickerson had talked to him just the month before about drawing one up.

"He said it was high time he did something about his estate," Helmsworth told DuBois.

"Did he give you any indication of how he was planning to dispose of it?"

"Not a clue. Nickerson was pretty tight-lipped."

"Absent a will, who inherits?"

"As far as I know, Ethan Grant is his next of kin. His sister's dead, and he's got no kids of his own. Under normal circumstances, the nephew would get everything. But the house is a special case. There's a stipulation in the original gift of the property to the Nickerson family that specifies it has to stay in Nickerson hands or it reverts to being part of the Chapin property. It's a kind of entail, requiring that the house be passed from son to son. No son, no house. It's a very strict stipulation and it's written almost as though the guy who wrote it *wanted* it to revert back to Chapin hands. I mean, who can count on having a son?"

"And Curtis Nickerson knew about this?"

"Sure. But I don't think he thought much about it. He certainly never indicated to me that he thought he should go out and have himself a son. Maybe he didn't care what happened after he was dead, or maybe he just thought it wouldn't stand up in court. A lot of these kinds of things, particularly if they're this old, don't. I'm not sure if he assumed the house was his to dispose of as he pleased, or if he assumed it wasn't, and he just wanted to talk about his personal effects."

"If he did think it was his to dispose of, do you have any sense of how he would have wanted to do it?" DuBois asked.

The lawyer shrugged. "No idea. Like I said, Nickerson was pretty tight-lipped. I don't know what he thought of Grant, but he had a strong sense of family, and it's hard to imagine he would have wanted to leave it to an outsider, even if he could." Helmsworth cocked his head to one side, considering. "If I had to guess, I'd guess he'd leave it to Ethan. But that's just a guess."

"One last question," Andrew said. "Would the fact that Chapin House is no longer in Chapin hands affect the will? Could the Nickerson house really go to Zoe Bell?"

"I couldn't tell you. The will specifies that it reverts to the 'Chapin estate,' but whether that would be interpreted to still exist after it's been sold is hard to know."

DuBois thanked him and left. He then called Grant to see if he was at home. He was, and DuBois asked if he could pay a visit.

Grant lived in a tiny cottage abutting a marsh. When DuBois drove up, he thought it was the guest cottage, or even a shed, and he looked around for the main house. Only when Grant came out the front door did he realize it *was* the main house.

The men shook hands, and Grant invited him in. He gestured to a sleek leather chair, out of place in the rustic surroundings, but DuBois shook his head. "I'll only be a minute. I found out about your uncle's will." He had come solely with the purpose of trying to read Grant's face, and he watched him closely as he said, "He died without one."

Grant nodded. "That's in character," he said.

"The estate has to go through probate, but as his next of kin you're the presumed heir of everything but the house."

"There's some kind of stipulation with the house, isn't there? It's supposed to pass down through the male line."

"There is, and that's my understanding of it."

"I assume I don't count because it was my mother who was a Nickerson."

"That's a question for the lawyers. There may have to be a legal battle."

Grant nodded again. "It's a beautiful house," he said. His tone was neutral. "But it's not worth a court fight. Is it okay if I go take a look at it?"

"The house itself is still a crime scene, and we've roped off some areas outside, but you're welcome to go see the place."

DuBois left, feeling as though his visit had gained him nothing. Grant also left, a few minutes after the detective, and drove over to the Nickerson place.

He'd known the house all his life, and he'd always had mixed feelings about it. He loved the setting and the sea. He loved the idea of living out on the beach, away from almost everyone.

It was that "almost" that was the fly in his ointment. He hadn't been fond of Clara Chapin, and the centuries-old relationship between the Chapins and Nickersons galled him. "It's archaic," he had told Curtis. "It's like the landed gentry condescending to the hired help."

His uncle had been philosophical about it to his nephew. "That relationship landed us this house, and a long tradition of meaningful work. Until you, none of us went to college, and this"—here he gestured to the house, the beach, and the water—"isn't a bad gig for a kid with a high school education."

Grant had conceded the point, but it had never stopped galling him.

He rambled over the grounds, along the beach, and then through the upland, absorbing the idea that the house might be his. He rambled a little too far and found himself within hailing distance of Chapin House just as Zoe was coming out the back door, a trowel in one hand and a cold drink in the other. Her fingernails were black, and there was a dirty streak down her cheek where she'd rubbed her hand on it. She'd been gardening, trying to clear some of the underbrush out from between the wild blueberry bushes that lined the side of the house.

She put down the trowel and held her hand over her eyes to try to identify her visitor. She didn't recognize him and was a little apprehensive. Although strangers wandered around the beach all the time, now the idea that a stranger might be a murderer was always in her mind.

Ethan waved. "Hello," he shouted, and walked up toward the deck. When he got close enough that he could make himself properly heard, he introduced himself.

She relaxed a bit when she learned he was Nickerson's nephew.

"I came to take a look at the house. I spent some time here when I was a kid."

Zoe stiffened just a little. Wouldn't he, as next of kin, inherit the house? And wasn't that kind of thing always the motive in murders? And why didn't she know him if he was here when he was a child? She judged that they were about the same age.

But he certainly didn't look threatening. He was big, but he spoke in a quiet, circumspect way.

"You've been digging in the dirt," he said.

"I've been trying to clear some space around those blueberries." She gestured to the corner of the house.

Ethan nodded. "Those have been there since I was a kid," he said. "There used to be a gardener who took care of all the landscaping, but I can see it's gone to hell."

Although Zoe herself would have described it that way, she wasn't sure she appreciated a stranger's coming here and saying it.

She thought it was in her interest to make sure she and Ethan got off on the right foot, though, so she said nothing. Instead, she asked him whether he wanted a glass of iced tea.

"I'd love one."

She invited him on the deck and went in for another glass.

She came out and found him standing at the rail, looking over the water.

"I spend a lot of time doing that," she said.

"No matter how much of my life I spend on the water, I never get tired of it."

"Do you spend a lot of your life on the water?"

"I lobster for a living."

"Oh." Zoe wasn't sure what to say about that. She didn't know the first thing about lobstering. But she knew that being a lobsterman wasn't like being a doctor or a lawyer, or even an aspiring painter, and she subconsciously slotted him into "blue-collar" in her mind.

After a pause, she said, "Do you live on the Cape now?"

"Yup. Just two towns over. I was born and raised here."

"And you've been here ever since?"

"More or less." He didn't mention that he'd left the Cape for college, and worked in Boston for a couple of years after his graduation.

Zoe found this conversation to be slow going, and she felt that Ethan wasn't holding up his end. Were all the Nickersons impossible to talk to? She decided that it was now his job to say something, and she asked him nothing else.

But Grant seemed perfectly content with silence. He drank his tea; he looked out at the waves and seemed to be at his ease.

If he was going to be her new neighbor, she wanted to be on friendly terms. It also hadn't escaped her notice that he was attractive, and her thoughts returned to Lorraine's injunction to keep her antennae up. But he didn't have much to say for himself, his social skills certainly weren't up to par, and this was not an auspicious beginning.

Finally, she looked at her watch. "I've got to run into town before the general store closes," she said. "I'm sorry to chase you off."

"I was the one who was trespassing," he said, handing her his empty glass.

"Will you be staying at the house?"

"No," he said. "It's still a crime scene. But I'll be going through his stuff as soon as DuBois gives me the go-ahead."

Zoe nodded. "I'm sure I'll see you around."

He nodded in turn. "Thanks for the tea." And he went down the stairs and off toward the Nickerson place.

Zoe did want to get to the general store before it closed, and when he was gone she got in the car and drove into town. She could see, as she approached the store, that Tom, Dick, and Harry were in their appointed spots.

She also saw that the population sign, which had been changed to 814 when she bought Chapin House, had been changed back to 813 now that Curtis Nickerson was dead.

She stood at the bottom of the store's steps for a moment, looking at the sign.

"Nickerson," said one of the men.

She nodded.

"Did you do it?" asked another of the three.

She shook her head. "Did you?"

That earned her a stifled guffaw. But she didn't want to talk to them about Nickerson. She wanted to find out the story of her ghost. She decided it was time for another assault on their storehouse of knowledge.

She walked up the stairs, leaned against a post, and looked at the three men. She smiled and nodded to the two she had met before, and turned her attention to the third, a wizened man with sun-damaged skin and an ancient fishing hat.

"You must be Tom," she said. "Or Dick, or Bartholemew."

"Or Harry," the little man said.

"Or Harry," Zoe conceded. "So, you keep everyone guessing so that, when one of you dies, nobody'll be quite sure which one, and the others can collect his Social Security?"

The two she'd met before—she was now thinking of them as Tom and Dick, strictly because of the chronology of her meeting them—looked serious, as though they might consider this scheme. Harry, though, cracked a smile.

"Not a bad idea," he said.

Zoe felt like this was a small triumph.

"So, Harry," she said to him, using the name decisively. "Do you believe in ghosts?"

"What's not to believe in? The place is crawling with them."

"So I'm not the only one with a ghost?"

"You've got a ghost of your very own?" Harry asked.

"I don't know if he's my very own, but he certainly is making a nuisance of himself."

"It's Robert," Tom said, leaning across Dick and addressing Harry.

Harry nodded sagely. "Ah. It's Robert." He shook his head and tsk-tsked.

"Do you know my ghost?"

"I knew your ghost before he was a ghost," Harry said.

Zoe was startled. Had she done the math, she would have realized that any son of Clara's who lived to be at least thirty would have overlapped time on this earth with anyone over about sixty. Harry appeared close to ninety.

"When did he die?"

Harry settled back in his chair. "Let's see," he said. "It was before I married Helen, so it must have been 1950 or 1951."

"And you knew him?"

"Oh, sure. Everyone knew him."

Zoe looked at Tom and Dick, her expression asking the question. But Harry scoffed. "Those two? They're wash-ashores. They haven't been in this town more than forty years, either of them."

Tom made a wry face, and Dick said, "I can see why you're so proud of never leaving this place your entire life. Makes for a life of excitement and sophistication."

Zoe wasn't sure if she was supposed to smile, so she looked at the floor to hide it.

"What was he like?" she asked when she looked up.

"He was no good." Harry scowled. "He was a trial to his mother, and I always thought he killed that poor Nickerson girl."

Zoe's eyebrows levitated in surprise. "He killed a girl?" she said.

"They never proved that," Tom said.

"You weren't there," Harry said. "He killed Molly, as sure as we're sitting here."

"What happened?" Zoe asked.

"He was engaged to marry her, but his mama didn't like it," said Dick. "She thought Chapins were Chapins and Nickersons were Nickersons, and she didn't want to confuse the bloodlines."

"So he killed her?" It seemed far-fetched to Zoe.

"It's not like he stabbed her or shot her or drowned her," Dick went on. "She got hit by a train."

"Did people think he pushed her?"

"Oh, it's a long story," Harry said slowly, and then looked out in the distance and rocked back and forth. Zoe got the sense that she wasn't going to get the story out of him, at least not today. But she had to give it a shot. "I figure, if it's my ghost, I ought to know."

"Maybe you'd better ask your ghost, then," said Harry, but not unkindly.

She knew a dismissal when she heard one, so she bought her groceries and headed back to Chapin House.

Zoe wasn't much of a cook, and when she made a meal for herself it was more assembly than actual cooking. She'd bought some chicken thighs and a big Chinese cabbage, and she pan-fried the chicken and put together a chicken salad with a soy-lemon dressing and some packaged fried noodles.

She took it out on the back porch, along with a beer. As she ate, she willed Robert to reappear. She wasn't sure he'd tell her what really happened, but she was eager to ask.

She didn't ask, though, because he didn't show. This was the first time she had really wanted him to come out, and she was disappointed that she couldn't summon him with her thoughts. She went to bed disappointed.

In the morning, though, when she wasn't thinking about him, there he was, in the form of breath on the back of her neck. She had gotten to the point where she thought she could tell when he was with her, although she realized he could probably be there without making his presence known.

For the first time, she started the conversation.

"Robert?"

He answered with warmth and a whisper.

She wasn't sure how to launch into her questions about Molly. Were you supposed to make small talk with a ghost? Say "good morning"? Ask him how his day was going? No, she thought, and launched right into it. "I heard about you and Molly."

There was a pause, and an absence. She waited, afraid he'd gone away.

It was a full minute before he said, *I loved her.*

And then he told her the story.

Robert Chapin and Molly Nickerson had been born months apart in 1922, and they'd known each other all their lives. Robert's father had died shortly after he was born, of a debilitating shrapnel wound he'd sustained in World War I, and which sapped his health until it took his life. His mother, Clara, depended on Molly's father, the Nickerson of the day, to maintain the house and grounds, a service for which she paid him well.

As children, Robert and Molly played together, swam together, sailed together, explored together. It was when they were eighteen, the summer between high school and Robert's going off to college, that they went from being playmates to being lovers.

It happened in a boat.

It had been a beautiful August day, the kind that you think of when you think of summer on Cape Cod. Robert had a little catboat that he sailed in the harbor that was just west of Chapin House, and on that beautiful August day he took Molly for a picnic on a little spit of land accessible only by water.

Since Clara had suspected that Robert's affection for Molly was taking a romantic turn, she had been trying to dissuade him from spending a lot of time with her, but Robert was old enough to have his own ideas about the people he wanted to spend time with, and he was very determined to spend time with Molly.

Still, he didn't want to incur more of his mother's displeasure than was necessary, and so he packed picnic provisions in a wicker basket on the sly, when Clara was out tending to her perennial garden.

He stashed the basket in the boat and fetched Molly from the Nickerson cottage. Out they sailed.

When they reached their destination, Robert saw that they weren't the only people who thought a picnic on the beach was a good idea— there were already several people there. So instead of landing, Robert sailed to the end of the spit, anchored about a hundred yards off the beach, and opened the basket.

They ate; they drank; they talked; they laughed. And then they stretched out on the floor of the boat.

It was a calm day, and it was inevitable that the gentle rocking of the sea would take them where they seemed destined to go.

They were eighteen, and they ached for each other. Robert felt his erection straining through his shorts, and the desire he felt was overwhelming.

He turned on his side and looked at Molly, lying on her back on the boat's wooden planking. He touched her cheek and, when he kissed her for the first time, he couldn't understand why it had taken him so long to do it. She tasted of sweet and salty sunshine, and her lips were warm from heat both within and without.

He kissed her as though she were the source of his sustenance, and she kissed him back.

She was wearing a light, sleeveless cotton blouse, and he unbuttoned it, starting at the top. He was a little afraid she would stop him, that she might not be ready for this, but her need was as acute as his own.

Her breasts were small, the nipples barely darker than the flesh surrounding them, and when Robert cupped one of them in his hand, he was momentarily afraid the mere feel of her skin would send him to orgasm.

He controlled himself with an effort.

This wasn't the first time he'd had a girl's naked skin up next to him, but his experience wasn't extensive enough that he was confident. Besides, other girls weren't Molly. His excitement, his arousal, his trepidation filled him to bursting.

He unbuttoned her blue cotton shorts, but wasn't quite sure where to go from there, so he bought time by pulling his own striped jersey over his head.

He had a boy's smooth skin, but a man's taut musculature, and Molly stroked its outlines. He watched her eyes as she ran them over his body, and then met them as she raised her head. She smiled. He melted. All would be right with the world as long as Molly could be his.

Her smile emboldened him, and he slipped her shorts and underpants off. She lay there, absolutely naked, tan and slim, firm and warm.

He touched her everywhere. He wanted to know what every square inch of her felt like. He wanted to know that the skin on her shins felt different from the skin on her forearms, that her thighs had give but her calves were firm, that she was ticklish.

Never in his life had there been anything of which he could not get enough, until this girl.

He took off his shorts and, as he lay on his side next to her, he marveled at the sight of his own penis, so familiar to him, lying up against the female hip, so unfamiliar.

Molly followed his eyes, propped herself up on one elbow, and tentatively reached for him. With one fingertip, she traced a line from the head of his cock down to its base, and then back up again.

For that one fingertip, he would have done anything. Still, he had to stop her. He knew his limits.

He couldn't look at her without wanting to kiss her, and so he kissed her again and again. He stroked her cheek and her hair and her breasts. He leaned over and kissed where he had stroked. He was completely absorbed by the feel of her, the look of her, the very idea of her.

He moved his hand between her legs, and they parted for him, welcoming him. He felt the warmth, and he felt the glistening dew. He wasn't quite sure how to navigate the complicated folds, but he went softly and slowly, and she moved under him to adjust his touch.

He knew he'd done something right when he heard a sharp little intake of breath, and her hips strained toward him of their own accord.

He got up and straddled her, his balls sitting high on the mound he had just been caressing.

"Are you ready?" he asked, and watched her intently as she nodded.

"We don't have to," he said. "I can wait." He wasn't sure whether that was strictly true, but he wanted it to be.

Molly reached up and took his hands.

"I've been ready," she told him. "Maybe for longer than you realize."

He was a little surprised at this, but it quelled any doubts he might have had about taking the virginity—for he assumed she was a virgin—of the girl he'd known all his life.

He knelt between her legs, and she guided him to the edge of her, and then in. He went in slowly, expecting that this would be painful for her.

If it was, she gave no sign. His whole length was in, and it seemed she felt nothing but pleasure. Her eyes were half-closed, her mouth half-open. Her hips rose to him.

He closed his own eyes and gave himself over to the best thing he'd ever felt in his young life. To be enveloped, to be held, to be welcomed. To feel her very being as he moved in and out. It was unbearably moving.

He stopped and took a breath. He tried to send his mind somewhere else so he could calm down. It worked, but not for long. An irresistible force compelled him to pull out, to thrust in.

And then, to his surprise, he heard her gasp and let out a long, high-pitched cry. He felt the spasm of her orgasm pull him deeper inside her, and it brought his own pleasure to a sharp, intense climax.

He made no sound, but his shudders must have told her all. The feeling was astonishing, all-encompassing. He had made love to a woman.

He lay down on her, his face buried in her neck, and she put her arms around him and held him. And then he wept. It wasn't a childish sobbing, but a dignified, emotional shedding of tears. He felt as though something important—even something momentous—had happened to them. On this warm August afternoon, they had closed the book on their childhood. It had been time.

They lay in the bottom of the boat, rocking with the waves, looking up at the clouds, saying nothing. They didn't head for home until the sun started to set.

He sailed the boat skillfully right up to the Chapin dock, and Molly jumped out to tie it fast. He lowered the sail, made everything shipshape, and then the two walked up the dock together.

She had to get home, he knew, and he kissed her once, softly, and watched her go.

This kiss was seen by Clara from the kitchen window, and told her all she needed to know. She knew she must separate them, but she knew it wouldn't be easy.

Life intervened to make her job a little easier. First, Robert went off to Harvard that fall, and she supposed, correctly, that he wouldn't marry Molly until he had graduated. Then, in his sophomore year, America entered the Second World War, and he immediately left school to enlist. Before he went overseas, though, he gave Molly a little pinkish white ring, carved out of a whelk shell. No formal words were spoken, but they both knew what it meant. Clara knew nothing about it.

It was only when the war was over, and he was back completing his studies, that the danger of his fulfilling his unspoken promise to Molly was imminent. He was as attached to her as ever, and Clara's campaign began in earnest. Try as she might, though, she couldn't talk him out of Molly. He loved her, and he was going to marry her as soon as he finished Harvard and Harvard Law, where he had already been accepted.

Clara's trump card was Chapin House, and the money that went with it. If Robert married Molly, she would disinherit him completely.

This threat stunned Robert. He had never thought his mother would go to those lengths. But he didn't care. He would stand by the girl, and they would make their own way in the world together.

That was what he told her, and he meant what he said.

Then, one night just after his law school graduation, they took a long walk on the beach. They ended up miles from home, and they quarreled.

The quarrel was about a job offer. Robert had been courted by a Chicago law firm, and they had put a very generous salary and benefits package on the table for his consideration. He had been inclined to take it, but Molly wanted him to stay on the Cape, or at least closer to home, for at least another year or two.

She was pregnant. And she wanted to have the baby close to home, with friends and family around her.

This took Robert by surprise. He'd thought Molly would rejoice at his success and want to join him in Chicago that fall as his wife. He had a hard time re-envisioning their lives in light of this news, and when he wasn't quick enough to give up his plan, or warm enough in his expressions of happiness that they were to have a child, Molly ran from him, saying she'd find her own way home.

They found her body the next morning, thirty yards from the tracks she'd been thrown from when the train hit her. The conductor hadn't even realized he'd hit something, and was astonished when he was told that his train had killed a girl the night before.

Robert never recovered. He never loved again, and not a day went by, for the rest of his life, that he didn't mourn the woman who was to have been his wife.

Zoe thought she should have been moved by this story, but the way it was being told to her—by a disembodied voice—and the nature of the boy-loves-girl tragedy gave it a fairy-tale quality that kept her from feeling real sadness. There was also that one question she had to ask.

"Why do they say you killed her?"

Because they don't know what happened.

Zoe persisted. "But what do they *think* happened?"

They think I jilted her, and she threw herself in front of that train.

It couldn't have been that simple, she thought, and she wanted to know more. Why did they think that? But she was stopped from asking the question by a knock on the front door.

CHAPTER NINE

S he opened the door to Andrew DuBois.

"I'm afraid I need to ask some more questions, Ms. Bell," he said. "Is this a good time?"

"Of course," she said, and asked him in. She found herself looking at him a bit differently since Lorraine suggested that he be the horse she got back on after her breakup with Sam.

"Is Mr. Stafford here as well?" he asked.

"No, he's in New York." She hesitated. "I don't think he'll be coming back."

DuBois nodded. "I can reach him at home if I need to," he said.

They went out to the back deck, and the detective took out his notebook.

"We've been able to narrow the time of Curtis Nickerson's death down to between four and four thirty a.m.," he said. "I know you and

Mr. Stafford were asleep together that night, but I have to ask you if you have any memories of that time. If you got up to use the bathroom, or you were woken up by any noise, anything."

Zoe thought back to that night. She knew she had been dead to the world, under the influence of sleeping meds. "I didn't notice anything," she said. "I slept right through."

"Last time, you mentioned that you had taken a sleeping pill. Are you generally a light sleeper?"

"I sometimes have pretty severe insomnia. That's what the pills are for." Then she added, "And there's something I should tell you."

DuBois looked up, receptive.

"Sometimes, when I take the pills, I sleepwalk. When I lived in New York, Sam said I did it several times, but I never left the apartment. Then, the night before the murder, I sleepwalked out of the house and down the stone steps." She pointed at the steps in question.

"I see," said DuBois. "And do you have any reason to think that you sleepwalked on the night in question?"

"The only way I know is if Sam tells me, and he didn't mention it."

"Did he say that you *didn't*, or did he not say anything?"

Zoe thought back. "He didn't say anything." And then she went on, as though being completely forthcoming about this would absolve her from the responsibility to tell him the details of the evening she'd spent with Nickerson two days before he died. "But he might not have known, even if I had sleepwalked. But I do know that, when I do, I tend to do it right about the time of the murder, at three thirty or four."

DuBois sat back in his chair and looked at Zoe. He'd never encountered a case with a sleepwalker before, although he knew something about the history of crimes being committed by them.

"To your knowledge, have you ever done anything while sleep-walking that surprised or upset you?"

"No," said Zoe. "The night I walked out of the house was the first time I went very far. I usually just wandered around the apartment a bit and then went back to bed." She looked down at the floor, and then up again, an idea occurring to her for the first time. "Is it possible for sleepwalkers to kill people?" Surely not, she thought.

DuBois nodded. "It doesn't happen very often, but there have been a few cases. It's called homicidal somnambulism."

"Do they kill people they have no motive to kill?"

"It's hard to say. Sometimes it seems that way, but who can be sure?" He shrugged. "You'd quarreled with Nickerson, and what might not translate to motive for murder in your waking life could work differently when you're asleep."

Zoe thought again of the shame she'd felt after the aborted kiss, and shuddered.

DuBois wasn't yet ready to ask Zoe about the stipulation in the will that meant that she might be in line to inherit the house. He wanted to know whether she knew about it, and he thought the best way to get at that information was to wait for her to mention it herself. She was certainly forthcoming about other things, so he thought she might bring this up as well.

She didn't. She simply looked at DuBois, and he could see that she was desperately trying to process the idea of somnambulistic homicide.

Try as she might, she couldn't. The very idea of it horrified Zoe. She simply couldn't believe she could do something like that, but the fact that she couldn't be absolutely sure made her stomach contract in an aching knot.

She looked at DuBois with such distress that his heart went out to her. "Was there any other evidence that I might have done it?" she asked.

"I can't discuss an ongoing investigation," he said. "So far, we haven't eliminated any lines of inquiry, so we're obligated to pursue this as well." This he said with as much compassion as he could muster.

He stood up to take his leave. "If you remember anything else from that night, even if it's just a flash of a memory, or something you might have sensed, please give me a call."

Killing a man while she slept had seemed like science fiction until DuBois had told her that it could happen. Now she sat there, trying to force her mind back to that night, to make herself aware of where she went and what she did. Some memory must lie dormant in the recesses of her brain, and she wanted desperately to pull it to the surface.

But there was nothing there.

She thought of Sam, and would have wished that he were there if she hadn't strictly forbidden herself to wish for such a thing. When she'd split up with him, she'd known it would be hard, at times, to be alone in this house. Besides, she wasn't quite alone.

She had begun to have a sense that Robert was there, watching over her, even when she couldn't sense his presence. At that moment, at least, she must have been right.

Don't be distressed. The voice had a soothing tone, but Zoe didn't feel soothed.

"Of course I'm distressed. There's a chance I killed someone!"

She felt a light pressure on her back, as though he were patting her.

The world will be a better place without him.

She looked around involuntarily. She wanted to see his face, read his expression.

"How can you say that?" she asked. "Maybe you didn't like him, but to want him dead?"

As she said the words, the possibility that Robert might have had something to do with Nickerson's death dawned on her. Could ghosts kill? If they could, presumably Robert wouldn't have waited so long.

What if they couldn't? What if they needed an earthly instrument? Like, say, a sleepwalker?

"Did you have anything to do with this?" She tried to keep suspicion out of her tone, to ask the question matter-of-factly.

I can't leave this property.

Zoe's eyebrows went up. She hadn't realized that ghosts had such limits. But would those limits prevent him from knowing?

"Do you know who killed him?"

There was a pause. *I don't.*

Zoe heard a reluctance in the voice. Was he telling her the truth? She couldn't be sure.

But he must know what went on inside the house . . .

"Did I sleepwalk that night?"

Yes, you did.

Zoe gulped. "Did I . . ." And then she balked, and swallowed. "Did I leave the house?"

Yes, you did. The voice was quiet and serious.

Zoe put her head in her hands. She tried to talk herself down. She'd sleepwalked just the night before, and she'd left the house without killing Nickerson. The odds were overwhelming that it happened again, just that way, the night he died. This didn't mean anything.

Don't be distressed, Robert said again.

But Zoe *was* distressed, and she wanted desperately to talk to someone. Again, she found herself almost wishing for Sam.

Instead, she picked up her bag and headed into town. She'd go back and see Lorraine.

She parked and walked over to the studio. She opened the door and waved to Lorraine, who was talking to a young couple Zoe didn't recognize. The man's "Cape Cod" cap and their well-groomed look gave them the mark of tourists, and Zoe didn't want to interrupt a sale. Although she'd seen them all before, she looked around at the mugs, vases, and plates while Lorraine chatted with her visitors.

After the couple bought two mugs, which they took with them, and a large bowl, which they had shipped, they asked Lorraine for a restaurant recommendation and then went on their way.

As soon as they were gone, she greeted Zoe warmly.

"I hope you don't think I'm going to make it a habit to drop in on you every single day," Zoe said. "It's just that Curtis's death has me shaken up, and I don't know who else to talk to."

Lorraine smiled. "First, I'd be delighted if you made it a habit to drop in on me every single day. Second, I'm in something of the same position about Curtis, so I'm glad to talk to you about him. Would you like a cup of coffee?"

Zoe was relieved to know she was welcome. "I'd love one."

She gestured to Zoe to take a seat, and she busied herself setting up the coffeemaker. When she was through, she sat down with Zoe.

"Now," she said, "talk to me."

"I don't think I'm going to be dating Andrew DuBois anytime

soon," she said. "I don't think he'd be interested in having dinner with a murder suspect."

"You?" Lorraine asked, surprised. "Why you?"

Zoe told her everything. She told her about the sleeping pills and that DuBois had told her that it did sometimes happen that sleepwalkers killed. She told her about her fear that maybe she had done this. She even told Lorraine about the evening she'd had with Nickerson, and her embarrassment over it. She told her what Robert had said about Nickerson, and how she was afraid that those thoughts had influenced her subconscious.

Lorraine listened, a look of intent focus on her face. "Can you remember anything, anything at all about that night?"

"That's just it! I can't remember a thing. I took the pill, I went to sleep, and the next thing I knew there was a cop at the door."

"It seems terrifically unlikely that you would have killed him," Lorraine said slowly, "and my first impulse is to tell you you're silly for worrying about it. But if I were in your shoes, I certainly wouldn't like having to deal with even the barest chance that I had done something like this."

Although Zoe hadn't gone to the studio with any expectations, Lorraine's seriousness surprised her.

"Do you really think it's possible?" Zoe asked, and then backtracked. "It's not fair to ask you that. You barely know me."

"I know you well enough to know that I *don't* think it's possible," said Lorraine, and reached a hand across the table to touch Zoe's forearm in a gesture of comfort. "I'm concerned about two things—your own anxiety, and the possibility that the police will believe you may have done it."

"I don't know that there's anything I can do about either of those things," Zoe said unhappily.

"But it's a temporary situation. I can't imagine it will take them long to solve the case, and when they arrest the culprit—who won't be you—all this will just go away."

This was cold comfort. What at first she couldn't believe, she now couldn't shake.

"If it makes you feel any better, I'm a suspect too," Lorraine said.

Zoe's surprise showed on her face. "You?"

"It's a matter of course. I was married to him, even if it was in the Pleistocene Age. Anyone who ever had any close connection to him is part of this investigation, and DuBois has been here twice to question me and has talked to my boyfriend as well."

Zoe looked dubious. "Is that the only reason? That you were married way back when?"

Lorraine shrugged. "If you had to bet whether the ex-wife did it to settle an old grudge or the next-door neighbor did it sleepwalking, the smart money's on the ex-wife."

Zoe had to laugh. She could see the point, and it helped her widen the lens on her anxiety and see that she was neither the only nor the most likely suspect.

She leaned in and said in a conspiratorial tone, "Who else do you think it might be?"

Lorraine leaned in too. "They'll suspect Greta Silva, his girlfriend, for the same reason they suspect me. And there's a commercial clammer with a vile temper whom Curtis had it out with a couple of times. And since Curtis leaves his door unlocked, it could be just about anybody wandering through."

"How about Ethan Grant? Isn't he supposed to inherit the property?"

Lorraine waved this suggestion away. "That kid's as straight-up as they come."

"So that's all?" Zoe asked.

"It's all I can think of, but I wasn't close enough to him to really know what was going on in his life."

The two women talked for quite a while, tossing out names of suspects, commiserating about the trouble each had had with Curtis, expressing sorrow for his violent death. It felt good to Zoe to talk freely, and to feel as though she had a friend.

That feeling of friendship emboldened Zoe to ask the question she'd been longing to ask. "Do you think . . ." she began, unsure of how to phrase it. "Do you think that the ghost was right about Curtis?"

Lorraine looked thoughtful, and Zoe went on. "I mean, I always just thought he was a decent, crusty, hardworking New Englander. Was there more—or less—to him?"

"Well," Lorraine said slowly, "he was certainly crusty and hardworking, and he was decent a lot of the time. But he always seemed to me to have a deep-seated need to feel superior. That was part of the reason I couldn't stay married to him. Whenever he felt like someone was looking down on him for being working-class, his hackles went up. And his hackles and his judgment didn't coexist very well. I've known him to do some unpleasant things."

Zoe leaned back in her chair. She hadn't expected this. Her view of Curtis Nickerson had been formed over decades, even though she'd had little to do with him in that time. When Robert painted a picture of his character so different from her own, it was easier for her to put it down to Chapin-Nickerson hostility than to believe her own picture was inaccurate. After all, the living, breathing Robert had never known the man. But Lorraine had been married to him. Presumably, she knew him well.

If Nickerson really had plied her with whiskey and then gulled her into trying to kiss him, that would certainly qualify as an unpleasant thing. It was looking more likely that Robert had been right.

"I don't suppose it matters anymore what he might or might not have done," Zoe said to Lorraine. "Good or bad, he certainly didn't deserve to die."

"And I hope neither one of us killed him," Lorraine added.

Zoe had long ago finished her coffee, and was glad to leave on a light note.

When she left Lorraine's, she felt better. There was a brighter cast to her state of mind, and she no longer thought that being alone in her house would make her feel uneasy. In fact, her mind turned to the blueberry bushes she wanted to finish working on, and the pathetically sparse tufts of sea grass around the back deck. Her landscape needed her, and she turned toward home.

She passed the general store and saw the three old guys in their usual chairs, but she wasn't in the mood for them and she waved and walked on.

They, apparently, were in the mood for her.

"Did you ask your ghost what happened?" called one of them as she was walking away.

She stopped and turned around. Did she want to tell them about Robert? The story he'd told her wasn't one she was inclined to share. It felt intimate, personal. She thought it was between the two of them.

But those three old guys might be the only ones in town who knew what really happened. They'd certainly know more about it than anyone else she knew. If she didn't talk to them, she'd have only Robert's version of the story.

She walked back toward them.

"I did, as a matter of fact."

"And?"

"I think he loved Molly Nickerson, and I don't think anybody killed anybody." She had a sense that she had wronged Robert when she doubted him about Nickerson, and she wanted to make it up to him by defending him to the rocking-chair trio.

Harry laughed in a vaguely sinister way. "Oh, my dear, lots of people killed lots of people."

"If he killed her, why wasn't he arrested?" She was staunch.

"It wasn't the kind of killing the law had anything to say about." Harry's tone turned sober.

Zoe was about to say that it was *real* killings the law had something to say about, and these folklore killings didn't seem to fall into that category, but she stopped herself. There were injustices of all kinds that the law had nothing to say about.

"And just what kind of a killing was it?" she asked. Her tone was flip, but she really wanted to know.

"It was the heartbreaking kind," said Harry. "And that's the worst kind there is."

"But he loved her," she protested.

"Whether he did or whether he didn't, he broke that girl's heart." All three men nodded.

"And you don't think her death was an accident?"

"No, ma'am, I don't. We'll never know exactly what forces were at work pushing her under that train, but I can tell you for certain that it wasn't an accident. She jumped, or she was pushed, but she didn't just stumble into an oncoming train. And whether she jumped or she was pushed, he's equally guilty. I'm telling you, he broke that girl's heart."

Zoe saw that, whatever the facts, the three old men were as sure as it was possible for men to be. She suspected there wasn't much more they could tell her.

"Whatever happened, it was a sad story," she said. Then she bade them good-bye and headed for her car.

Had she stayed outside the general store just a few minutes more, Zoe would have seen Lorraine drive by, headed south out of town. When Zoe had left her studio, she'd made a phone call. "Are you done for the day?" she asked.

"I can be," said the voice on the other end.

She locked up her studio and flipped the OPEN sign over to CLOSED. Half an hour later, she was in Chad Helmsworth's office.

She'd been seeing the lawyer for the better part of a year. It had started with a chance meeting at a restaurant where they'd both been lunching alone. They struck up a conversation and in a remarkably short time discovered that they shared certain proclivities.

They were proclivities that she didn't share with Tim, her boyfriend, and she thought of Chad not as a man she was seeing behind Tim's back, but as a device to save Tim from her seamier side.

The tools of their proclivities were kept in a locked drawer of a file cabinet in Chad's office. When Lorraine arrived, Chad locked the office door and unlocked the drawer. He held it open for Lorraine, and she surveyed its contents.

She pulled out a set of restraints, a worn leather whip, and a peacock feather.

They had fallen into the habit of not talking much. Their time together was something separate, something outside their normal lives, and they seldom brought their normal lives to their encounters. Part of the appeal of their interludes was that they lived, for those hours, in a fantasy world. Talking about the weather, or their work, or current events spoiled the illusion, and they seldom did it.

"Are you ready?" she asked Chad.

He nodded, and started to undress. First his jacket, which he put over the back of his chair, and then his shirt and tie, which he put over the jacket. He folded his pants carefully and put them on his desk. Shoes went under the desk, socks inside them. He stood there in his blue-and-white-striped boxers and took a deep breath.

Lorraine loved the moment when she went from being Lorraine, small-town potter, to Lorraine, mistress of ecstasy.

That moment came when she told Chad to take off the boxers.

He did.

"Lie down," she said. Her tone wasn't substantially different from her normal conversational tone, but it had a hardness around the edges.

He lay down, faceup, spread-eagled on the floor. She tied his hands together, and then to one of the legs of his desk behind his head. His legs she tied to the credenza.

When he was secured, she stripped down to black panties and bra, and pulled a pair of very high heels out of the drawer.

Lorraine was almost fifty, and if she had let her body go she would have felt ridiculous in that kind of getup. But she had stayed fit and slim and was conscious that, even at her age, she looked damn good in her underwear.

This consciousness was at the heart of why she enjoyed domination games. The confidence that came of looking good wasn't sufficient to deal with the vagaries of real life—the failed marriage, the pointless career, the financial setbacks—but it was all she needed behind the locked door of Chad Helmsworth's office. Here, she was in complete control.

She stood over the lawyer, who was naked and clearly aroused. While she understood perfectly the urge to dominate, submission was harder for her to understand. He had tried to explain it to her, but she couldn't see how the ceding of control could be as erotic to him as the taking of it was for her. But she was certainly glad it worked out that way.

"I want silence," she said to him. Then she took the peacock feather and ran it from the base of his balls to the tip of his cock. It was clearly difficult for him to be silent.

She did it again, and this time the smallest groan escaped him.

"It was silence I required." She took the whip and flicked it on his chest. Then she took up the feather again. This time he couldn't even hold out once. The feeling of the feather against the hardness of his erection, titillating the nerve endings that were already on edge, was more than he could stand in silence. The groan was full-fledged this time.

And so was the crack of the whip.

He couldn't help but cry out, and so she whipped him again.

This time he was quiet, and she went back to the peacock feather. This game went on for quite a while. As it did, Lorraine felt her own response building. She felt the pressure in her cunt, the moisture deep inside, the compulsion to be filled.

But she resisted for now.

She watched as he pulled against his restraints, eyes shut tight. She kept the touch of the feather light, so it fed his arousal but didn't take him to climax. She stroked him rhythmically, and then stopped, with the tip of the feather just touching the head of his cock.

He opened his eyes. She stroked again, and he cried out.

This time she whipped his legs. When he made no noise, she let the end of the whip, which was several strands of leather, do the work the feather had been doing. She dangled it over him, tracing the outline of his cock as it lay at full attention on his belly.

Then she used the whip with a little more force, sliding the length of the leather strands over the length of him, over and over, faster and faster.

"Open your eyes," she said to him. She made him watch as she put her hand in her panties and massaged her own clitoris, already hard under her touch. She stepped off him long enough to take her panties off so he could have a full view of her pussy and the glistening finger that ran in, out, and around it.

He watched, riveted. He rocked side to side—the only motion he could make—and he had his lips clamped firmly between his teeth in the hopes that it would prevent him from making a noise that would make her stop.

He succeeded, and Lorraine knew he had gone beyond that magic point, that point from which there was no turning back. She sank to her knees, and he was inside her in one motion. He was noiseless no more. His groans were in sync with her motion, and then the eruption came. The long, even cry told her not just that he was there, but how deep and how long his orgasm was.

She slid him out of her, and then moved so her cunt was over his mouth.

"Lick me," she said, with more urgency than dominance.

He did, and the barest sensation of his tongue on the spot of her pleasure brought her own orgasm roaring to life. She stayed on him for one, two, three strokes as her climax built to a climax of its own, and then pulled away to let it overtake her.

It did overtake her, leaving every fiber first tense, and then relaxed. She lay on the floor beside him as she caught her breath and came back to reality.

She came back reluctantly. Reality meant her studio, her mortgage, and selling mugs to tourists. It also meant Tim. He was a fine man, and she loved him, but in a tame sort of way. None of her reality added up to what she had thought she might be by this time in her life.

But she was brave, and she was tough. She got up, she got dressed, and she went back to her life.

CHAPTER TEN

❦

"I just don't get why there's this one pathetic little fingerprint fragment," said Veronica McSweeney, who had just finished enhancing the image of it so she and Andrew DuBois could have a shot at identifying it.

"Yeah, it's odd," he said. "There are a number of possible explanations."

"Like what?"

"The killer might have wiped the thing clean of fingerprints before using it, and then worn a glove with a hole in it to do the deed."

"Who wipes something clean *before* they kill the guy?"

"Anyone who realizes the thing's going to shatter so you can't clean it afterward," said Andrew.

"But why bother to clean the fucking thing if you're going to use gloves?"

"Maybe you were there earlier in the day, and touched it, and you didn't want your own prints on it."

Veronica scoffed. "From what you tell me, absolutely everyone knows that absolutely everyone touches the damn thing every time they walk into the house."

"But maybe you're the murderer and don't know how often Nickerson cleans it, and you told the police you hadn't seen the guy in days, but it turns out he cleaned it the morning before he died and yours are the only prints on it. Cleaning it's the only safe thing to do."

"So you're thinking so clearly that you clean it before you bonk old Nickerson on the head, and then you do something stupid like go and wear gloves with a hole in them?" Veronica was incredulous.

"Or maybe he touched it accidentally, or maybe he used a towel or something instead of gloves, and got one finger on the statue when it slipped, or maybe he cleaned it but missed this one spot and the fingerprint isn't his at all."

"I doubt that last one," she said. "There would have been smudges and streaks on the edge of it, and there weren't any."

"Or maybe the killer wore gloves, but didn't clean it at all. Nickerson could have cleaned it that day and had a visitor who left that one print. There are lots of ways it could have happened. Once we know whose fingerprint it is, we'll have a better shot at figuring out how it got there."

Veronica looked critically at the fingerprint image. "That's probably not enough to send to get us an ID out of the database, but it may be enough to confirm a match if we've got the fingerprint in front of us."

She showed him that the fragment had a distinctive tented arch pattern, and enough minutiae points that a positive ID ought to be possible.

"I think it's unlikely many of Nickerson's visitors would be in the FBI database, anyway," said DuBois. "As for the killer, if I had to bet, I'd bet this was the first crime he ever committed."

"Or she," said Veronica.

"I'm the last living proponent of the generic 'he,'" DuBois said, smiling. "In this case, our list of suspects contains almost half women."

"Is it a long list?"

"As these things go, not really. The most obvious two would be the heir and the girlfriend, but in this case the girlfriend seems to have no motive whatsoever, and the heir is complicated."

"How so?"

DuBois explained the situation with the house to her.

"So let me get this straight. If the original will holds, the house goes to Zoe Bell, and if it doesn't, it goes to Nickerson's next of kin, which would be Ethan Grant?"

"That seems to be the story. It will be for the probate court to decide."

"Do both Bell and Grant know the situation?"

"Grant does, and I have to say he doesn't seem to care very much one way or the other. As for Zoe, I don't know yet. I didn't ask her directly, because I thought the best way to find out whether she knew would be to wait for her to say something about it, but she hasn't."

"Huh," said Veronica. "Either one of them have alibis?"

"Nobody ever has an alibi for the middle of the night. Everyone's always asleep. Grant says he was asleep alone. Zoe says she was asleep with her boyfriend, but she admits taking sleeping pills that have been known to make her sleepwalk."

"A sleepwalking murderess!" exclaimed Veronica. "Outstanding!" DuBois rolled his eyes.

"Who else you got?" she asked.

"There's the ex-wife, although she's had so little to do with him over the years that I'd say she's a long shot. The guy who found the body probably couldn't have lifted the murder weapon. The only other one on the list is a commercial clammer who seems to have had an ongoing feud with the victim."

"You like the clammer?" asked Veronica.

"I don't know yet."

"Oh, for chrissake," she said. "You've got to have a feeling about it."

DuBois gave a little shrug. "I try not to have feelings about these things. Most of the time, feelings steer you wrong."

"But you can't help having them, can you?"

"You can help listening to them." His ideas about feelings and hunches put him at odds with the rest of the police force, most of whom believed they had a sixth sense for ferreting out criminals. Andrew had seen too much zealous prosecution of the wrong guy to believe in anything but the facts on the ground. Those, too, could steer you wrong, but following facts was less likely to get you emotionally committed to a mistake.

"Do you always refuse to listen to your feelings?" Veronica walked up to him with a little swagger, stood close, and looked up into his face. The two had a history of flirtation that she was doing her part to continue.

He moved almost imperceptibly closer to her and simply said, "No."

"So," she said huskily, putting her hand on his chest, "do you feel like you want me to go out and help you get some fingerprints?"

He grinned. "That's exactly what I feel like, and it's a feeling I'm listening to."

He reached for his badge and gun, but Veronica stopped him. "Wait," she said. "First, how about a friendly wager?"

"A wager?"

"Yeah. Wanna bet whose fingerprint this is?" She held up the card with an image of the enhanced print fragment they'd gotten off the statue.

"What are we betting?"

"Dinner, of course. What else?"

He nodded and held out his hand. They shook on the deal.

"I'm taking the nephew," said Veronica.

Andrew made a show of thinking carefully about his choice. "I'll take the clammer."

"So you do like the clammer," she said.

"I don't know how much I like him, but I can tell you I definitely don't like the nephew."

"Now you tell me! Why don't you like the nephew?"

"Just a feeling."

She hit him on the arm, and they went out to try to collect fingerprints from everyone involved.

~❧~

Four hours later, they'd gotten everyone but the girlfriend, and they were headed to Greta Silva's house to complete their rounds.

Absent a warrant, they couldn't take fingerprints without permission, but none of the people involved had refused. DuBois hadn't told them that there was only one print on the statue, but had asked for fingerprints "to make sense" of what they found, implying that Angie was full of prints, as anyone would expect her to be.

Everyone but Steve Cromwell, the clammer, had touched the statue and would have expected to have left prints. "I've never set foot in that house," Cromwell had said as Veronica inked him, "so you won't be finding anything of mine in there."

Greta, though, balked. More than balked. Rebelled.

"I've been there once or twice a week for two years!" she said. "My fingerprints are on everything! First I lose Curtis and now you come to me asking for my fingerprints so you can figure out who touched that statue? Let me help you out. I touched that statue. I also touched every doorknob, every kitchen utensil, every piece of furniture, and the toothpaste."

"But if we know those fingerprints are yours, we don't have to spend more time trying to figure out if they're some stranger's, or the murderer's," said Veronica, with as much patience as she could muster.

"Don't talk to me about your time when you're spending it trying to decipher a murder weapon that must have fingerprints from everyone in town. You can't seriously think that's going to get you anywhere. Meanwhile, whoever killed Curtis is still out there while you fuck around with fingerprints! Get a real clue, and then maybe we can talk."

She slammed the door in their faces. Literally.

"Ouch," said DuBois.

"Good thing I didn't take the girlfriend. I don't like her at all," said Veronica.

"You don't like her because she won't give her fingerprints?" DuBois himself hadn't suspected her from the start, and now he was almost sure of her innocence, but he was curious to find out what Veronica's take was.

"If she killed the guy, she would have let us print her, and been as cooperative as she knows how to be. She's got every excuse in the world to have fingerprints all over the place. The only reason she wouldn't give us prints is that she's really upset. That makes her irrational."

"I think that's right," the detective said. "Let's go see if we can find a match with what we've got."

⁓⁂⁓

When Zoe got home from the village, after Lorraine had told her that Robert might have been right about Nickerson, she headed straight for the garden shed for a trowel, rake, and wheelbarrow. She was beginning to feel that the grounds of Chapin House should be her next project, that the landscape could be her way of accomplishing something constructive while she decided on what she'd do with the next phase of her life.

She took the tools to where she'd left off with the blueberries, and then went inside to get her gardening clogs and gloves. They were right by the door, and she put them on and was about to head back out when she felt the familiar soft draft on the back of her neck that told her Robert was there with her.

She turned around. "Robert?" she said softly.

There was no answer from him, but she felt his presence encircle her. It was warm, it was safe, and it was comforting. She felt watched over, protected. Maybe even loved.

When Robert had first appeared to her, she had been disconcerted and felt like she was an interloper. But he had welcomed her to this house; he had made her a part of it. The mystique the house had had for her when she was young, the sense she'd had of Chapins as the closest thing to Brahmins as America had to offer, was now becoming part of her own history. She was of it, and of them.

The one glimpse she'd gotten of Robert, in the bedroom mirror, had become an indelible image. She saw it in her mind the way she'd see a portrait—his smile, his sweater, his wide-set blue eyes. He had become part of her fascination with the place, and he had opened the door to its past in a way that made her a part of it.

Strangely, she felt now that Nickerson's death had helped to solidify her feeling that she belonged in the house. When he had been there, next door, he'd been a tangible reminder that she was living in the present of Chapin House, and that its past was over and done with. His cantankerousness and his disdain had been undeniably here and now. Now they were a part of the past, a part she had known personally.

She felt this warm, enveloping presence lift her to her feet. It took her hand and loosened her grip on the trowel, so she dropped it in the blueberry bed. And then it led her inside.

It pressured her gently through the kitchen and up the stairs, as though he were giving her a tour—his own personal tour. And even though she'd been through every room many times, she sensed that he wanted her to see it differently, to see herself as part of it even as he was still part of it himself. To see it as theirs, together.

When she'd gone through the house by herself, she'd looked everywhere for clues to its previous inhabitants, for evidence of its history. She hadn't found anything more interesting than a receipt, dated 1972, for a television set now long gone. The only room that had anything in it was the small room in the basement where Sam had found the candles, but it contained only mundane household things. The receipt had come from the drawer of the old desk that had been moldering in there, probably for decades. It was the only substantial piece of furniture that had been in the house when she took possession, and she had hoped its drawers would offer up something more interesting.

But she had been looking as an outsider, a stranger. Now that she felt as though she'd crossed a line and was of the house, she thought it might give up its secrets to her.

That was why Robert was leading her upstairs. That was why she found herself standing in the large, airy bedroom on the northwest corner of the second floor. It was a beautiful room, and she had almost chosen it for her own bedroom. It had lost out to the bigger room in the center of the house primarily because its one closet was small and airless.

She had decorated the room with what few items of furniture she had from her childhood. There was a single bed with the tattered counterpane she'd slept with all through grade school. There was a simple oak desk, a matching dresser, and a large, ornate rocking horse.

The horse had been a gift from her grandparents for her sixth birthday, and she had loved it. It wasn't the kind with rockers; it was attached to a heavy wood frame with springs. It was to this horse that Robert led her.

She probably hadn't sat on the horse in fifteen years, but as soon as she got on, it felt familiar, even though her feet reached the floor and her thighs barely cleared the frame. She moved gently up and down, and felt the springs move the horse under her.

And then the horse started to move of its own accord, and she felt Robert's presence as though he were sitting right behind her. She felt the warmth and the pressure of his chest right up against her back, and she leaned back into it. She felt a tendril of a caress come around her waist from either side, as though he were putting his arms around her.

She closed her eyes and she felt the embrace as though it were real. A small sigh escaped her as she basked in it.

And then she felt herself pushed forward, as though to make more room for her behind, and the horse moved under her, in a combination of back-and-forth and up-and-down that gave her a giddy sensation. Giddy in a good way.

Zoe felt her temperature rise and her fingers tingle as the motion and the warmth engaged all her senses. She felt his breath—his kiss?— on the back of her neck.

She was far enough forward on the horse that its mane came right between her legs, and when the horse moved in a particular way, her clitoris brushed against it. She opened her eyes in surprise at the pleasure of it, and then closed them again and moved with the rhythm of the horse.

She was suffused: with pleasure, with wetness, with the wonder of the power of a presence she couldn't see. Gradually, the horse moved in bigger waves, and the mane hit her more firmly and more often. She felt herself straining toward it and, at the same time, leaning backward into the presence behind her.

The movement was smooth, almost soothing, and it was in contrast to the urgent aching she was feeling radiating from her center. She leaned all the way back, trusting that he would support her.

He did.

She felt a caress on her breast and a warmth on her cheek as she lay back on the horse, suspended in midair. The caress, the warmth, the support all came out of thin air. The only real physical touch was the horse between her legs, and that seemed to make it even more intense.

Somehow, and she didn't know how, she was aware of his arousal too. Maybe the warmth was that much warmer; maybe the touch was that much firmer. But she felt his need matching her own.

She felt herself coming to a climax, and she slowed their pace and forced her thoughts to bring her down a notch. As soon as she scaled it back, it began to build up again, though, stronger and faster.

Throughout, the only sound had been the gentle squeak of the springs, punctuating their rhythm. And soundlessly, she hit her peak. She felt it begin deep inside her and spread. And spread. Every nerve, every cell was suffused with an orgasm that was strong but not sharp— it was rounded and full.

She didn't know whether ghosts could feel things like that, but she hoped they could.

She felt herself gently raised so she was sitting upright on the horse again, with the presence still there against her back. And after a moment the presence lifted, and then pulled her to her feet. It took her to the middle of the room and stopped, as if to say, *Look around.*

She looked around, and then she knew. She knew that this had been his room. She felt a shiver as she imagined him inhabiting it. Living there as a real, live man. In her mind's eye, she could see it full of his life. His clothes tossed carelessly on the bed, sailing trophies, maybe, on top of a bookshelf. Photographs on his desk, instead of hers.

She could almost see him at the window, looking out at the water.

She knew he was there, but he wasn't talking to her in his usual way. Perhaps she was projecting her own contentment, but she felt as though he simply wanted to be in the room with her.

And then the closet door opened of its own accord, and she felt the lightest possible pressure pushing her in that direction.

She understood, and she walked over to the closet. She looked in, but saw nothing. There was a bar for hanging clothes, and a shelf above it. That was all.

The pressure pushed her just a little farther in, and then she felt it lift her left hand and guide it to the closet wall, just to the left of the door.

She stepped all the way into the closet so she could see the wall. There was a tiny nail in it. Hanging from the nail, on a decaying silk cord, was a little shell ring, pink and white.

She took the cord off the nail, and it practically disintegrated in her hand. She slipped the ring off it and held it between her fingers. It was smooth and delicate, almost translucent.

"Molly's ring," she said.

It was.

Zoe slipped it on the ring finger of her right hand. It was almost too small, but once she got it over her knuckle it was a comfortable fit. As she held her hand out in front of her and admired the simplicity of the ring, she felt suffused with contentment. This was where she belonged. In this house, with this man. It was almost unaccountable, in the light of Nickerson's death and her breakup with Sam, but she was happy.

Her happiness was interrupted by the sound of a car pulling up in the gravel driveway. She wasn't expecting anyone, and she went downstairs and opened the door just as Andrew DuBois was about to knock.

Her contentment was immediately overshadowed, and her heart sank. "Detective," she said, "we're seeing a lot of each other." She nodded at Veronica McSweeney. "Hello again." It had been only that morning that the two police officers had been there to take her finger-prints, which she had freely given.

DuBois asked if he and Veronica could come in.

"Of course," Zoe said, and led the way into the kitchen.

"I don't suppose you've been able to remember anything else about the night Curtis Nickerson was killed," DuBois said when they were seated.

"I'm afraid not," said Zoe, beginning to be concerned about the nature of this visit. "Is something wrong?"

She realized how foolish that sounded and hastened to add, "I mean, it's obviously wrong that someone killed Curtis, but has something happened that involves me?"

"Something has," said DuBois, and told her about the statue. "We expected a big jumble of prints, but there was only one, and it was yours."

"Mine?" She was incredulous.

Both police officers nodded.

"I touched it when I was at his house, and that was"—she thought back—"two days before he died."

"If the print we found was from that visit, we would have expected a full set, or at least more than just one, as well as the prints of everyone else who touched it. What I need to explain is why there was only one print, and why it was yours."

Zoe felt a kind of panic begin to rise in her chest. "I have no idea." She held up her hands helplessly. "I have no idea at all." And then she started to think about it. "But if I had killed him while I was sleep-walking, wouldn't there be a full set of my prints on it anyway?"

"Not necessarily," said DuBois. "You could have picked it up with a towel, or been wearing gloves with a hole."

"Do people who kill while they're sleepwalking have that much foresight?" she asked, genuinely puzzled.

"It's hard to know," said DuBois.

"People who *claim* to be sleepwalking often have that much foresight," said Veronica McSweeney.

Zoe was taken aback. Up until that moment, her interviews with DuBois had been friendly, without any hint that she wasn't being taken at her word. This interview had a completely different dynamic. If this woman was here as the fingerprint expert, which was how DuBois had introduced her, what business did she have speculating about what happened that night? She glanced from McSweeney to DuBois, and it crossed her mind that there might be something between them.

"Look," she said to Veronica, her irritation at the woman's presence showing clearly in her tone, "I've been racking my brain trying to remember what happened that night, and I'm coming up blank. It's been driving me crazy that there's some chance, however remote, that I did this while I was asleep. But I know there's *no* chance that I did it when I *wasn't* asleep. If you think I woke up in the middle of the night and sneaked out of the house to murder a man I barely knew but didn't have any real reason to even dislike, you're out of your mind."

"We have to consider every possible scenario that fits the facts," said DuBois, in a conciliatory tone.

"And what facts would motivate me to *kill* somebody?" Zoe's voice got high and shrill as her indignation grew. "You can't seriously believe I just show up in town, buy a house, and murder my next-door neighbor before the week is out?"

"As I said, we have to consider every possible scenario that fits the facts as we know them." DuBois used a tone softer and lower than he had before, implicitly suggesting that reasonable people didn't raise their voices when they talked about serious things. "We don't know what kind of history you may have had with Nickerson personally." He looked at Zoe closely. "And it's possible that, with his death, his house reverts to being part of this property." He gestured around him.

"What?" exclaimed Zoe, baffled. "How could it? That house has been in the Nickerson family for generations."

"It would be for the courts to decide, but there's a stipulation in the original gift that might mean you get the house if Nickerson dies."

"But what about Ethan Grant? He's a Nickerson."

DuBois shrugged. "But he's not Curtis Nickerson's son. He's Curtis Nickerson's *sister's* son, and the will stipulates that the house be handed down through the male line. But, as I said, it would be for the courts to decide."

None of this made sense to Zoe. Surely, in this day and age, something as old-fashioned as a male-line entail wouldn't be enforced.

"But even if a will like that stands up, wouldn't it be"—she didn't know the legal word—"no good anymore once the property got sold to me?"

"Again, it's a question for the courts. It's possible the house will go to Ethan Grant, but it's also possible it will go to you."

"But I had no idea about that," protested Zoe. "This is the first I'm hearing about it."

"If you did know about it, and it was a murder motive, it's likely you wouldn't have seen fit to mention it to us." Here DuBois paused, and then added, "I'm speaking hypothetically."

Zoe put her elbows on the table and her head in her hands. What they were suggesting was so far-fetched that she was having trouble believing that *they* could believe it.

She took a deep breath and moderated her voice. "Technically, I've known Curtis Nickerson all my life, but when I was a kid, he was just one of the adult faces I saw around here. My adult acquaintance with him dates back to the day after I bought this house, a little over a week ago. There's no "personal history," as you call it, between us. And, as for the house, I simply had no idea. No idea."

And then they went through it all again, with DuBois asking about the details of her dealings with Nickerson, and Zoe trying to remember every last little thing either of them said. As before, she left out his rebuff, but that was her only omission.

When they finally left, Zoe was drained. For the hundredth time, she tried to pull up details of the night of Nickerson's death, and for the hundredth time, she came up empty.

"Whaddya think?" Andrew asked, as he and Veronica drove back to the barracks.

"Either she didn't know about that house thing, or she's Greta fucking Garbo."

He laughed. "I tend to agree. But why else would she do it?"

"Maybe she walked in on Nickerson and her mother when she was ten, and she's never forgiven him."

He snorted.

"Who knows?" Veronica went on. "I could come up with a list of a dozen possible motives, and so could you."

"I don't see it," said Andrew. "She's not like any murderer I've ever known."

"So what you're saying is, you have a feeling about it."

He laughed. "I have a feeling about it."

"I'll tell you one thing: If you ever had your eye on her as a girl and not as a suspect, you pretty much sank your ship with that interview. She won't be forgiving you anytime soon."

DuBois laughed. "Actually, I think it's you she won't forgive."

"That's okay; I didn't want to date her."

"Neither did I," said DuBois. "So no harm done."

Veronica looked at him and waited for him to take his eyes off the road long enough to glance at her before she spoke again. "I know neither of us won dinner on the fingerprint bet," she said, "but we could have dinner anyway."

He smiled. "We could."

They did. They went to a clam shack called Clem's Shack of Clams, which looked like an old-fashioned fried-clam joint but was really an upscale seafood house started by a well-known Boston chef. They had lobster rolls.

"What's in this?" Veronica said between bites. "I mean, it tastes like lobster, but it has just the faintest hint of something else and I can't put my finger on it."

"It's fennel," he told her. "Just a little bit. Finely chopped."

"It's fucking perfect."

Over the course of the meal, and the bottle of Viognier they drank with it, it became clear to both of them where their ongoing flirtation was headed.

When they got in Andrew's car, he asked her simply, "Will you come home with me?"

She nodded, and they didn't say another word in the few minutes it took to drive to his house, a small, neat saltbox on a quiet residential street.

The front door was barely closed behind them when they were in each other's arms. The tension between them had been building all day—as it had each time they'd worked together over the past several years—and their energy was explosive.

They kissed deep and hard, and their embrace was so tight that Andrew found himself lifting her off the ground without realizing that he was doing it. She wrapped her legs around him almost automatically. He put his hands under her ass and took the two steps to the nearest wall so he could brace her up against it.

They kissed deeper and harder, as though each were trying to reach the essence of the other. Her hands were on the back of his head and she was running her fingers through his hair. Her legs tightened their grip around his waist, and her own body cleaved to his.

He wanted desperately to touch more of her, and so he carried her into the bedroom and put her down.

They each took a breath, a little overwhelmed by the fierceness of those first moments. And then she reached up to his shoulders and took his jacket off. Her movements were slow and deliberate, as though she were trying to change their pace together.

They were dressed almost identically: khakis, crisp button-down shirts, jackets. He marveled that she made it look so feminine. After he shrugged out of his jacket and tossed it over the back of a chair, he returned the favor, matching his pace to hers.

They both had handcuffs and guns in shoulder holsters, and they each took off their own. As they were putting them on the desk, though, Veronica took Andrew's handcuffs from him. "I think we can use these," she said, holding one set in each hand.

His eyebrows went up, more in anticipation than surprise.

He unbuttoned her blouse, revealing a plain white bra and smooth, pale, freckled skin. He rubbed the back of his hand against her muscular belly, and then slid his fingers under the waistband of her pants to unclasp them. She stepped out of them, revealing cotton panties with orange and white stripes.

DuBois smiled. "I'd like to see the matching bra to those," he said.

"There is no matching bra. I gave up on matching underwear years ago. If you get panties that fit, the bra pinches, and if the bra fits, the panties ride up your ass. Now I just get bras and panties I like, and to hell with it."

DuBois was used to women who wore premeditated matched sets, and it hadn't occurred to him that they'd endured discomfort in the service of sexiness.

He liked Veronica. He really liked Veronica.

"Men are lucky," she said, as she unbuttoned his shirt in turn. "Just the one piece of underwear." She pulled his waistband away from his body and peered down his pants. "Boxers."

He nodded.

"Do you ever find that they don't provide enough support?"

He laughed. "They work for me, but maybe I don't have the equipment to put them to the test."

She peered down his pants again. "I wouldn't say that's a problem."

She unbuttoned and unzipped, and he stood naked in front of her.

He watched as she reached behind her, unhooked her bra, and wriggled out of her panties. He reached for her waist to draw her to him, but she backed away.

"Just a sec," she said, and picked the handcuffs up off the desk.

"Do I handcuff you? Or do you handcuff me?" he asked.

"Oh, please," she said. "Let's have none of that."

She reached for his hand and cuffed his wrist. Then she put the second cuff on her own wrist, connecting her hand to his. She connected their other two hands with the second set of cuffs.

"Now we're in this together," she said.

He stood looking at her, trying to figure out what to do with his hands. He had to reconsider every move he would make, knowing that her hands were tethered to his. If he put his arms around her, she'd have to put her own hands behind her back. If he touched her cheek, her hand would dangle awkwardly below her chin.

He took her hands in his, interlacing his fingers with hers. That, at least, felt more natural. He brought her hands up to his lips, and kissed each one in turn. He reached down and, with the index finger of each hand, traced an arc on the underside of each of her full, heavy breasts.

She unlaced the fingers of her right hand and guided his hand down to his own cock, fully erect. She laid his hand on top of it, and put her own hand underneath. She gently stroked its underside as his hand ran along the top.

He found this both strange and intensely arousing, and as she stroked just a little faster, it became more arousing still.

Before it became too arousing altogether, he took her hand again. He took one of her fingers in his mouth and sucked on it. He flicked his tongue around it, and watched with satisfaction as she closed her eyes and gave a little moan.

He then guided her hand down between her legs, and used that finger to find just the right spot. It wasn't hard, since she knew where it was and it was her finger. Once there, he rubbed her finger back and forth, back and forth. Her breathing was getting faster and he could feel the heat coming off her body.

He backed her toward the bed and sat her down at the edge of it. She took his hands in hers and looked up at him. Her eyes were an unusual shade of blue-green, and those eyes held him.

He really liked Veronica.

"I'm very glad I couldn't figure out that fingerprint by myself," he said.

"So am I."

She scooted back on the bed and pulled him down over her. He lay on top of her, propped on his elbows, holding her hands so that his thumbs were in her palms.

He kissed her. Gently at first, but then with increasing intensity. The passion that had fueled their first kiss by the front door came flooding back to both of them, and they strained toward each other.

He moved his hips up so he could slip inside her, and reached down to guide himself in, forgetting that he was handcuffed to her. She pulled back on the handcuffs.

"We can do this hands-free," she said.

She tilted her hips to meet him, and in a moment he was inside.

He groaned with the sensation of his first thrust. The heat, the moisture, the pressure on his cock. It was almost unbearably good. He gasped with the pleasure of it, and then stilled himself so he could focus on the sensation. He didn't want to be carried away with the urgency, with the passion. He wanted to prolong it, to heighten it.

He didn't move. He looked at her and felt what it was to be inside her, and marveled at his good fortune.

And then she moved, just a little. She tilted her hips up just slightly, and he felt the movement of her against him. She did it again, and he rocked with her. All the while, he held her gaze. Neither of them closed their eyes. This was personal.

Their rocking slowly grew in intensity, in force. He withdrew until just the tip of his cock was inside her, and then pushed in so he was subsumed in her. And then again.

He saw that her mouth was open. He felt that her muscles were taut. He sensed from her moisture and her heat that she was there with him. And he felt the first inkling of his orgasm begin at the base of his cock. As it started to spread down his legs, he heard her moan and felt her tighten around him. That spasm sent him over the edge, and he felt a warmth, an ecstasy, so complete that it turned him liquid.

It seemed to him that it wasn't just his climax. It was hers as well. Her whole body seemed gripped around him, and she made a low-pitched, breathy gasp that lasted a very long time. When she was finally silent, he kissed the very corner of her mouth.

"You've made it hard for me to use handcuffs with a straight face."

She smiled and propped herself up on her elbows.

"The hard part is getting over there to the desk to get the key without falling all over each other," she said. "Why is it that we never think about our dignity until afterward?"

They managed to get up and to uncouple.

"Now that we're done with that print, I have to go back to Boston."

"Do you have to go now?"

"I have to show up at work in the morning."

"Do you mind an early drive?" He gestured toward the alarm clock on the nightstand.

"I prefer an early drive, considering the alternative," she said. "Set it for six o'clock."

CHAPTER ELEVEN

B y six o'clock, Zoe was already on her second cup of coffee. She had flushed her sleeping meds down the toilet and vowed to never take them again, and she had paid the price in a restless night. At three in the morning, when night thoughts were at their darkest, she'd seen herself being convicted of murder and locked away for the duration of her natural life.

When the sun came up, her fears eased with the brightening day, and that second cup of coffee dispelled her sluggishness and strengthened her resolve to do something constructive with her time, and not just hang around worrying about whether she might have murdered Curtis Nickerson in her sleep.

She'd been finding the landscaping work she'd started around the property to be therapeutic. Despite the fact that she had started, built, and sold a gardening business, it had been a very long time since she'd had her hands in the soil, and it felt good.

It was already well into June, and she wanted to get some vegetables in for the season, so she'd gone to the hardware store for supplies to build raised beds next to the driveway, on the south-facing side of the house.

She took the requisite tools and started marking out the plots. An hour later, she'd forgotten the chill in the air, the troubles on her mind, and the murder next door in the effort of leveling and clearing the ground. By the time she started hammering the boards together to make the boxes, the sun was warm enough that she took off her outer layers and was working in shorts and a T-shirt.

She was so intent on her work that she didn't see Ethan Grant until she stood up to stretch her back. She'd thought she was alone, and was startled—and a bit irritated that he hadn't made his presence known.

He'd seen her start, and before she could say anything, he apologized. "I wasn't trying to sneak up on you. I wasn't sure which way of getting your attention would be least likely to startle you, and you caught me trying to decide." He smiled a little sheepishly, and she forgave him on the spot.

"Hi," she said, with a hint of a quizzical tone. She wasn't sure why he was there.

"I was over at my uncle's, and I heard the hammering. I thought it might be something I could help you with."

She expressed surprise that the noise would carry that far, and he explained that, since the prevailing wind was from the southwest, loud sounds would sometimes reach the cottage. And then he gestured at the partially constructed bed. "Vegetables?" he asked.

She nodded. "It's a little late in the season, but I think I can get a few things to grow."

"It's not as late as you might think," Ethan told her. "Because of the water, we get a cold spring and a warm fall, so our growing season starts late but extends well into the fall."

She looked at him. Of course, it made perfect sense, and she couldn't have told herself why she was surprised that he would know it. "That's good to know," she said.

And she took him up on his offer to help. With two people, the work went much faster, and they had two beds done before noon.

"Hard labor earns lunch, if you'd like to stay," Zoe said. As she said it, she found herself hoping he would take her up on her offer. Although the work had absorbed them, and they'd been focused on whether the ground was level and the angles square, she had been aware that she was becoming sensitive to his presence. She realized that she was attuned to how close he was to her, what he was doing, the sound of his breath.

"I'd love some lunch," he said.

They went inside and Zoe surveyed the contents of her refrigerator. She put together a makeshift spread of olives, cheese, bread, and some sliced tomato, and the two sat down at the kitchen table.

"Are you staying at your uncle's house?" Zoe asked him. It had only just occurred to her to wonder what he was doing there.

"Off and on, I think," he said. "Andrew DuBois told me they'd cleared it as a crime scene, and I could start trying to sort things out as long as I didn't remove anything."

"Is there a lot to sort through?"

"There is, but it's in pretty good order. My uncle was an orderly man."

Zoe looked down at her plate, swallowed, and said, "I'm a suspect in his murder, you know."

Ethan looked at her, clearly taken aback. "It's hard for me to imagine you killing my uncle."

"It's hard for *me* to imagine it," she said, and then told him the whole story.

He listened to it without interrupting her, with the exception of a question or two.

When she got to the part about her interview with the two detectives, in which Veronica McSweeney all but accused her of lying about sleepwalking, he leaned back in his chair and looked at her.

"You can't possibly be worried about this," he said.

Zoe didn't understand. "Of course I'm worried. I'm suspected in a murder case. They've found my fingerprint—and only mine—on the murder weapon. There's some weird thing about the house and maybe I inherit it instead of you!"

Here Ethan nodded. "I know about that."

But Zoe barely heard him. "And they've hinted that I could have some motive that dates back to my childhood. They think I'm lying about sleepwalking." As she said it, her worries moved once again to the forefront of her mind, and she had to take several deep, deliberate breaths to prevent herself from getting upset all over again.

Ethan leaned forward, reached across the table, and put a hand on her forearm. "Look at me."

She did.

"Were you lying about sleepwalking?"

"No, of course not."

"Did you know anything about who would inherit the house?"

"No."

"Do you have some old family grievance against the Nickersons?" Here he couldn't completely suppress a smile.

She smiled back. "Most definitely not."

"In that case, the fact that they found that one print, and it was yours, should make you feel better, not worse."

She looked at him blankly, not comprehending.

"Think about it. If you're the police, even if you suspect you"—he pointed at Zoe—"the most likely explanation is that you're lying about sleepwalking and you did this deliberately. It's hard to come up with a scenario in which a sleepwalker would leave just the one print, yes?"

"Yes."

"And *you* know you're not lying about sleepwalking, and *you* know you didn't know anything about the house, and *you* know you don't have a motive that dates back to your childhood, and *you* know you didn't go over there in cold blood and kill him, right?"

"Right."

"What you were afraid of was that you killed him and you didn't know it. I would think that was a pretty far-fetched theory to begin with, and this makes it even more so. Right?"

She saw his point. "Right."

"So, at this point, you should be absolutely confident that you didn't kill him, which should make you feel better—not worse."

"But the police don't know that I didn't go over there in cold blood. They still suspect me, and that's what I'm worried about."

"You should have enough confidence in the system, and in DuBois, to know that they're going to figure out what really happened." He paused. He wasn't sure he had that much faith in the system himself.

"Or at the very least, they're not going to prosecute someone innocent who's as unlikely a suspect as you are."

To Zoe's surprise, she found this reassuring. Ethan had reasoned it out in a way that her high-running emotions had prevented her from doing. She felt her gut unclench just a little. And then a little more.

She leaned back in her chair. "Maybe you're right."

And then she leaned forward again. "Thank you."

This man was beginning to get her attention. There was something about him that made her feel safe in his presence. He seemed so sure of himself, as though he were in control of the world around him.

Just as she started to wonder where this lunch might go, Ethan looked at his watch. "I want to get out on the ebb tide," he said, "so I should get going." He stood up. "Thanks for lunch."

"You earned it," she said. "And I can't tell you how much I appreciate your talking me down. It's hard to see it clearly when you're knee-deep in it."

"I'm glad I could help, and I really don't think you have to worry about this. I'll be next door a lot, and I'm happy to talk you down anytime you'd like. Just come by."

"I will."

⁓⁂⁓

When Ethan was gone, Zoe went upstairs and turned on the shower. She waited for it to run hot, and then tossed her dirty clothes in the hamper and stepped in. At first, the heat felt like it was almost too much, but as she got used to it she made it hotter and hotter.

It was when the bathroom was completely steamed up that she felt

Robert's presence. He didn't say anything, and she didn't feel his touch, but she knew he was there. She felt a tingling excitement and an awareness of her nakedness.

She waited to feel the warmth of his caress, the feel of his breath, but neither came. Still, she could sense his presence. She felt her body begin to respond to the thought of that caress, that breath, and the dull ache began to spread from her core outward.

She stood directly under the showerhead and felt the water cascade from her shoulders, and she felt the meandering rivulets that found their way down her body. Her own heat seemed to match the heat of the water.

She had the soap in one hand, and she rubbed it across her belly and then down. She ran it between her legs and felt its slippery, hard surface against her pussy. And then she did it again.

She put the soap back in the dish, and reached for that magic little spot with her middle finger. She rubbed her finger across it, back and forth, slowly, and felt the shooting pleasure emanate out toward her legs and back. She leaned against the tile wall, still cool despite the hot water, and closed her eyes.

That was when she felt his touch. It came between her hand and her cunt, taking over. It was the same motion she used herself, light pressure, back and forth, only it seemed to come out of nowhere. The feeling was eerie and erotic at the same time, and she groaned.

The light touch got a little harder and the stroke a little faster, and she felt her muscles begin to tense. And then it slowed and lightened again, and her quickened breath slowed a bit with it.

She felt the caress move up, lightly, gently. Up her belly, up between her breasts, to her collarbone, to her chin.

It tilted her head up, and she heard a whisper. Only this time, she actually heard it. With her ears. Like a real voice. "Open your eyes."

She did, and there he was.

She gasped with the shock of seeing him standing before her. For a split second, she felt exposed, vulnerable. And then he smiled, and she melted.

His eyes, his face, his hair were all just as she remembered them from the one glimpse she'd had. But he was tall, taller than she'd thought, and she had to tilt her head to look at him.

He was every bit as beautiful as she'd thought him the last time.

His body was smooth and taut, almost hairless. He was tanned, and it occurred to her to wonder whether a ghost's tan ever faded.

He ran his hand down her arm and took her hand in his. He brought it to his own chest, and she touched him. He felt almost, but not exactly, like a real, live man. Had she had a chance to guess what he'd have felt like, she would have imagined she could put her hand right through him, that he'd be a mirage, an apparition. But the opposite was true. He felt, if anything, harder than a living being. He was firm, solid, and very, very real.

Just touching him unleashed a fountain in Zoe. She'd felt drawn to him in all their encounters, but now that he was standing in front of her, she was overwhelmed with pure desire.

She ran her hand down his chest, feeling every ridge, every muscle. She touched his cock, which was as taut and hard as the rest of him, and she found that it responded to her. *He* responded to her. He groaned and reached for her.

His kiss electrified her. His tongue, his lips, his very proximity. She felt the full length of her hot, soapy body against him, his hands behind her, pulling her to him. She felt the length of his cock against her belly and her breasts pushing against his chest.

She pulled away, just a little, so she could look at him. As a voice and a touch, he had captured her imagination, but he had been incomplete. As a whole man, he was truly compelling. She wanted to have him, and to give herself to him.

He pulled her close again and ran his hands down her back, over her ass, and back up her sides. He reached for the soap and ran it all over her body and his own.

They embraced; they caressed; they explored. They discovered each other's bodies, and Zoe felt an intensity and a level of arousal that she could barely contain. Her body responded to him like a wire pulled tight. His touch, wherever it landed, vibrated the whole of her.

She marveled at the perfection of him. His beauty, the grace of his movements, the smooth, well-defined musculature. She touched every part of him, as though to commit him to memory. Even as he stood in front of her, she wondered whether he'd ever be real to her again. She wanted to remember every detail, from the way his compact nipples pointed slightly out to the way the palm of her hand fit in the dimple on the side of his ass.

She knelt on the floor of the bathtub so she could touch his thighs, hold his balls, rub his hard cock against her soft cheek. Her tongue flitted out and brushed the underside of his penis, and she felt it flutter and stiffen just a little bit more.

She stood up and looked at him. She tried to see into him, to know what he was by looking into his eyes. She saw brightness and clarity in their perfect blue.

He reached down and put his hand under her ass and lifted her.

She wrapped her legs around him and reached down for his cock. She stroked it, soapy and rigid in her hand, and then guided it into her.

They moaned at the same time, in the same pitch, with the astonishing pleasure of it.

Held hard between Robert and the wall of the shower, Zoe gave herself up to the feeling of his erect penis inside her. She felt the length of him plunge in and ease out. She relished the warmth of the water, the hard surface of the tile, the slide that the soap gave to the touch of skin on skin.

Her orgasm was unstoppable. She felt herself going toward the edge long before the edge was in view, and she knew nothing could come between her and it. It started soft and small, and it grew. It expanded, it gained momentum, and then it came.

It filled her so completely, so intensely, that she cried out.

And then it had a second wave that took her completely by surprise, and she cried out again, astonished that her body could have so much left to give.

As that second wave subsided, she felt him shudder and then tense. He groaned, softly but deeply, as his orgasm picked up where hers left off.

Finally, she felt his shoulders and his arms relax as he recovered himself.

For a moment or two he held her there, up against the tile. The water flowed over them, keeping them warm as their bodies started to cool. He put her down, and she turned in to the shower to rinse off her face.

When she turned around again, he was gone.

No, not quite gone. His body was gone, but she still felt him there. And then she heard him in her head. *You have to be careful.*

It took her a moment to readjust to this way of talking to him. "Careful of what?"

There are things about the Nickersons that you don't know. It was barely a whisper inside her head.

Her attention, which had been lingering on the image of Robert in the flesh, shifted back to Nickerson's murder. "What don't I know?" she asked sharply.

One of them committed murder, and the rest of them conspired to cover it up.

"Murder? Who was murdered?"

I was.

Zoe was surprised into speechlessness. Her mouth hung open. She turned around and shut off the shower as she tried to process this, and stepped out of the tub and reached for her robe.

She had known he'd died young, because Tom, Dick, and Harry had told her. But she'd been so absorbed by the story of Molly's death that she hadn't given much thought to Robert's.

"You were murdered?" she finally said, incredulous.

That's why I haunt this house.

She finally had the presence of mind to do the math. "But Curtis Nickerson wasn't even alive when you died."

He didn't kill me. His father did.

This took a moment to sink in. "What happened?"

He told her the story.

Everything changed between the Chapins and Nickersons the night Molly died.

No one knew what had happened until the next day, when Molly's parents found her missing and saw that her bed hadn't been slept in. They came to Chapin House to see whether she was there, or if Robert knew where she was. He said they'd had a quarrel and that Molly had run from him when they were several miles down the beach. He hadn't seen her since.

Search parties were mobilized, and it wasn't more than an hour or two before her body was found near the train tracks, where she'd been struck by the mail train, which had come through a little after midnight. There had been an investigation, and Robert had told the police the story of his fight with Molly.

There were only three possible explanations for Molly's death. Either it was an accident, a suicide, or a murder. If it was a murder, Robert was, of course, the prime suspect.

The police found very little to go on. The train's engineer had witnessed nothing. The body had been so mangled by the train that it was impossible to tell whether there had been a struggle. The sandy soil held nothing that could be identified as a footprint. All they had was Robert's version of the quarrel, and a dead girl.

Eventually, the death was ruled an accident, but not everyone was satisfied with the verdict. Molly's family, particularly, thought that there was more to the story.

Because Clara had made no secret of her opposition to her son's engagement to Molly, everyone in town knew she'd been waging a campaign against the marriage, and that she had used every weapon at her disposal, including the threat of disinheritance.

There were those in the town who believed that Robert, if he had to choose between Molly and all that the Chapin coffers had to offer, would choose the latter. Although it was clear to everyone that he loved her, his enemies thought him weak and false, and didn't think his love could withstand that kind of test.

Those enemies took sustenance from the story of one of Robert's law school classmates, in whom he had confided. He'd told his friend about his mother's threat and confessed that it was a hard choice. He cursed his mother for putting him in that position and said that he found himself vacillating.

His friend had been quite clear that Robert had never said he'd give up Molly; he said only that he had thought about it. But that was enough to convince a lot of people, including Molly's older brother, Paul.

The week after Molly died, Paul came to Chapin House and asked to see Robert. Robert came down to meet him on the back deck, and Paul handed him the little shell ring. He told Robert that Molly would have wanted him to have it back, since he broke his engagement to her, and he turned around and went home.

From that day, Robert felt nothing but menace from all the Nickersons, but from Paul in particular. At first, the situation was uncomfortable enough that he thought about taking the Chicago job and leaving town, but his mother also felt vaguely threatened, and he didn't want to leave her alone.

He stayed, and eventually feelings on all sides were blunted by the passage of time.

It wasn't until three years later that Paul took his revenge.

Robert still had the catboat that he and Molly had taken the day they first made love. He didn't use it much, because it brought up too many difficult memories, but every now and then, on a good day with a steady breeze, he'd take it out into the bay.

And that was what he did one day in September 1950.

He wasn't out long before he heard the drone of a motor and saw Paul Nickerson waving to him from his fishing boat, the *Nick of Time*. He signaled that he wanted to pull up alongside, and Robert motioned him in.

From there, it was the easiest thing in the world. When Robert leaned over to ask what he wanted, Paul simply bashed him over the head with an ax handle, rendering him unconscious. He tossed him in the water and drove away.

Anyone would have assumed he'd been hit by the boom and fell overboard. And that was exactly what everyone did assume. That it was a terrible accident was never questioned.

Paul, the oldest of the Nickerson children, didn't marry until several years later, when a girl from New York, whose family summered in Danmouth, caught his fancy like no other girl ever had. Their first child was a girl, and five years later they had a son. They named him Curtis—his mother's maiden name.

∼❦∽

When Robert finished the story, Zoe took some time to absorb it.

"But how can he be guilty of covering it up if he wasn't born until more than ten years later?"

He knew. From the time he was a teenager, he knew. And now he's finally paid.

There was something about his tone that made Zoe wonder whether Robert had had something to do with Nickerson's death.

"Did you . . . ?" She wasn't at all sure how to phrase the question. Her mind was going over the possibilities. Could Robert himself have killed him? Surely not, or he would have done it a long time ago, and probably would have killed Paul instead. Could he have been waiting for an earthly instrument? A flesh-and-blood human he could manipulate? For *her*?

Surely not.

Zoe wasn't sure what kinds of rules existed for human/ghost interactions, but she didn't think ghosts could make people kill other people. But maybe it was there in the fine print: that it worked only if the human was sleepwalking, the way you could kill vampires only at midnight. Or when the moon was full. Or something.

But this wasn't just any ghost. This was Robert.

Still, she wanted to ask the question. She needed to ask the question.

"Did I . . . ?" she started again.

But she realized he was gone.

CHAPTER TWELVE

The idea that Robert might have had something to do with Nickerson's death cost Zoe another sleepless night, and the next morning she couldn't shake her anxiety about what she had done that night.

She tried to distract herself with gardening, but it didn't work. She took a walk along the beach and then tried settling in with a book, but those activities didn't work either. She couldn't make the little knot in her gut dissipate.

She decided to take the bull by the horns and trace the steps she would have taken if she had sleepwalked to Nickerson's cottage. Perhaps that would trigger a memory—if there was a memory to be triggered.

She started in the bedroom and walked down the stairs. Out the back door, across the deck, down the stone steps. Then off to the right, to the path through the sand and scrub that led to Nickerson's house.

She took it slowly, looking for anything that might be a clue, might tap into the inaccessible depths of her memory.

Nothing did.

She got to the house and stood at some distance to it. She didn't know whether Ethan was staying there, but if he was, she didn't want him to catch her casing the house.

She looked at the door that led into the foyer where the ceramic statue had been. She tried to imagine going through it in the middle of the night, picking up the statue, and bashing Curtis Nickerson over the head. She couldn't.

She was dismayed when the door opened and Ethan walked outside.

"Hello," he said. "I thought I heard something."

She felt herself blush.

"I'm sorry. I didn't know you were here." After he'd been so sensible and rational talking her down yesterday, she was reluctant to admit that her anxiety had resurfaced. But anything else sounded like she was stalking him, so she decided she'd better tell him the truth.

"I know it sounds silly," she said, "but I was hoping that walking down here the way I would have done if I'd been sleepwalking might trigger something, might help me remember." She shrugged and gave a half smile.

She breathed an inward sigh of relief when Ethan said, "That sounds reasonable."

"Well, whether it's reasonable or not, it didn't work," she said. "It's just a blank. The whole night."

He opened the door and gestured inside. "Come in. Do you want some coffee, or a glass of iced tea?"

"No, thanks. I should get back." There was no need for her to get back, but she didn't want to make him rehash all the reasons she shouldn't worry about what happened that night. She knew the reasons, but they couldn't chase away the fear.

"Oh, come on," he said. "It's a beautiful day to have iced tea on the porch. Besides, I owe you one for the one you gave me the other day, not to mention the lunch."

She hesitated. She wanted to stay, but she didn't want to come off as an idiot.

He opened the door wider and stepped aside so she could walk in. She did.

There were piles of papers, photographs, and files on the kitchen table.

"That looks like a lot of work," she said by way of heading off any further discussion of what, in Ethan's presence, seemed again like a ridiculous scenario. She couldn't, she told herself, have possibly killed Curtis Nickerson, so there was no need to discuss it.

"It is, but it's interesting work. Some of that stuff dates back over a hundred years, and there's lots more where that came from." He pointed up to the attic.

Ethan took a pitcher of iced tea out of the refrigerator and poured two glasses. They went out on the small porch overlooking the water and sat down in the twin rockers.

Had she known him better, Zoe would have asked if she could see what was up there. She was intensely curious to find any artifacts of the stories Robert had told her.

"I wish Chapin House hadn't been cleared out so thoroughly before I bought it. The stories it could have told."

"Are you interested in the history of the place?"

"I couldn't imagine buying an old house like that without being interested in its history. It's a big part of the appeal. And Chapin House has particular significance for me, because I've known it all my life. My family vacationed here when I was a kid."

Ethan nodded. He'd known that, but he didn't say.

"It's funny," she went on. "I wanted to do some work on the house, just some things to make it more comfortable and efficient, bring it up-to-date. I thought it was all in the spirit of the place—I mean, I bought it to preserve it—but your uncle thought it was a kind of blasphemy."

She looked down at her glass, talking as much to herself as to him.

"I think he saw me as just one step removed from the rich city people who come here, flash their money around, and tear down the cottages to build their luxury summer homes."

"I think that's the way he saw everyone who wasn't born here."

Zoe gave a soft laugh.

"What did you want to do, add a three-car garage?" he asked.

"Not exactly. I wanted granite countertops and new windows."

"He could hardly have objected to those."

"I think it was the glass cupola that put him over the edge."

Grant smiled. "That, I could see."

"Now that he's dead, I suppose I'll have to find someone else to manage the work." She looked up at him. "Do you know anyone?"

"I know some people. But if you're not doing much, you could manage it yourself and just hire the people to do the individual jobs. It's not hard."

Zoe looked skeptical. "I've lived in an apartment my entire adult life. This is the first home I've had that's more than seven hundred square feet. I don't know that I'm up to being my own general contractor."

He paused. "Do you want to show me what you're thinking about? I could probably help you. It looks like I'll be spending time over here."

This surprised Zoe. She barely knew him, and he hadn't seemed particularly interested in the house. He did, however, seem competent.

"Sure," she said. "Do you have time right now? We could go take a look."

As they walked the quarter mile back to Chapin House, Zoe told him about all the things she'd discussed with Nickerson. He neither approved nor condemned; he simply listened.

When they got there, they did the same tour she'd done with his uncle, starting in the basement and working up through the house.

They talked about replacing the windows, refinishing the floors, and taking out a couple of walls. Zoe had a strange sense that she was repeating herself with a kinder, gentler Nickerson. Ethan agreed with her about the windows and thought it perfectly reasonable that she wanted a couple of larger rooms on the second floor.

When they got to the kitchen, though, she hesitated. All of a sudden, she saw what Curtis had objected to in granite countertops and a pot-filling faucet.

She stood in the middle of the room, her arms folded, looking around. Ethan said nothing.

She saw an old-fashioned kitchen with Formica countertops from the 1950s and white appliances several decades newer. The cabinets, solid maple, were also white. More than that, though, she saw the light. It had a cool, bluish tinge from the water. Light colors, warm surfaces were what the house needed. A counterpoint to the outdoors.

"You know," she said, turning to Ethan, "I think he might have been right."

He gave a barely perceptible nod. "That doesn't mean you have to live with Formica. What do you think about butcher-block counters? And maybe a cork floor instead of tile?"

She looked around, trying to imagine it. She could, and she liked it.

At that moment, she felt at one with the house. She hadn't realized she'd been fighting it, but now she understood she had been. She'd been trying to reconcile its spirit with her sensibilities. She could see that was a losing battle, and the smart thing, the appropriate thing, was to let the house tell her what it should be.

She looked at Ethan. What was it about him? Whenever he was with her, she felt calm, grounded. He made the world seem like a benign and manageable place.

Over the course of the hour they'd spent talking about the house, he'd made her feel its essence. He hadn't battled with her, or contradicted her, or even made many suggestions. But he had made her see the house through his eyes.

Those eyes met hers, and didn't look away.

After a couple of heartbeats, he said, "Have you looked in the shed?"

Zoe had been expecting something a little more personal, and the contrast made her smile. "I have. In fact, I just cleaned it out this morning. It's mostly some *very* old gardening stuff, and there are a couple of lobster pots."

"Let's go look," he said, with more animation than he had shown thus far.

The shed was about eight feet by ten, some fifty yards from the house on the west side. They went out and opened its door. It was as she'd said; there was some very old gardening stuff and a couple of lobster pots.

Ethan walked in and brought one of the pots out into the sunshine. He looked at it critically. It was probably a good twenty years old, but it hadn't been used much and still looked serviceable. The wire mesh had some rust spots where the plastic coating had ripped off, but he thought it would hold.

"Have you ever lobstered?" he asked Zoe.

She shook her head.

"Do you know how one of these works?"

She shook her head again.

Ethan explained to her how the entrances to the trap started wide and then narrowed, so the lobster had an easy time getting in but a difficult time getting out.

"You put the bait in a bag and hang it here." He pointed to a couple of wires in the middle of the trap's top. "You close it up, you sink it, and you wait."

"How do you know where the lobsters are?" she asked.

"Ah, isn't that the question? Usually, it's just experience. You put traps down and if you don't get lobsters, you don't go there again. You get lobsters, you stick around. Now we've got equipment that tells us something about the seafloor, and we can make educated guesses, but experience still counts for more than anything."

"Who used these pots?" Zoe couldn't picture old Clara Chapin hauling them up from the depths, and they clearly postdated Robert.

"My uncle used to set them for Clara. There's a place on the jetty where it gets deep very quickly, and you can put them in without a boat. You've been out there, haven't you?" The jetty was near the west end of the Chapin property, and Zoe had walked out on it many times.

"Have you seen the two big iron rings in the rocks?"

She nodded. "I always wondered what those were for."

"You hook the lines from the pots onto the rings so they don't get swept away by a storm."

Zoe loved the idea of putting her own lobster pots out on her own property, and dining off what she could catch in her own backyard. And Ethan's clear enthusiasm for lobstering was catching.

"Could we put them out?" Zoe asked.

"Sure, but we need bait."

"What do lobsters eat?"

"They love oily fish, like herring or bluefish. I don't suppose you have any on hand?"

"There's some smoked bluefish in the refrigerator. Does that count?"

Ethan laughed. "I'm not sure lobsters would take to that. They don't have much experience with smoked foods, so why don't you save that for yourself. But if you want to make a quick run with me over to my boat, I can get some bait and a couple of bait bags."

As she told him she'd love to do that, if he was sure he didn't mind, it occurred to her that, for the first time since she'd bought the house, she was having fun. If someone had told her that morning that Ethan Grant, whose first appearance in her life had been so inauspicious, would be the source of her first fun there, she wouldn't have believed it.

"I know you do this for a living, and so it's not very exciting for you, but it's great fun for me." She looked at him and gave him a smile that made him believe her.

"It's still exciting for me," he said. "Every time I pull up a line of pots, I don't know what I'll find. It's exciting every time. That's why I keep doing it."

They grinned at each other like children, both of them enjoying their little adventure.

"Let's go to the boat," he said, and pulled his car keys out of his pocket. Zoe felt like taking his hand and running, but thought better of it.

Less than an hour later they were back, with two bait bags and a cooler filled with frozen chunks of mackerel.

"Now comes the hard part," Ethan said. "Each of these weighs about forty pounds, and we have to get them all the way to the jetty. Can you carry one?"

Zoe wasn't sure, but she was willing to give it a try.

As it turned out, she could carry one, although she had to stop and rest a couple of times along the way. When they got to the jetty, he showed her how to fill the bait bags and string them up inside the traps. When the pots were baited and closed, Ethan walked to the very edge of the jetty and threw the traps, one at a time, as far from the rocks as he could.

There was a rope attached to each pot, with a clip hook on the end, and he hooked them to the two iron rings set in the rocks.

"And now we wait."

Zoe looked at her watch involuntarily. "How long?"

"Overnight, at least."

She found herself disappointed. She was eager to catch her first lobster.

They walked back along the beach slowly. Zoe asked him how he ended up being a lobsterman. "Was your family in the business?"

"My father was an accountant, and he was bitterly disappointed that this was what I did with my college education."

"You went to college?" Zoe asked, before she had a chance to think about the kind of prejudice the question revealed.

Ethan raised one corner of his mouth in a half smile. "You think only people who don't have choices choose work like this?"

Zoe reddened. "N-no . . ." she stammered a bit. "It's not that. . . ." And then she thought for a moment. She stopped walking so she could look him full in the face. "Actually, yes, it *is* that. Exactly that."

His look encouraged her to go on. "I've never met anyone who had choices and chose work like this. The people I know chose to become doctors or investment bankers or architects, or they went into business for themselves." She thought of Sam, and added, "Or they tried to be artists of some kind—painters, writers. Manual work was something that going to college meant you didn't have to do."

"Have you ever known *anyone* who's chosen work like this?" he asked, but in a way that indicated that he wanted to know, not that he was pointing out what a sheltered life she'd led.

She thought a moment. "No," she said. "I don't think I have."

"You might be surprised. There's a particular satisfaction that comes with doing physical work. It's tangible; it's exhausting; it's satisfying. But most manual work has an element that's not manual at all. Lobsters are actually pretty interesting, and we don't know much about them. I've done some work with the marine biologists down at Woods Hole to study them. If I were a carpenter, I'd be interested in all the kinds of wood and their properties. If I were a mason, I'd know about bricks and cement and concrete—concrete's fascinating, by the way."

He paused to see if she was still following him. She was, with interest. She thought about how much she'd enjoyed the simple act of building raised beds, and how that kind of work contrasted with the behind-the-desk type that had consumed her when she ran her seed business.

"People who do manual work end their day with something to show for it. I come in with a hold full of lobsters, something that feeds people. What do I go home with if I'm an investment banker?"

"Besides the paycheck?"

"Besides the paycheck."

They started walking again.

She couldn't put her finger on why Ethan seemed so . . . so . . . solid. Everything about him was reassuring. He was stable; he was confident; he was directed. His focus was outward, to what he thought was important in the world.

She couldn't help but compare him not just to Sam, but to Robert. He made both of them seem almost unreliable. Not to be counted on.

She also compared Ethan to herself. In a way, she had also carved out her place in the world, but she had always felt like she'd just been lucky. She started an Internet business because that was what everyone was doing at the time, and the fact that her business succeeded when so many others failed was due more to chance, she thought, than to her brilliance or hard work.

Regardless of whether or not that was true, she knew she had never felt the kind of direction or commitment that Ethan seemed to feel about his chosen life.

It hadn't occurred to her that the life she had planned, spending summers in Danmouth and winters in New York, living off the income of the proceeds of her business, would be unsatisfying. After the work she'd put in on the business, a life of leisure had sounded awfully good.

She was going to have to rethink that. Now that she didn't need the money, she was free to do whatever kind of work she wanted.

They went on in silence for a while, and it was only when they stopped talking that she noticed that her body, independent of her mind, was having a reaction to his presence. She felt the edginess, the awareness, as though her nerves were standing at attention. There was a yearning, and it was growing.

They reached Chapin House, and they stood looking at it from the beach. The Nickerson cottage was just visible off to the east. She invited Ethan to come up to the deck, and they walked up the stone steps together.

"Have you heard anything about what's going to happen to the cottage?" Zoe asked. "Do you know any details about the original will that gave it to the Nickersons?"

"I know a little. The house is supposed to pass from son to son, but I'm not sure those kinds of things are enforceable. It's been in the family for over a century now, and I'm no lawyer, but I think that counts for something." And then he shrugged. "But maybe it doesn't. I don't know."

"Don't you care?" Zoe was surprised at his nonchalance.

"I guess I do. I'd rather have it than not have it, but I was doing fine without it."

They sat for a few minutes in silence, looking at the water, and then Ethan got up to leave. "I've still got a fair amount to do over there." He nodded in the direction of the cottage. "And I think DuBois wants me to spend time there to discourage any curious souvenir hunters."

Zoe thought about asking him to stay for a while, to see what they might be able to whip up for dinner, but then she thought better of it. If this was going to develop into something, she wanted to give it space and time to do it at its own pace.

She thanked him for showing her the lobster pots. "Do we get to check them tomorrow?"

He grinned. "We do. Maybe we can have lobster rolls for lunch."

"I'd like that."

When he was gone, Zoe opened a bottle of wine, sat on the deck with a glass, and thought about him. He'd made an impression on her, but it wasn't like the impressions other men had made. When she'd met Sam, she'd been taken with him immediately. His charm, his circumstances, his good looks all conspired to make him irresistible. And he hadn't been the first man she'd fallen for almost at first sight. It had happened to her often enough that she'd gotten the idea that that was what attraction was—an immediate connection, a faster heartbeat, a sexual tug.

Ethan Grant made her see her love life with a new clarity. When she first met him, she hadn't much cared for him. She hadn't thought him particularly attractive, and she certainly felt no quickening of her pulse. Their conversation had been a slog, and she had thought him ungainly, a bit odd.

Now, though, after spending time with him, she felt profoundly drawn to him. His quiet confidence, his comfort with himself, his physical size and strength, made him seem so manly. And so desirable.

Zoe had always had confidence in her ability to attract the men who interested her. She knew how to deploy her vivacious good spirits, her ready wit, and her good looks to get attention. But she wasn't confident that she could attract Ethan. And, the more she considered it, the clearer it became to her that attracting Ethan was what she wanted to do.

Could she? She wasn't sure. For the first time in her life, she asked herself whether she was good enough to win a man. A very particular man.

The idea that he might not be within her grasp had the predictable effect of making him that much more desirable in her eyes. She lay down on the swing on her deck, closed her eyes, and tried to conjure the vision of him. She could see specifics—his close-cropped dark hair with scatterings of premature gray, his wide brow and the thoughtful dark eyes beneath it—but the pieces wouldn't come together in a faithful whole, a picture of the man.

She played back some of what they'd done that day, hoping to sneak up on a memory that would bring him into focus. There was Ethan opening the door at the Nickerson cottage, Ethan looking at her kitchen counters, Ethan pulling his car keys out of his pocket. Still, her mental image was hazy. It was maddening.

In lieu of the whole, she focused on the parts. The way his jeans had hung easily from his waist, the smooth bulge of a biceps below the sleeve of his T-shirt. And his hands—she thought she'd never seen hands like that. Hard, strong, calloused, and capable, they were the kinds of hands she could imagine touching her, lightly and then not so lightly. On her face, around her waist, and then everywhere.

She imagined the pressure, just where it mattered most, and then she thought she felt the pressure. She reined in her imagination to focus on her physical sensations, and there it was. A gentle pressing on the inside of each of her thighs, and the familiar prickling on the back of her neck.

She wondered whether Robert knew she'd spent the day with Ethan. He'd told her he was consigned to the house he haunted, and didn't have jurisdiction outside its grounds. Regardless, she counted herself lucky that he couldn't read her thoughts, which were, at that moment, decidedly intimate.

When Robert had appeared to her in the shower, he'd taken her breath away. But the contrast between Ethan and Robert was more than the difference between a living man and a spirit. Ethan's concreteness wasn't just literal. Zoe thought she could lean against him figuratively, as well.

Between the warmth of the setting sun on her face and the fog of the first stages of arousal that her thoughts of Ethan had brought on, she wasn't reasoning very clearly. Right then, lying on the swing, enjoying the afterglow of a wonderful day, she didn't want to sort it all out. She didn't want to make any decisions. She just wanted to bask, to relax, to enjoy.

Happy? was the question the voice in her head asked, as the pressure became a little firmer and more deliberate.

"Mmmm," was Zoe's response. She wasn't sure whether there had been sarcasm in the question. And she was happy.

He's a Nickerson, you know. Apparently there had been.

"Mmmm," she said again. Basking, relaxing, enjoying. She wouldn't be drawn in. She loved the strangeness of the ghostly caress, and she lay still on the swing, focused on the sensation. She didn't want to talk.

Apparently, neither did he. Not then.

She felt the whisper of a touch on her neck, and she imagined it as Ethan's breath. The surrounding pressure on her breast was his hand, cupping her. The force was on her skin, under her clothes, and it became, in her mind, his skin, his touch.

She lay absolutely still, all her energy concentrated on the fantasy in her mind.

It began as a kind of massage touching every part of her, from the soles of her feet to the tips of her earlobes. It was a gentle touch, but it seemed to have a backbone of strength. She had the idea that, if she struggled against it, she would lose.

She didn't struggle.

She was completely relaxed, with just the soft beginnings of real desire, when the pressure became a little more intense, more purposeful. It would start in one part of her body and then move, unexpectedly, to another.

She felt it encircling both her breasts and then concentrating at her nipples until she felt a direct line from them to the increasingly moist spot between her legs. Still, she didn't move.

Then it jumped to her waist and went around it almost like a lasso, tightening and loosening, tightening and loosening. Would Ethan's hands go all the way around? She wasn't sure.

Her arousal was beginning to build, and some of her muscles were tightening of their own accord. But she didn't want to lose her sense of relaxation, and so she deliberately unclenched them. She imagined herself inert and passive, floating in a sea of sensation.

That was what it felt like. It was like no human touch in that it grew in size and strength to envelop her completely. She was submerged in a bath of something heavy, something in constant motion. It was a continuous, all-over caress.

It was getting more difficult to maintain her passive relaxation in the face of mounting desire. The caress developed little hot spots—they felt like fingers—where both pressure and temperature increased. She felt them first pinching the narrow spot behind her ankles, a spot she never would have thought could be sexy, but it definitely felt that way now.

They moved to the back of her knees, and then radiated up the insides of her thighs. They traced every aspect of her intimate anatomy, coaxing her juices out. Then one of them was inside her. Far, far inside her, touching her where no man had ever gone. It was an astonishing sensation. The hot spot came back out, and then went in again.

In her mind, it was Ethan, making love to her for the first time.

She moaned, but she didn't move.

As one of the hot spots traced the inside of her, another traced the outside. A third found the hard little button of her clitoris and stayed with it, nudging it gently to the right, and then to the left.

It was a feeling that no two-handed human could have managed, and she reveled in it. She sank deeper into the fantasy of making love to Ethan, even though he wouldn't have been able to do quite what this spirit was doing to her.

The three hot spots continued, getting just a little faster and just a little harder, never interrupting their rhythm.

She was aching for a climax, but she still kept her body relaxed. She didn't want to hurry it. She wanted to let it happen. She was passive, inert, surrounded.

And she felt what wasn't the beginnings of an orgasm, but was rather the first sign that the beginnings were imminent. There was a rich, full feeling in the backs of her calves, and it started to spread.

It ran up the back of her legs, and then, as it spread, it turned into ecstasy. From her toes, which curled involuntarily, to the tips of her fingers, she was consumed by pure pleasure.

She marveled at its strength, only to feel it get stronger. From what she thought was its peak, it gathered new momentum, and a fresh wave broke over her. And then a third.

It was the longest, strongest orgasm she'd ever experienced, and it took her breath away.

As she came down the other side of it, the touch receded. It softened and cooled, and then disappeared altogether.

Only then did she open her eyes. She didn't know whether Robert was still there, but she felt the shell ring, still on the ring finger of her right hand, twist.

Then she was sure he was gone. He'd made his point.

CHAPTER THIRTEEN

❧

The next morning, Zoe was up early. She felt fresh and energized, and attributed it to the day she'd spent with Ethan. It crossed her mind that the session on the porch swing might have had something to do with it, but in the bright light of morning, she wanted to think about real, live people.

She was burning with curiosity about the lobster traps. Was it possible that there were lobsters in them so soon after they had set them? She considered walking over to the Nickerson cottage to see whether Ethan was up, but she didn't want to appear quite that eager.

Well, okay, then, she'd just have to pull them herself.

She wasn't confident that she could. She'd had a great deal of trouble just carrying one, and hauling one up from the murky depths wasn't going to be easy. They were at least thirty feet down.

She could try, at the very least.

She found a sturdy pair of gardening gloves and a large bucket for any lobsters she caught, and she headed out to the jetty.

She stopped at the first iron ring and put on the gloves. She picked up the rope and pulled. At first it didn't feel that difficult, but that was just because she was taking up the slack. As soon as the pot left the seafloor, it was much, much harder.

She pulled with a will, holding on to the rope and walking to the far side of the jetty, leaning in with all her strength. Then she made her way hand-over-hand back to where the rope disappeared over the rocks and did it again. Each pull got her about five feet.

After only four pulls, she was tired enough that she wrapped the rope around a jutting rock and caught her breath.

On the next pull, she felt the trap clang against the rocks. She peered over the edge. There it was! And something was moving inside it.

Suddenly she wasn't tired anymore, and she pulled the pot up the side of the jetty in a series of four or five good tugs.

There was something moving, but it wasn't a lobster. It was three crabs—two small and one enormous, with only one claw. She was terribly disappointed, and she had no idea what to do with them. She didn't know what kind of crabs they were, or whether they were edible. She wanted to ask Ethan, but she couldn't very well just leave the crabs there until she could come back with him, and she knew she wasn't strong enough to throw the pot the way he had.

She opened it and took out the crabs one by one, tossing them back in the water. She closed the pot—there was still bait in the bait bag—and left it on the edge of the jetty.

Was it worth it to pull the second one?

She wasn't looking forward to the effort, but if she went home now she'd wonder all morning what was in there, and she didn't like the idea that she'd have to tell Ethan she pulled one but then quit.

She picked up the rope.

The second pot felt harder than the first, probably because she was already tired. She had to rest twice before she got the pot up over the waterline.

Again, something was moving. She felt her heart beat faster, but she told herself not to get her hopes up.

As she pulled the pot up, though, she could see that the something looked a lot like a lobster. A pretty big lobster. She was surprised as she felt the flush of adrenaline. She never would have thought pulling a lobster pot would be so exciting.

She hauled it up to the jetty and saw that it wasn't a lobster—it was two lobsters!

Two lobsters! She almost jumped with the joy of it. She'd caught two lobsters in her own backyard.

She opened the pot and gingerly transferred the lobsters from the trap to the bucket. There were also two crabs in the trap, and those she consigned back to the water.

She couldn't wait to show Ethan, and as she made her way homeward she found herself skipping like a little girl. She couldn't believe how good it made her feel to have been up early, done some hard work, and accomplished something so concrete. Somehow, the complexities of the modern world, the nuances of her various relationships, even the looming threat of being a murder suspect, all fell away in the simple pleasure of catching a lobster.

She went straight to the Nickerson cottage, but hesitated before she knocked on the door. It wasn't even eight o'clock yet, and she didn't want to wake Ethan, or even catch him unawares. But as she paused, she heard stirrings within, so she gave a brisk couple of knocks.

Ethan opened the door and she held out the bucket of lobsters, beaming.

He looked at the bucket, and he looked at Zoe. And then he smiled the widest smile she'd seen on him yet.

"You pulled the pots!" he said.

"I did."

"I would have thought they'd be too heavy for you."

"They're heavy, but I managed." Her excitement hadn't left her. "I got two lobsters!" She held the bucket out so he could see them up close.

"So I see!"

He was clearly impressed, and she positively basked in his admiration.

"What should we do with them?" she asked him.

"Well, we could keep them as pets, but I'd recommend we eat them."

She grinned. "I've never cooked a lobster before."

"I've cooked hundreds, so you're in good hands. Bring 'em into the kitchen." He opened the door wide and stood aside for her to pass. "We'll have them for breakfast."

They went into the kitchen and put the lobster bucket on the table. Ethan took a big pot down from the top of the cabinets. "We should cook them in seawater."

They went down to the shore and filled the pot about two-thirds of the way. "You should have a lot of water in the pot so it returns to the boil immediately after you put the lobsters in. You want them to die as quickly as possible."

"Do they feel pain?"

"We don't really know. Whether a lobster's nervous system is capable of what we think of as pain is a controversial question in the lobstering community. I'm not sure at all. Some people put a knife through the back of the head to kill it before they put it in the water, but I'm not convinced that hurts any less."

They went back to the cottage, and Ethan put the pot on to boil. While they waited, they drank coffee and she told him about pulling the pots.

When the time came to put the lobsters in the water, Ethan took the pot off the lid and motioned that she should pick up one of the lobsters.

"Take the big one first. It looks like it's about two pounds, and it should cook in about twelve minutes. The second one's smaller, so we'll put it in two minutes later."

She gave him a look that clearly said she'd rather not do this.

"If you're going to take creatures out of the ocean, you owe it to them to see it through to the end," he said, a little didactically. And then, with more compassion: "I know it's no fun, but it's got to be done."

She steeled herself and picked up the bigger lobster.

"Head in first," he told her.

She slipped him into the water and looked away.

He put the lid back on. "It's not so bad, once you get used to it."

"I'm not sure I want to get used to it."

"If you eat lobsters, this is part of the process. Some people refuse to eat them because of it, but I always think that if you're going to eat them, you ought to be able to do the dirty work."

After two minutes, he opened the pot again, and she put the second lobster in.

"Ten minutes to lobster," he said. "But we'll need butter."

He took some out of the refrigerator, cut off several thick pats, and put them in a small saucepan to melt over low heat. He took out plates, lobster crackers, and two tiny, skinny forks. A big bowl for shells, a huge pile of napkins, and they were ready.

When the lobsters were cooked and cool enough to handle, Ethan put the larger one on her plate.

"No," she protested. "You take the big one. I'll eat the little one."

"Lobsterman gets the big one," he said, and refused to switch.

"So, ah . . ." Zoe began, looking at the big red crustacean on her plate, "where do you start?"

"Wherever you want," said Ethan, and then noticed her bewilderment. "Is this your first lobster?"

"I've eaten lots of lobster, but this part has always been done before it gets to me," she said.

He was surprised. "But you came here every summer as a kid. You really never had a lobster?"

"We didn't have the budget for a lot of lobster, and even when we did I went for the fried clams. I was a little squeamish about food when I was little."

"Are you still?"

"No," she lied. It was still hard for her to deal with some kinds of food, but she didn't like that about herself and she tried to get over it.

"Well," he said, "I start with the claws."

They started with the claws, and he showed her how to break the shell at the joints and extract the meat in big pieces. He told her about lobster anatomy, and how to tell a male from a female. He showed her the little nooks and crannies where small morsels of meat were hiding.

They dipped the pieces in butter and ate them with relish, paying no attention to the butter that dripped onto the table or the pieces of lobster that went flying when they cracked the tails. They sat side by side, watching each other eat, and giving themselves completely to the pleasure of the meal, and of eating it together.

It was one of the most intimate activities that Zoe had ever experienced.

When they'd eaten the claws and tail, he opened the carapace and showed her the green tomalley inside. "It's the liver," he explained.

"People eat that?" she asked. She couldn't help making a disgusted face.

"People don't just eat it; they love it."

His enthusiasm made her feel like a food sissy. It took some fortitude, but she told him she'd taste it.

He took a small forkful and fed it to her, watching for her reaction. She was braced for something slimy and disgusting, but she found it surprisingly good. It was mild, with just a little earthy flavor, and its texture was creamy.

His enjoyment of her enjoyment was written on his face.

She cracked open the other carapace, and a white gob of lobster fat landed on Ethan's cheek. She laughed and reached out to brush it off with her thumb. When she had, he took her hand and held it to his cheek. He turned his face into it and took her thumb in his mouth.

He held her eyes as he sucked gently, and then he let it go.

Zoe felt her heart leap. She had thought she felt the connection and the sexual tension between them, but she wasn't sure. She didn't trust herself to read him accurately, and she was relieved and elated to find that she had. He had broken the barrier between friendship and something more, and now they were through. She was filled with a sense of anticipation.

"You taste like lobster," he said.

"And small wonder." She licked one of her own fingers and then nodded, confirming.

"All that's left are the legs." He turned his attention back to the remains of his lobster.

"Is there meat in them?" Zoe asked.

"There's a little, but you have to work for it."

He showed her how to break the legs at the joint and work the little bite of meat out of the long segment with her teeth.

She ate two of the largest legs, but didn't think the rest were worth the effort.

"Come on," Ethan said. "You can't qualify as a lobster eater unless you eat them all." He broke off one of her lobster's legs, cracked it, and held it out to her. She put both her hands around his, still holding the leg, and worked the meat out of it.

Then she took the empty shell out of his hand and kissed the end of his thumb. "There's not much to choose between them," she said, holding his thumb in one hand and the lobster leg in the other.

For a moment, they just looked at each other. Neither of them was in a hurry to get where they seemed to be going. They were enjoying the moment, each other's company, and the promise the morning held.

When they had finished every last morsel of both lobsters, they cleaned up and took a last cup of coffee out to the porch.

They were about to sit down when a boat came roaring around Chapin Point. Zoe recognized it as the gunboat-gray boat of the clammer who had given Nickerson the finger on the first day she'd met him, right out on this beach.

This time the boat slowed, and Steve Cromwell waved at Ethan.

"Hey, Grant," he shouted over the sound of the idling engine, "I'm sorry about your uncle."

Ethan nodded his acknowledgment, but said nothing.

His silence seemed to make Cromwell uncomfortable. "I mean, I can't say I liked the guy, but I didn't want him to get his head bashed in or anything."

Again, Ethan nodded.

"He just never understood what it was to make a living from the sea," continued Cromwell. "I didn't want to have to fight with the guy."

Ethan walked down the steps of the porch, toward the beach, but still said nothing.

Cromwell seemed to feel compelled to keep talking. "You know what it's like being out there every day, how tough it is. A guy's gotta do what a guy's gotta do to make a living."

"I know what it's like being out there every day, how tough it is," he finally said. "So you don't need to tell me."

That was all he said. He stood on the beach, arms crossed in front of him, just looking at Cromwell. He didn't say anything either challenging or conciliatory. He just watched.

Cromwell didn't know what to make of this, and he was visibly uncomfortable. He made a halfhearted attempt to return stare for stare, but it lasted only a couple of moments. Eventually, he gave a wave that was part good-bye, part dismissal, and he roared off.

"I can't stand that guy," Ethan said to Zoe as he came back up the porch steps. "Anyone who takes off-limits clams or short lobsters or out-of-season oysters dishonors the profession and disrespects the sea."

"It was your uncle who taught me about poaching," she said, and proceeded to tell Ethan the story of getting caught clamming on a Thursday when she was six years old. "That was the first and last time I ever poached anything."

"You get a free pass when you're six," he said.

They sat for a while in silence, enjoying the breeze off the water. Zoe wanted to tell him about how pulling the lobster pots made her feel, but she was a little afraid of sounding silly, and she wasn't sure how to begin.

"You know, after this morning, I think I understand why you do it."

He looked at her and nodded encouragement.

"I mean, I know they were the first and only lobster pots I've ever pulled, so maybe I'm talking through my hat. It was really exciting, waiting for the surprise of what was in the trap, but I don't think that's it."

"You're right. That's not it."

"I've spent my whole career doing work that gets done from a desk. The closest I came to hard labor was putting seed packets in envelopes and taking them to the post office. Whenever I've gotten exercise, it's been at the gym. Today I was up almost at dawn, and all I could think about was going out to get the pots. I went out by myself, and I did something that was *hard*. But I came home with something to show for it."

"And that's what it is, isn't it?" he asked.

"That's what it is. Maybe humans get a primal satisfaction out of providing sustenance." She thought for a moment. "I built a business that got bought out for enough money to leave me financially secure for the rest of my life, and I'm proud of that. But the feeling of strenuous work that puts food on the table is so . . ." She wanted just the right word. "It's so *constructive*."

She colored, sensing that she was drawing a conclusion from very limited experience, and remembering that she was talking to someone who provided sustenance professionally.

"I suspect I'm overreaching." She backtracked. "I mean, pulling two lousy lobster pots doesn't give me license to blather on about the nobility of the work to someone who's been doing it for a decade."

He laughed softly.

"Well, I think I've earned the license, and I agree with you down the line. I started lobstering by pulling those same two pots on that same jetty, and the first time I hauled one up and found a lobster in it, I imagine I felt exactly the way you did this morning."

Zoe nodded. "The only time I've ever had a feeling like it is when I'm gardening. Somehow, it seems like I'm creating something from nothing, order from chaos. I'm getting dirty, and I'm accomplishing something."

"If that's how you feel about it, maybe you should do more gardening," Ethan said, and stood up.

He held his hand out to Zoe, and she took it. He pulled her up and, without dithering or ceremony, took her in his arms. And then he kissed her.

Zoe felt her body give in to him immediately. Over the last couple of days she'd been imagining his touch, his kiss, his closeness, but nothing she'd imagined came close to the completeness she felt being with him. There was certainly arousal, but there was something more—a rightness, a wholeness.

Her hands moved over his body, and she found that there was no softness on him. Every surface was firm and defined. There was nothing extra.

His hands were doing some exploring of their own, and she felt every part of her body come alive to his touch. When he reached under her shirt and she felt his calloused hands on her waist and her ribs, she felt her body yearn for him.

He stepped back and looked at her, and then led her into the house, through the kitchen, into the living room. He sat down on the couch and pulled her into his lap. She sat straddling him, her arms around his neck. She couldn't get enough of just looking at him. His eyes, kind and intelligent, looked back at her.

They sat like that for a long time, not talking. Their hands played over each other's body, learning the contours and textures. And then Ethan reached under her T-shirt and pulled it over her head. He traced the line where her chocolate brown bra covered her soft white skin.

She returned the favor, pulled his shirt over his head, and ran her fingers over the musculature of his chest. He was a beautiful man. His body was all muscle, but it wasn't the kind of definition that came from the gym, with six-pack abs and chiseled arms. It was the solid form built by physical work. It was a form that functioned, that lifted and hauled and pushed, that did some of the world's work. It had an authenticity to it.

"If it were winter," he said, "I'd like nothing better than to make love to you in front of that fireplace, but it seems a little silly on a summer morning."

He lifted her off his lap, stood up, and took her hand. They walked together into the bedroom.

Although this was their first time together, there wasn't the urgency or the frenetic pace of some of the first encounters Zoe had had. There was a calmness, a sense of taking their time and making the most of each moment.

Ethan unzipped her jeans, and she stepped out of them. He sat down on the edge of the bed, his hands on her waist. "You're very beautiful," he said, and kissed her belly just above the line of her panties.

Then he pulled her close, burying his head between her breasts.

Zoe ran her hands through his hair as she felt his breath, warm and damp, on her skin. Then she stepped back and pulled his hands so he stood up. She had his jeans and boxers off in a moment, and she stood in front of him, admiring his body.

His shoulders were broad, but then his shape tapered to a surprisingly narrow waist. She could see the outline of the muscles in his thighs, coming to a blunt point just above his knees. His cock stood straight out, reaching for her.

"You're very beautiful," she said, and smiled softly.

She pressed him down so he was lying faceup on the bed, and knelt beside him, her legs tucked under her.

He had his hands under his head, and his body stretched, exaggerating his leanness so a hollow triangle formed under his rib cage. She put her hand there, stretched her fingers wide, and touched the edges of his ribs. She moved her hand down, brushing the side of his cock and then stroking his thigh.

He started to sit up and reach for her, but she put her hand on his chest and pressed him back down. "I want to learn your body," she said.

She ran her hand to his knee and reached around behind it to one of those little patches, a smooth crease. She traced it with her index finger.

She ran her palm down the length of the bone at the front of his calf, and then back up. From there, she moved up the inside of his thigh, and he spread his legs a bit to accommodate her.

She reached his balls and held them in her hand. She manipulated them, rubbing them against each other, and he groaned.

Zoe leaned down and ran the tip of her tongue up the length of his penis. She held it between her palms and rubbed. Ethan didn't make any noise, but she could tell by the tension in his core that he was heating up quickly. He stroked her hair and cheek, and Zoe felt an electrical tingling at his touch.

She sat up and unhooked her bra. She took it off, wriggled out of her panties, and lay down beside Ethan. She stretched her body next to his and sighed with pleasure at the warmth of his skin next to hers, the entire length of her.

"You fit me," Ethan said.

He worked his leg between hers and she nestled against it. He rubbed his thigh against the soft mound of her pubis, and the gentle pressure was exquisite. He flexed the muscle rhythmically, and she found her excitement, which had been building slowly, suddenly spiking. With each motion, more of her body was involved until she felt as though every nerve were engaged, every muscle attuned.

Suddenly, their pace changed. They had taken their time and savored their moments, but now they needed each other. They held each other and kissed as though they wanted to taste each other's essence. Their legs were intertwined, their movements in sync, their excitement building.

She paused to take a breath and take control. Ethan turned her on her back to let her arousal ebb just a bit, and admired her body in much the same way she had admired his. She was small and curvy, not so much thin as taut. Her body was firm and functional, but with a softness his lacked.

He put his hand between her legs and nudged them apart. He felt the fine down on her thighs against the back of his fingers as he moved his hand closer and closer to where her legs met. He could feel the moist heat coming out of her, and she found herself rocking side to side in anticipation of his touch.

When it came, she groaned aloud. He thrust his middle finger deep inside her, and held his palm against her, hard. Then he moved it in and out, and in and out again, changing the pressure on her clitoris from strong to soft, strong to soft.

She moved her hips against him, and felt the excitement welling inside her. He took his hand away, sensing her urgency.

"I want us to make love," he said to her. "Is that what you want too?"

She propped herself up for a moment so she could look him in the eye when she answered. "Yes. Yes, it's what I want."

And then he was on top of her, the full length of his penis buried inside her.

For a moment they both lay still. And then, slowly, he began a motion that wasn't so much a thrust as a rock. His chest was on hers, his mouth buried in her neck. Only his hips were moving out and in.

He was heavy, but his weight contained her in a way that contributed to the building pleasure. All of her senses were filled with him: the smell of him, the feel of him, the weight of him, and the motion of him.

They grew toward climax together, but he didn't move any faster or thrust any harder. It was a slow, steady build, and she knew exactly where it was headed.

She let out a long, low moan when the floodgates opened and the pleasure suffused her body. He was a heartbeat behind her, and noiselessly rode the wave of their orgasm with her. For Zoe, it was as though they melted together into one being. She felt the ecstasy in her own body, but she felt his too. For those few seconds, they were an inseparable whole.

She lay there, relishing all of it—not just the peak, but the little waves that came afterward. She didn't move until the last sensation had left her fingertips and all that was left was a suffusing relaxation.

Ethan lifted himself up on his elbows and looked at her. He brushed a wisp of hair off her face and kissed her forehead. "That didn't just feel good," he said. "It felt right."

They lay on top of the covers, letting the coolness of the room temper the warmth of their bodies, and then Ethan leaned up on an elbow.

"After all that talk about how useful lobstering is, I would be remiss if I didn't attend to it. I should try to get out on this tide."

"By all means," said Zoe. "I'm the last one to keep you from useful work." She smiled at him and gave him a gentle push on the chest.

But he didn't get up right away. He reached his hand to her hip and drew her close to him one more time. "Thank you," he said, and kissed her, softly, on the cheek.

❧

As she walked back to Chapin House, she replayed the morning over and over. She wanted to remember the feel of his touch, the contours of his body. She wanted to remember his smell. Mostly, though, she wanted to remember his face. She wanted to be able to call up his image at will, to see him clearly in her mind.

She knew she was falling in love, and she was afraid it was precipitate. She could count the hours she'd spent with him on two hands, yet she had a feeling of certainty about where it was going, and she wanted it to go there.

But it wasn't just Ethan himself. It was that he had made her see, with a clarity she thought she'd never had before, what had been missing not just from her relationship with Sam, but from all her old relationships—it had been missing from her *understanding* of relationships. She'd been involved with a number of interesting, attractive men. She had liked all of them, and loved some of them. But she hadn't *admired* any of them. Respected, yes, but not admired.

She knew for a certainty that if she was going to spend the rest of her life with a man, he had to be someone she admired. It might be Ethan, or it might not. What was most important about him right now was that he had made her understand something fundamental about herself.

❧

While Zoe had been enjoying the fruits of her lobstering, Andrew DuBois had been making inquiries that went back some twenty years, to Zoe's childhood. His first stop had been Greta Silva.

When he asked her whether Nickerson had ever mentioned Zoe's family, or anything particular about his interaction with them, she scoffed. "You didn't know him, did you?" she asked pointedly.

DuBois admitted that he hadn't.

"If you had, you wouldn't have needed to ask. He almost never talked about his past, and if there had been anything disreputable, or sordid, or even just private, he never would have said a word about it."

DuBois tried another line of questioning. "Do you know whether he was thinking about making a will?"

Greta shook her head.

"Did he ever talk about who would inherit the house, or whether the condition in the original will, that it be passed from son to son, meant it might revert to the Chapin estate when he died?"

She shook her head again. She was singularly unhelpful, and he sighed in frustration. At that, Greta softened a bit.

"I realize this isn't useful to you, but there's nothing I'm not telling you. He was a very private man, and even though I was very close to him, there were many, many things he never shared with me. And I never asked. That was part of why we got along."

He nodded. He believed her. He had a few more perfunctory questions, and then he took his leave to go to Lorraine Nickerson's studio.

She was there, and her shop was filled with vacationers looking at pottery. It took only three or four to fill the tiny shop, and she asked Andrew if she could see to them before she sat down with him.

"By all means," he said, and busied himself checking his phone messages and arranging his notes while she attended to her customers.

It was a good fifteen minutes before she was finished.

"I'm so sorry," she said. "It's just that the busy season is my only chance to make what passes for a living, so I don't like to let a single sale go."

"I understand completely." And he did. He wasn't put out by having to wait.

He had some hopes of getting more from her than he had from Greta. After all, she had actually been there, at least for a while, when Zoe was a child. "What do you remember about Nickerson's relations with her family?"

"I don't remember that he had any relations with her family. He knew them by sight, he knew Zoe's name—at least, I think he did—and that was about all."

He probed a little deeper, but got nowhere.

"Did he ever mention the house and the stipulation that it be passed from son to son or it would revert to the Chapin estate?"

"Sure, he did," Lorraine said. "And I think he believed the stipulation was mean-spirited, and he was damned if he was going to try to have a son just so the house could stay in the family." She smiled at the memory of it.

Just then, another group of tourists came in, and Lorraine excused herself for a couple of minutes.

While he waited, DuBois wandered around the shop, browsing. He had vivid memories of his mother's work, and of his own attempt to throw pots, and he stuck his head around the corner to where the wheel and kiln were, to see where she worked. It made him want to sit down with a hunk of clay and see what he could do.

He heard Lorraine ringing up a sale, and was turning to go back into the shop when a little spot of color between the floorboards caught his eye. He noticed it because it was the same peculiar shade of green that Nickerson's statue was. He leaned down, dislodged the little shard of clay with his pen, and pocketed it.

When Lorraine's customers were gone, he picked up his conversation where he'd left off.

"So Nickerson believed that the stipulation would stand up in court?"

"I don't think he gave it much thought, but I guess he assumed it would. I always assumed it would. Clara Chapin certainly believed it would, and she went out of her way to tell me it would. I imagine she told Curtis the same thing. But whether it would or whether it wouldn't, it's not something he would fight. He hated lawyers."

"I didn't know him, but my understanding is that he valued tradition and wanted to keep things as they were. He had a real sense of family pride, and he was acutely aware that both Nickersons and Chapins go back hundreds of years on the Cape. Is that accurate?"

"I think so."

"Do you think his feelings about that stipulation would have changed once Chapin House went out of Chapin hands?"

Lorraine shrugged. "I really have no idea. I haven't exchanged more than pleasantries with the man in twenty years."

DuBois nodded.

"Thanks for your help," he said, and got up to go. But as he was about to walk out the door, he turned around and took the little shard out of his pocket and held it up to the light.

"Where did this come from?"

Lorraine was clearly surprised, and the color rose to her face.

"I've been experimenting with that glaze again, the glaze I used to make that statue, the one that killed Curtis," she said, sounding flustered. "I know it sounds macabre. I always liked that glaze, but I'd forgotten about it until Curtis was bashed in the head with Angie." She shivered a little at the thought. "I wanted to see if I could still get that same effect, even though it's pretty morbid in light of what happened." She looked a little sheepish. "I wasn't going to try to make anything salable with it until this whole thing had blown over."

DuBois nodded again, thanked her again, and left.

CHAPTER FOURTEEN

Lorraine was unsettled by Andrew's asking her about the glaze. It would still be almost an hour until her usual closing time of six o'clock, but, after a moment's hesitation, she put up the CLOSED sign. Then she picked up the phone to call Chad Helmsworth.

He was just leaving his office when the phone rang, and he was going to let it ring until he saw Lorraine's number flash on the caller ID screen.

"Chad Helmsworth," he said into the receiver. He always identified himself this way, no matter what showed up on caller ID. You never knew who might be using someone else's phone.

"It's me," she said. "Can I stop by?"

"Sure," he said, "but I've got an eight-o'clock dinner."

"I'll be there in twenty minutes."

Chad had just opened the file cabinet drawer when Lorraine walked in. He was about to lock the door behind her when she surprised him by sitting down in the chair facing his desk.

"I think Curtis's death is getting to me," she said.

His eyebrows went up. She seldom talked much to him. He sat down in his own chair, across the desk from her.

"I suppose that's natural," he said. "After all, you were married to the guy."

"Yes, but it was a thousand years ago. I barely remember it."

"I don't think we're good at predicting how a death will affect us," he said, with a compassion that surprised her a little.

"I'll feel better when they find out who killed him."

"I think we all will. Andrew DuBois in particular."

She nodded. "He's been around asking me questions about Zoe and her family, and whether Curtis had anything to do with them back when she was a kid."

"He came here asking me about the will," Chad said, "wanting to know if that old Chapin entail would stand up."

She waved her hand. "It's ironclad," she said.

He was a little surprised at this. Given that he was the lawyer in the room, he would have expected her to ask his opinion. "What makes you think so?"

"It got explained to me by old Clara Chapin over tea one afternoon, right before I was going to marry Curtis. It was just the two of us, and it was bizarre."

Chad's personal and professional curiosity were both piqued, and he listened with interest.

"I think she was trying to be kind to me, to welcome me to the whole Chapin/Nickerson alliance, but it came off as incredibly conde-scending and almost like a warning. She explained to me that the house had been a gift, which I already knew. Then she told me it was passed down from son to son, which I also knew—"

Helmsworth interrupted. "Did Curtis already have the house?"

"He did. His father had moved down to Florida just the year before. And Curtis had told me about the will, but it sounded so weird and archaic that I thought it couldn't possibly be true. But Clara told me all about it, and she even produced a copy of it."

"Really? She showed you a copy?"

"Yup. And she pointed to the section that talked about it, and it seemed like she wanted Curtis to get hit by a bus so she could get his house back. God, I hated that old lady. She told me she'd taken the will to Boston and gotten expert opinions and everybody said it was crystal clear, and could withstand any challenge."

Chad snorted. That certainly wasn't his opinion of it.

"But why did she tell you all this?"

"Supposedly, it was to make me aware of my obligations upon becoming a Nickerson. It was as though I'd married into English gen-try and the matriarch took me aside to tell me I had to visit the farm-ers' wives every Sunday afternoon. Really, though, I think it was a kind of reverse psychology. I swear she thought I'd be less likely to have a son if I thought it was expected of me to have a son. That's the kind of girl she thought I was."

"That's the kind of girl *I* think you are," said Chad matter-of-factly.

"I suppose that's the kind of girl I am," said Lorraine. "But I still can't believe that I'd let something as petty as that influence me when it came to something as important as having children. If Curtis and I had lasted long enough, I expect we would have had them anyway."

Chad leaned back in his chair, taking it all in.

"Is what's bothering you that Zoe Bell's going to get the house?"

She cocked her head, thinking. "I guess partly. But it's more than that. The guy I was married to gets brutally murdered, Chapin House goes out of the family, and it just feels like the natural order of things is all upset."

"Maybe it's progress," said Chad. "Maybe it's high time that whole feudal thing between Chapins and Nickersons went away. It never seemed to me like a healthy kind of relationship."

Lorraine considered this. "Maybe so. In any case, it doesn't have anything to do with me, so I suppose I should just get over it." She looked at him, her eyes narrowing just a bit and the beginnings of a playful smile showing. "You think you can help me get over it?"

Chad looked at his watch. "I think I can just fit you in."

Lorraine got up and walked over to the drawer, and they picked up as though they had never had the discussion.

Without ceremony, he took off all his clothes as she rummaged through the drawer. She took out two three-foot-long cords with nooselike loops on each end.

"Lie down on the floor." Her tone was commanding; she had slipped into character.

"Facedown!" she barked, as Chad was about to lie faceup.

He turned over.

"Hands at your sides!"

He put his hands down.

She took the ligatures and fastened his hands to his feet, with each hand connected to the foot on the same side.

She stripped down to black panties and bra, as she always did, and took the familiar high-heeled boots out of the drawer. She also took something that looked like a billy club—a short, stout stick with a handle.

She put on the boots and stood over Chad, and she felt the surge of confidence, the sense of power, that their sessions always gave her.

"Look at me!" she said. Chad had had his face to one side, his cheek to the floor. He turned his head so his chin was down and he looked straight ahead at her. Or at her boots, at any rate. He couldn't use his hands to prop himself up, so his range of motion was limited.

Lorraine sat down on the floor about a foot from his head, one leg extended on either side of him. He had a full-on view of the crotch of her panties.

Lorraine owned the crotchless kind, but hadn't had the foresight to wear them. Instead, she reached over to the top of Chad's desk and borrowed his scissors. She cut a slit through the panties.

She moved closer to Chad's face, and, with an effort, he lifted his chest up and strained toward Lorraine's pussy, inches from him. He started to wriggle toward her, but she rapped him on the shoulder with the baton. "Stay where you are!"

And then, slowly, she moved toward him. Toward his open mouth. Toward the tip of his tongue, just peeking out from between his parted lips. For a moment she stayed there, anticipating the warm, wet touch. And then she moved so her hips were beneath him, his mouth in full contact with her cunt.

She watched, propped up on her elbows, as Chad ran his tongue around her. He circled and swooped, dove and darted. She felt the gushing response deep within her.

"Stop," she commanded.

He did as he was bidden, but the only way he could prevent himself from being in contact was by arching his back and holding his head away from her. It didn't look like a comfortable position.

"Resume," she said, after a few moments.

He did, and she closed her eyes and focused on the sensation. It always seemed odd to Lorraine that, no matter how aroused she was, no matter how acute the sensation, she never lost hold on the character she played when she was with Chad. She inhabited the mistress of ecstasy so thoroughly, and left Lorraine so far behind, that she stayed in character even in the throes of orgasm.

It was then that she heard just about the only thing that could have turned her back into Lorraine: a knock at the door. And then, a moment later, the door opened. She was surprised and alarmed, in part because she thought the door had been locked, and in part because the man who looked in the open door was Tim.

He gaped, openmouthed, at the tableau before him. It took him several moments to get his mind around what it was he was looking at, and then he quickly withdrew and shut the door.

Lorraine moved away from Chad, and was considering whether she ought to go after Tim when the door opened again. He had apparently decided that he deserved an explanation, and he came in and closed the door behind him. He stood there, hands on hips, trying to form the appropriate question.

"*What . . . ?*" He gestured to Chad, naked and facedown on the floor.

Lorraine scrambled to her feet. "Tim . . ." she said, mainly for Chad's benefit. The two men had never met, but Chad knew of Tim's existence.

Tim looked mutely from Lorraine to Chad, and back to Lorraine. "I saw your car." He pointed in the general direction of the building's parking lot, as though that made it clearer. And then he looked at Chad again.

"What . . ." he said, a second time. But then he seemed to recognize the futility of asking questions.

Lorraine wasn't sure what to say to him. She and Tim had never had an explicit agreement about not seeing other people, but they spent enough time together that she knew it was almost implied. She decided to simply tell him the truth.

"I was trying to spare you this," she said. "We tried a few"—here she paused—"unconventional things early on, and it was pretty clear it wasn't quite your speed." She looked at him with obvious frankness. "I'm sorry you had to find out this way."

Tim couldn't help being angry at finding the woman he was sleeping with was with another man, but he also couldn't help seeing that there was some small element of justice in what she said. Lorraine had never made any promises to him. She had indeed tried some of those unconventional things with him, and he had not responded with enthusiasm. That she would try to find another outlet was not so very surprising.

Besides, he couldn't help wondering just what they were up to. The sex he and Lorraine had had the morning DuBois had told them about Nickerson's death had opened his eyes to the idea that he had been limited in his appreciation for what sex had to offer. There was more out there.

Lorraine could see the spark of curiosity. She followed his eyes as he looked at Chad, and then back to her.

"What *is* this?" Tim finally asked, and it actually sounded like he wanted to know.

"It's a game; it's a role; it's a diversion," said Lorraine softly. "It's separate from my real life."

Tim looked at her with incomprehension mixed with unmistakable interest, but he certainly wasn't going to talk to her with a naked stranger on the floor. He reached for the door handle.

"Don't go," said Chad.

Tim paused, surprised.

"It *is* just a game," Chad went on. "Three can play."

There was a whirlwind of emotions in Tim's mind. He felt anger at being cuckolded, but also curious and even vaguely, faintly aroused. Through his conflicting feelings and thoughts, though, he had to admit to himself that Lorraine looked damn good in black underwear and high-heeled boots. Damn good.

Lorraine saw him hesitate, and handed him the baton.

"He spoke without being spoken to." She pointed at Chad. "That's not allowed."

Tim looked at the baton in his hand, and looked at Chad. He hefted the club in his hand and slapped it against his palm, feeling its weight. He wasn't sure he should participate. He felt some genuine hostility toward the naked man on the floor, and he wasn't sure real emotion should play any part in this game.

Still, it was a chance to hit him. He leaned over and whacked him across the ass.

Tim was a gentle man and he didn't hit very hard, but there was a red line where the baton had been.

"That's not much punishment," said Lorraine.

Tim hit him again, just a bit harder.

"When we punish, and we're sure the punishment has made an impact, we always find a way to say it's over and done with." Lorraine squatted down and rubbed the red line on Chad's ass. Then she stood up and gestured for Tim to take over.

A little dubiously, he squatted down and put his hand on Chad's buttocks. He rubbed.

And he marveled. This was the first time in his life he'd touched a man's backside for longer than it took to give a congratulatory, manly slap. Chad's ass was firmer and softer than any woman's he'd ever known. It was cool to the touch, high and round, with perfect dimples on either side of it. There was no excess flesh, no sagging perimeter. It was lovely.

Almost before he knew what happened, he had a full-blown erection. He looked up at Lorraine, and she could see that he would play.

"Take off your clothes," she said to him.

"Spread your legs," she said to Chad, in a different tone.

She told Tim, now naked, to kneel between Chad's legs.

"Up on your knees," she commanded Chad, who moved so that his ass was in the air, just in front of Tim's cock. This took some doing, as his hands were tethered to his ankles, but he did it.

She gestured to Tim to move just a little closer, so his erection lay nestled between the cheeks of Chad's ass. He moved back and forth, using his hands to close the firm buttocks around his cock. Chad pushed backward, sandwiching Tim's cock between his own ass and Tim's abdomen. Tim gasped at the pleasure of it.

"Stop!" said Lorraine, and Chad instantly released the pressure.

Lorraine went back to the position she'd been in when Tim had first walked in, her hips under Chad's face.

"Now me," she said, and Chad obediently began licking her now-drenched pussy.

"Now him," she said, and banged her hand on the floor.

Chad backed his ass back up to Tim and rubbed up against him.

"Now me," said Lorraine after a minute, and Chad was back to her.

Lorraine sent Chad back and forth, and she and Tim alternated their enjoyment of his services. Tim watched as Lorraine lost herself in the feeling of Chad's skillful tongue, and she watched in turn as Tim felt the pleasure of a new sensation.

Through it all, they stayed focused on each other. It was almost as though it were just the two of them in the room, with the world's most sophisticated sex toy.

As the arousal built, the temperature of the room went up, and Chad was sent back and forth in shortening intervals. And then Tim pushed Chad flat on the floor and went down on his elbows so his cock rested on Chad's ass. He could feel the muscles in Chad's ass contract as he rubbed his own erect penis against the plush carpeting.

Together, the three of them found a rhythm. Lorraine lay back and closed her eyes. Chad rocked toward Lorraine just a bit, and then back toward Tim, smelling and tasting her wet cunt on one end, and feeling the pressure of Tim's hard cock against his ass on the other.

At this point, Chad was in control of the pace, and as all of their excitement mounted to a climax, he moved faster and faster.

And then they were there. All three, together. The energy in the room swallowed up all of them, and each was, for a few moments, lost in the throes of pleasure. It was like nothing any of them had ever experienced before.

It took a while for them to come down. Tim was the first to stand up, and he reached for his pants and took a handkerchief out of his pocket. He used it to clean off Chad's back, and then waited for him to get up so he could turn his attention to the carpet.

Lorraine untied the ligatures, and Chad rubbed his wrists and ankles. Then he extended his hand to Tim. "Chad Helmsworth," he said with a smile.

Tim took his hand a little sheepishly. "Tim O'Donnell." The two men shook hands, and then began to dress.

Tim wasn't sure what etiquette required in this situation. Should he wait for Lorraine, or should he leave her alone with Chad? He decided on the latter, only because he would have felt awkward standing in Chad's office as she put away the baton and boots and got herself dressed.

"I'm going to go," he said. Should he say thank you? He had no idea. So he opened the door and was about to walk out when Lorraine asked him to wait. "I'll just be a minute."

It was just a minute; she dressed in no time. Then she said goodbye to Chad and walked out with Tim.

He wasn't sure what to say to her. Some of his anger had returned, but he felt as though he had given up his right to it by participating.

"That was weird," he said.

Lorraine laughed at full volume, and the tension dissipated.

"I suppose it is a little weird, but I hope you enjoyed it." She said it tentatively. "You seemed to."

"I did," he said. "To my surprise."

"The world is full of surprises," she said softly.

He nodded and gave a half smile.

"Are you still angry?" she asked.

"I don't know," he said. "My thoughts are a little muddled at the moment."

They got to her car, and she unlocked it. "I'm sorry you had to find us like that, but I'm not sorry that you know. I didn't like having a secret."

"I'm going to let this settle a bit in my mind, and I'll talk to you when I know what I think."

She nodded, kissed him on the cheek, and got in the car.

CHAPTER FIFTEEN

⁂

The next day, Zoe woke up still feeling the glow of Ethan. After she had some coffee, she spent the morning doing mindless tasks, things that would keep her hands busy while freeing her mind to go over the details of the day before.

It wasn't until well into the afternoon that she left the house and went into town for supplies. She wasn't planning to talk with Tom, Dick, and Harry—she had other things on her mind—but, to her surprise, Harry stood up as she came up the stairs of the general store, and made a low bow with a cartoonish flourish as she walked by.

She stopped, not sure what to make of it. Was she being made fun of?

She decided to work with it. "To what do I owe the honor of your obeisance?" she asked in a queenly voice.

"It is merely a mark of my respect, O lady of the lobster."

Zoe laughed and smiled broadly at him.

"So you heard about my little adventure with the lobster pots."

"We did indeed," said Tom. "And we must admit, we cruelly misjudged you."

Harry nodded. "We thought you a citified sissy," he said.

"A citified sissy!" Zoe exclaimed.

Harry nodded again. "A citified sissy."

"But we cruelly misjudged you," said Tom.

"I'm glad to know you've come to see the error of your ways," Zoe said gravely.

"We always admit when we're wrong," said Harry. "We're big that way."

Tom and Dick nodded.

"So, did you get the story out of your ghost?" Harry asked.

"I did," said Zoe. "For a ghost, he seemed remarkably forthcoming."

"He always did have an outgoing personality."

It still seemed strange to Zoe that Harry had actually known Robert, the real Robert.

Zoe sat down on the top step of the porch stairs. If Harry was in the mood to talk, she wanted to hear what he remembered from that time. "I think he really loved Molly," she said.

"Oh, he loved her, all right," said Harry.

"How can you be so sure?"

Harry didn't answer for a moment or two, and then he looked down and said softly, "I loved her too." He looked up at Zoe. "She was my best friend."

Zoe was astonished. Not only did Harry know Robert, but they were rivals for the same girl. It was very hard for her to get her mind around the melding of present and past. "Wow," was all she could think to say.

Tom looked over at Harry. "Tell her the story, Bart."

Only then did Zoe remember that his name wasn't really Harry.

Bartholomew leaned back in his rocking chair and told her the story.

He had been a year older than Molly and Robert, but they were in the same grade in school, since he had started late. Bart's family lived in town, where his father made a living fixing cars and machinery. When he was very young, their family was quite poor, but as more and more people had cars, his father's business grew and prospered.

Like most of the local kids, he spent a lot of time at the beach. He and his brothers would bicycle down to the public beach just east of Chapin Point, and wander out to the point from there—necessarily passing the Nickerson house. Like Robert, Bart had known Molly all his life.

And he had loved her almost as long. But from the time they were teenagers, he knew he was no match for Robert Chapin. Robert was the golden boy from the golden family. He was beautiful; he was rich; he was charming and charismatic and athletic. Every girl in Danmouth dreamed of Robert Chapin.

But Robert wanted no one but Molly. From the very beginning, he never expressed an interest in any other girl. The whole town believed the two were meant to be together, and Bart never believed he had a chance to win Molly.

So he never tried. Instead, he settled for being her friend. He was always in her background, ready to step in if she needed anything. He helped her with everything from homework to bicycle repair. He listened when she talked, comforted her when she was upset, cheered her when she was unhappy.

Some of his happiest memories dated to when Robert was away at school, and he had Molly all to himself. She talked about Robert a lot, but that was a small price to pay for her company.

The day she showed him the little shell ring and told him she and Robert were going to be married was one of the worst he'd ever had. He forced himself to smile and to congratulate her, but his voice faltered. He would never forget the way she looked at him, how he realized she was understanding for the very first time how he felt about her.

From that day on, their relationship was constrained. They still saw a lot of each other, but they didn't talk with the same freedom, and she rarely mentioned Robert—until things started to go wrong.

At first, when Clara Chapin began her all-out effort to get Robert to break off his engagement, Molly wasn't worried. She was secure in Robert's attachment to her and convinced that his mother would come around. Robert told her that nothing on earth would induce him to give her up.

As time went on and Clara didn't relent, though, his assurances started to take on a less reassuring tone. When she started to read hesitation and doubt in his voice and his eyes, it was Bart she turned to. She told him she thought Robert was wavering. She told him Clara was waving the Chapin money and the Chapin home in front of him, and he was wavering. She was afraid—she was very afraid—that he was going to give in.

It pained him to see her sad and confused, but he couldn't prevent a little spark of hope from kindling inside him. He didn't want his opportunity to have to come from her heartbreak, but if Robert turned out to be the kind of man who jilted a girl because he was threatened with disinheritance, then she would be well rid of him.

And then she had told him she was pregnant.

He couldn't help being surprised. Back then, getting pregnant out of wedlock was a much more serious affair than it came to be in the decades following, and Bart had to admit to himself that he hadn't thought Molly was that kind of girl.

But her distress at the possibility that Robert would not just leave her, but leave her with a baby, trumped any disapproval he might have felt. He felt her anguish, and he vowed to himself that, if he had the chance, he would take the baby with the girl, and love that child as though it were his own.

And that was what he told her the night before she died. He held her two hands in his and confessed the depth and breadth, the profundity of his love. He told her he wanted her to be happy, and if she could find happiness with Robert he would wish her well and look elsewhere for his own. But if she couldn't, she had only to reach out to him. He would be there. He would always be there.

She burst into tears. She told him how much it grieved her to make him unhappy, but that if she couldn't be with Robert, she didn't think she could be with anyone. He had the sense that his confession, rather than giving solace, only increased her woes.

When she had left him that night, she kissed his cheek and thanked him. Whoever became his wife, she told him, would be a very lucky woman, and she was infinitely sorry that it couldn't be her. Her heart had already been given, and if Robert wouldn't take it, life wouldn't be worth living.

That had been what she said. Life wouldn't be worth living.

The next night, she was dead.

⋇

When he finished telling the story, Zoe sat silent, absorbing it. She had taken it as an article of faith that if Robert had truly loved Molly, he wouldn't have abandoned her. Perhaps love wasn't as powerful a force as she'd thought.

Tom leaned over to look at Zoe. "You see, he was a little shit."

Bart—she couldn't think of him as Harry anymore—nodded. "He was a class-A little shit."

Zoe looked at Bart. "I'm so sorry," she said.

He waved his hand. "Don't be. It was sixty years ago, and I went on to marry a wonderful woman. Molly was my first love, but Helen, my wife, was the better woman." He gave a sad smile. "Turns out Molly'd rather die than marry me—that doesn't say much for her judgment, now, does it?"

Zoe was surprised that he could talk about her this way, but then she remembered that it was a very long time ago. "Did you tell people what Molly said to you? Did you tell the police?"

"You bet I did. I was devastated by her death, and I would have liked nothing better than to see his little shittiness held up to a bright light. Either he pushed her in front of that train, or he jilted her and she threw herself in front of it. As far as I'm concerned, those are the same thing. Even so, as much of a shit as he was, I don't think he pushed her. He was too much of a coward. My money's on the jilt, and that's killing her, sure enough, but not the kind of killing the law has anything to say about."

"He denied it."

"He denied it to his dying day."

Speaking of which, Zoe was very curious to know whether Bart knew anything about that particular day. "Do you remember his death?" she asked, with all the innocence she could muster.

Bart nodded. "Oh, do I."

"He died on his boat, didn't he?"

"No," said Bart. "He died off his boat, and the only question was how he got from on his boat to off his boat."

"Wasn't it an accident?"

At this, Bart smiled enigmatically and shrugged theatrically.

Zoe waited a beat to see whether his willingness to talk about the past would extend to sharing what he knew about Robert's death. Apparently, it didn't, and Zoe stood up to go into the store. "Thanks for telling me," she said. "And if any of you gentlemen ever want to come pull lobster pots, I'll be happy to take you out to the jetty with me."

As she went in to get her groceries, she felt real gratification. Beneath the silliness of Tom, Dick, and Bart's making much of her pulling the lobster pots was a real acceptance, even a respect.

When she'd had enough of congratulating herself for earning the trust of the locals, she thought about what Bart had told her. She had believed Robert's version of the story, and she had believed in him as a man who had been true to the girl he loved. And Bart, as a rival, would necessarily see the worst in Robert, and any criticism Molly made of him at the time probably would have been amplified in his mind over all these years. Was he really a more trustworthy source?

She got home just as afternoon was turning to evening, and she felt herself reacclimating to her house and her setting as she put the groceries away. She thought it was a bit too early to open a bottle of wine, but then she did it anyway.

She went out on the deck and sat on the swing. She didn't think she would ever get tired of that view.

For almost the first time since she'd bought the house, she felt at peace. Although breaking up with Sam had been difficult, she knew she was better off for it. And her worries about being a murder suspect were fading with every hour with no word from Andrew DuBois. If he were hot on her trail, presumably she'd hear from him.

And then there was Ethan. She sighed and smiled. She even considered going next door to see whether he was there, but she thought better of it. She didn't want to rush this. The anticipation was delightful, and she thought she could enjoy at least another day of it.

When she felt the familiar prickling on the back of her neck, her first feeling was irritation that her reverie was interrupted. But then she thought this would be a chance to ask Robert about what Bart had told her.

Welcome home.

"Mmm," she said, thinking about how best to approach her subject. And then she just went straight for it.

"I talked to Bart today." She realized she didn't even know his last name, and hoped Robert knew whom she was talking about.

Ah! And he told you his story about Molly and me, no doubt.

"He did."

You're welcome to believe it. His tone was a mixture of sadness and disdain, and it surprised her. She expected a spirited defense, a denunciation of the accuser, an avowal of his loyalty to Molly, but she got none of that.

"I don't know what to believe. Whom to believe."

I think you do. He said it so soberly that his loss was real to her once again. This story, that happened so long ago, seemed as if it were still real to him, as if the pain were still sharp, the memories still vivid. Her heart went out to him, ghost though he was.

She heard the door into the house, which she'd left open, suddenly slam shut, and she turned around. At first she saw nothing, but then her gaze moved to the kitchen window, and she saw him there, looking out at her.

He *was* the golden boy, she thought. He looked every inch what he was. His careless beauty, his confident smile, his air of ease all marked him as aristocracy, or the nearest thing. He embodied—to the extent that something disembodied *could* embody—what compelled her about the Chapins and Chapin House.

She stared and stared. As long as she looked at him, he couldn't disappear, she thought. He wouldn't vaporize before her very eyes, she was sure. And he didn't. He looked back at her, and there was a frankness, an honesty in his eyes. She smiled sadly.

Then she felt the little shell ring on her finger twist, and she looked down involuntarily. She knew, when she looked back up, that the window would be empty.

When he had appeared that evening, she hadn't wanted him, but now that he was gone, she wanted him back. She wanted to ask him about Molly, ask him about that night, ask him about Bart. His presence in the house had somehow become a part of her attachment to it.

She stayed on the deck, sipping her wine. She twisted the ring. She even said his name. She waited for a sign that he was still with her, but none came.

CHAPTER SIXTEEN

꩜

Andrew DuBois had thought much about the green shard of clay he'd found wedged between the floorboards of Lorraine's studio. She said she was experimenting with the glaze, but he hadn't seen any samples in her workroom. Had there been any, he surely would have noticed, attuned as he was to that particular color.

He brought out the reassembled statue and compared the color. It was precisely the same. Why was she re-creating this particular glaze at this particular time?

He decided to ask her face-to-face, so he drove out to her studio. She was alone, in the back, sweeping the dust, crumbs, and shards off her workroom floor.

She heard the bell on the door and came out. "Oh, hello," she said.

He nodded his greeting and took the shard out of his pocket and put it on the counter.

"I can't figure this out," he said.

"There's nothing to figure," she said mildly. "It was just a practice run for that glaze."

"How did it go?"

"Surprisingly well, actually, for a color I hadn't tried in decades."

"What did you make out of it?"

She thought for a moment. "Shallow dishes. Three of them. I didn't want to make anything difficult, because I wasn't confident it was going to work out."

"May I see one of them?"

"Oh, I didn't keep them. I thought if I had them lying around, someone might be offended. Everyone knew the statue that killed him, and the color is distinctive. If dishes that color suddenly appeared in Curtis Nickerson's ex-wife's studio, it wouldn't have gone over well."

"What did you do with them?"

"I gave them away. They weren't good enough to sell, but three nice ladies from Nova Scotia came in, and I gave them one each. They were delighted."

"So where did this shard come from?"

"Whenever I try something completely new, I do the very first firing on unworked clay. It's only if that works out that I move on to the tests, like the dishes. Those just get tossed when I'm finished with them, and one of them must have broken."

"Do you have anything this color left? A test, a sample, a piece?"

"I don't think so, unless there's an escaped shard in a dusty corner somewhere."

DuBois nodded and looked around the studio, as if to find the escapee.

"I like the glaze," she said, "and I'm looking forward to making some interesting pieces with it once a decent interval has passed."

The detective looked at her, trying to read her face.

"If you're so fond of it, why haven't you been using it?" There was no hostility in the question. He was just curious.

"I completely forgot about it. It was a long time ago, and I spent many years not making anything at all. When I came back here, I was focused on making pieces I could sell."

He nodded again. He often found that, if he nodded but said nothing, the people he was questioning would continue to talk, filling the silence.

It didn't work with Lorraine, though. She simply looked at him, waiting for his next question.

He didn't have another question. What he had was a feeling, but after explaining to Veronica why feelings weren't to be trusted, he certainly wasn't going to go ahead and trust his.

"Thank you," he said. "I think that about does it."

He drove back to the barracks and set the statue and the shard on his desk. There was something they weren't telling him, and he willed them to speak. He went over the statue with a magnifying glass, looking for something, anything, that he might have missed. He tried the shard in every crevice where a piece of the statue was missing, but it didn't fit any of them. The unglazed part of the clay wasn't even the same color; it clearly hadn't come from the statue.

He looked, and he thought, and he tried to look and think from different angles.

And then, suddenly, out of nowhere, he understood.

He picked up the phone and called Ethan Grant, but got his voice mail.

He left a message saying he'd like to meet Ethan out at the Nickerson cottage at his earliest convenience, and then he could do nothing but wait.

First thing in the morning, Andrew met Ethan out at his uncle's house.

"I only need to see if we can find some photographs."

"Photographs? Of someone in particular?"

"Of some*thing* in particular. I'm looking for photos of Angie."

Ethan's eyebrows went up.

"I would have tried looking for them myself last night, but I thought you'd have a much better idea of where we might find them."

Ethan looked around the house, considering.

"If there are any, there are only one or two places they're likely to be." He pointed to a top shelf with some old shoe boxes on it and indicated it as one of them. "Can I ask why you're looking for them?"

"I'm afraid you can't," said Andrew. "Or rather, you can, but I'm afraid I can't tell you just yet."

"I suspected as much," said Ethan as he pulled a step stool out of the pantry.

He took down two of the boxes and put them on the coffee table in front of the couch. Each man took a box, and they started going through them. For Ethan, it was slow going. Although he was looking for Angie, he knew a lot of the people in the photographs, and he couldn't help but spend a little time with each.

"My God," he said, as he picked up one of them. "That's my mother."

It was a yellowed picture of Curtis and his sister, two tan and slim teenagers. He showed it to Andrew. "May I keep this one?"

DuBois nodded, and they kept looking.

There were several pictures of Curtis and his friends and guests where Angie was in the background, but none where DuBois could see the statue clearly.

"There's another box up in the attic," Ethan said, and went up to get it.

He brought it down and opened it. It wasn't just photos. There were papers, postcards, and even a pressed flower. They both rummaged through it.

In a moment, Ethan held up a picture, triumphant. It must have dated to Curtis's marriage to Lorraine, and it showed the twenty-something Nickerson holding the statue and grinning.

"Perfect," said DuBois. "Just what I needed." He pocketed the photo, thanked Ethan, and took his leave.

When he was gone, Ethan looked at his watch, checking both time and tide. He had to get back on the water, but he had at least half an hour before he needed to leave. He'd been so busy with work that he hadn't seen Zoe since the morning of the lobster breakfast two days before, and he wanted to ask her if she'd have dinner with him that night.

He thought about calling—that was what people generally did, he knew—but he preferred to walk over to Chapin House and see her in person.

He went around the back and up the stairs to the deck. He knocked on the kitchen door, but there was no answer. He checked around the front, and her car was there, so he tried the front door, louder this time. He heard sounds inside, and she opened the door.

She was wearing an old pair of cutoff jeans and a worn T-shirt, and she was covered with dust. She beamed when she opened the door and saw who it was.

She greeted him and opened the door wide to invite him in. He kissed her, lightly, on the very corner of her mouth, and then took a step back to look at her.

"What are you doing, cleaning out the farthest reaches of the basement?" he asked.

"That's exactly what I'm doing. I've been tackling it little by little, and it's almost done." She wiped her nose with the back of a hand, suppressing a sneeze. "Since you're here, though, could you give me a hand with something?"

"Sure," he said. "As long as it only takes a few minutes. I've got to get out on the water, but I wanted to stop by to see if you'd have dinner with me tonight."

"I'd love to," Zoe said. "And I promise to dress better. As for the help, there's a giant desk in a little room in the basement, and I just want to move it so I can clean under it. I can have you out of here in five minutes."

They went down to the basement, which, to Ethan's eyes, was cleaner than any basement on the planet. Zoe led him to the little room with the desk. "I just want to move it from where it is to over there." She pointed to a corner she'd already cleaned.

Ethan took one side and Zoe the other. The only way to get a grip was to take it from the bottom, and they both bent over.

They lifted. It was very heavy, and Zoe could barely hold up her end.

They were moving it only three steps, but after two she lost her grip, and her side of the desk crashed to the ground. Ethan had no choice but to let go.

The desk, heavy as it was, couldn't survive that kind of handling. Everything to the right of the kneehole came detached from the top and sat lopsided on the floor.

"Shit," said Zoe. "Sorry. I lost my grip."

"Don't apologize to me. It's your desk."

She looked at it ruefully. "I kind of liked it."

"It might be repairable," he suggested.

She sat down on the floor and peered into the collapsed portion. "I'm dubious," she said. "But on the bright side, at least we got it far enough so I can clean where it was." She looked at the dusty spot where the desk had stood.

Ethan looked at his watch. "I hate to leave you with the job half-done—"

She interrupted him. "You have to go, I know; please don't worry about it. Besides, I think the job is all done. I don't see this desk ever moving again, until it moves in pieces up to the fireplace."

"Will you come over to the cottage around seven?" he asked.

She smiled and nodded. "I look forward to it."

"So do I. But I've got to run." He leaned over and kissed the top of her head. "I know my way out. I'll see you tonight." And he was gone.

Zoe got to work on the floor, scrubbing on her hands and knees. When she'd gotten it done, she thought she might be able to work the desk into the corner by moving one side at a time, and she gave it a mighty shove.

The thing didn't budge. So she tried the other side, the side that had come apart. This time, success—sort of. The frame moved, leaving the section with the drawers behind. If the desk hadn't been a total loss before, it was now.

She looked at it, trying to figure out what to do, when she noticed a piece of paper sticking out of the back of one of the drawers. She was surprised, because she'd been through the desk several times and was sure it was empty. She reached around to retrieve the paper, but it was stuck.

It was caught under the broken desk, and she had to feel around the back of the drawer to figure out how to get it out. She didn't see why she couldn't just reach into the drawer and pull it out, and then she finally figured it out: There was a compartment at the back of the drawer, blocked off by a panel.

An actual secret compartment! She couldn't believe it.

There must be a release somewhere, she thought, but it probably didn't survive the crash. She felt around for a moment to see if she could find it, but she wasn't sure she knew what she was looking for, and it seemed like an ordinary drawer. She went upstairs and got a screwdriver to break through the panel.

It was hard to find the angle that would give her leverage on the panel, but she found it eventually and got the panel out. She reached into the back of the drawer and discovered that it wasn't just a piece of paper. The compartment was crammed with papers.

She took a few out carefully. They seemed old, and she didn't want to damage them. After her previous search of the house, she prepared herself for something utterly mundane. They'd be bank statements or laundry lists.

It took only a glance at the first one to know they weren't mundane at all. They were letters.

The first one she picked up was dated April 7, 1946. Its salutation was *Dear Mother*. It was from Robert to Clara. Her heart beat faster as she started to skim it.

But then she stopped. There were other letters. She wanted to sort through them before she started reading. She thought they would tell her a story, and she wanted to begin at the beginning.

She took all the letters out of the compartment and spread them out. At first, she thought there were only Robert's letters to his mother, but then she found a few of hers to him. There were about thirty, and all were dated, so it was easy to put them in chronological order.

The earliest were from his days at Harvard, before the war, and that was where she started. She read straight through those, and then his letters from overseas, during the war. Then on to his postwar return to Harvard and law school.

At first she read with eager interest. She expected the letters to make the man come alive. This was his handwriting! These were words that came out of his pen! But her enthusiasm ebbed as she read. It took her at least five letters to admit to herself that they were dull. Robert's to Clara were almost form letters: reports of his health, his classes, and even the weather. Hers to him were motherly sets of instructions and concerns. When Zoe got to the part where he was instructed to wear his flannels, she positively rolled her eyes.

She started skimming through, and got him in the army in no time. He apparently never saw combat, because his typing skill, of all things, landed him a plum job as assistant to a general who oversaw strategy from afar. He had nothing to say, apparently, about the war itself or even of army life. She fast-forwarded to his return in the hopes of something personal, or at least interesting.

She'd almost given up hope when she found it. It was there in the last four letters, the first from Clara and the following three from Robert.

There it was, in Clara's spiky, old-fashioned handwriting. *To my sorrow, I will feel obligated to leave the estate away from you if you choose to follow through on your planned wedding.* When Zoe saw it, she took up Robert's last three letters and read them carefully, alert to any nuances.

They were different from his previous letters. Apparently, the threat of disinheritance stopped the flow of filial chatter. In the first letter he told his mother, in no uncertain terms, that he loved Molly and he would marry her; let her do what she would.

Zoe didn't find any reply to this, and Robert's next letter was dated several months later. He still professed his love for Molly, but there was something equivocal, almost mealymouthed, in the way he said it.

She picked up his last letter, almost holding her breath. Would it tell her what really happened?

It was very short, and it read, in its entirety:

Dear Mother,

I do not believe it is to your credit that you repeatedly insist that I abandon the girl I have engaged myself to. Nevertheless, I have concluded that I must do as you ask. You leave me no choice. I cannot be severed from my family and my home.

I trust you have the decency to feel no triumph over this victory. There
is only sadness.

Your son,

Robert

Zoe put that last letter in the pile with the others.

So that was why those letters were hidden away in a secret compartment. They proved that Robert had lied about what happened the
night Molly Nickerson died. He had thrown her over. The letter
served as confirmation of Bart's story of what Molly had told him, and
it added up to something very unpleasant. No one would ever know for
sure how Molly ended up on the train tracks, but Robert was guilty, at
the very least, of jilting his pregnant fiancée to protect his inheritance,
and at most, of throwing her in front of a train. Zoe sat on the basement floor, processing what she'd read.

Either way, Bart was right: He was a shit. For all his talk, for all his
professions of love, he ditched Molly for the money. "Family and home,
my ass," Zoe said under her breath as she reread the letter. It was all
about the money.

She held up the letter and shook it at the empty room. "You're a
shit!" she said.

And then she felt the prickling. This time she felt a sense of fore-
boding. But she would not be cowed by a spirit who had lied to her. He
seduced her, he charmed her, he won her over, and it was all a sham.

"You're a shit!" she repeated, louder. "You ditched her for the
money, and she died for you!" She stood up and waved the letter as
though she were waving it in his face.

There was no response, but the room went suddenly cold. Bitter cold. Icy cold.

Zoe felt the goose bumps rise on her arms. She looked around, trying to find some sign of Robert's presence, some direction in which she could direct her anger. But there was none. There was only the cold. As she breathed it in, she felt as though it were freezing her very blood, making her heart beat slowly and her breath come with effort. She felt as though she were being smothered by cold.

"You can't scare me away from here," she said, not loudly but with grim determination. "This is my house now, and you're no longer welcome here." But the cold closed in. She was gasping now, and shivering, but still she would not leave the room. She had the sense that this was their showdown, and she was determined that she was going to win. She was flesh and blood, the rightful owner of this house, and he was a liar and a jilt. Not to mention dead!

She stood her ground, looking angrily around the room. "You . . . are . . . not . . . welcome . . . here," she said through tight lips, with a deliberation that underscored her fury.

She felt the cold as if it were walls closing in on her in a grip that was tightening little by little, and she didn't know how to make it stop.

"Get out of my house!" She screamed it at the top of her lungs, but the cold kept coming.

She stamped her foot in anger and frustration. She looked around for a weapon, but what weapon did you use against a ghost?

And then she thought of the ring, the shell ring, Molly's ring. She yanked it off her finger, threw it on the floor, and ground the heel of her shoe into it. Nothing happened.

She looked around for something hard. In the corner was a

rudimentary shelving unit made of boards and cinder blocks, and she took the top shelf off. She picked up one of the cinder blocks, held it high, and dropped it on the ring.

It shattered into a pile of pink-white dust.

The cold was gone. The prickling was gone. Robert was gone.

She stood there for a few moments, waiting and listening. Would he be back, or was he gone for good? She was tensed for the feeling at the back of her neck, but it didn't come.

He was gone. He was really and truly gone.

CHAPTER SEVENTEEN

O nce Robert stopped appearing to her, Zoe had some trouble believing he was ever real. Although she remembered much of what he had said, and many of their intimate moments, she couldn't call up a reliable memory of what his voice had sounded like. Because his words to her had been insinuated, rather than said aloud, she couldn't reproduce their sound.

She remembered his face, but it was as though she were looking at a snapshot, not a person. It was always the same smile, the same sweater, the same casually ruffled blond hair.

Now that he was gone—and she was sure he was gone for good—it was as though he had never been.

She spent the day reclaiming the house. Although it was still Chapin House in her mind, she wanted to possess it in her own way, as a new chapter in its life rather than a part of its history. Robert's presence, and her preoccupation with him, had kept her from inhabiting it fully as her own. She had been trying to be of it, rather than making it be of her.

But now she would make it hers. Chapins, she'd discovered, were overrated. As far as she could tell, they were greedy and venal and utterly convinced of their own superiority.

She didn't tear down any walls or paint the exterior or even rearrange the furniture. She didn't do anything physical to the house. But as she walked through it she thought of it differently. It was a house, not an aspiration. It didn't represent family or roots or respectability. It was a beautiful seaside house, and she reveled in the fact that it was hers.

As she walked over to the cottage to have dinner with Ethan, she considered whether she ought to tell him about her encounters with the ghost of Robert Chapin. It was much on her mind, and she would have liked to have talked about it, but she was pretty sure that would be a bad idea. It sounded so far-fetched, and she didn't want Ethan to think she was a babbling lunatic.

She knocked on the door with the determination that she could tell him all about the letters and what Bart had told her about Robert, but she would say nothing about the ghost.

Ethan opened the door, and a lovely smell came wafting out.

"Hello," he said, and kissed her with a soft, welcoming kiss. "Come in."

"What is that smell?" she asked with some enthusiasm.

"It's just the onions from the creamed collard greens. I sauté them in butter and they smell up the whole house."

"Creamed collard greens?"

"Like creamed spinach. It goes great with lobster pot pies."

Zoe grinned broadly. She'd never even eaten a lobster pot pie, let alone had a man go out of his way to make one for her.

"Can I get you a glass of wine?" he asked.

She nodded, and he poured two glasses of a beautiful amber Riesling from a bottle he had on ice. He handed one to her and held up his glass. "To the new owner of Chapin House," he said.

They clinked glasses and Zoe took a sip of the wine. It was surprising, sweeter than she'd expected, but also crisp and clean. "This is wonderful," she said.

"I'm glad you like it. It's an Alsatian Riesling. It's my favorite wine with lobster." After a moment he added, "And I've gotten to experiment a lot."

He pulled out one of the kitchen chairs. "It's more comfortable in the living room, but I've still got some things to do and I was hoping you'd keep me company."

"You can't seriously think I'd sit alone in the living room while you make my dinner?"

"Not for a moment."

She sat down and he turned back to the garlic he was chopping. As he worked she told him about the compartment that their attempt at moving the desk had disclosed, and the letters that had been in it.

When she told him about the last letter and how it revealed that Robert really had jilted Molly, Ethan wasn't surprised at all.

"You know the story?" she asked him.

"Of course. I'm a Nickerson, remember."

"And you've believed all along that he did it?" Zoe asked.

Ethan shrugged. "I thought everyone did. Who told you he *didn't* jilt her?" he asked.

Zoe was flustered. She didn't want to risk telling him that Robert himself had told her. "I thought nobody knew what really happened."

"Well, in a sense, nobody does. Robert and Molly were the only ones there that night, and the rest of us are left to infer what happened based on what was known about him and his character. I'm sure I'm biased, because I was fed the Nickerson side of the story with my mother's milk, but I can't say I'm surprised that you turned up evidence that backs up our version."

His tone was so matter-of-fact, his assessment so cut-and-dried, that Zoe felt silly for ever having believed anything else.

From there, the talk turned to other things. Ethan told her about lobstering, and Zoe told him about her business. They conversed with ease and interest, and Zoe felt comfortable, as though she'd known him much longer than she had. He could talk, he could laugh, and he could listen.

And he could cook! The lobster pot pies were wonderful. The filling was mostly lobster and cream, with a little bit of sherry and a few sweet green peas, and the top was puff pastry. They looked huge when Ethan put them on the table, but Zoe ate every last crumb.

When she looked up from the very last bite, Ethan was watching her, smiling.

"I guess I liked it," she said, gesturing at the empty plate.

"I love watching a woman enjoy a meal," he said. "If there's one thing I can't stand, it's a reluctant eater."

"Nobody's ever accused me of that," Zoe said, putting down her fork.

She got up and started to pick up the dirty plates, but Ethan reached out and put a hand on her wrist. "You're the guest," he said. "I'll just put them in the sink and do them later."

Once he'd cleared the table, he took two small glasses out of a cabinet, and a bottle of port from a shelf. He held the bottle so she could see the label. "'Seventy-seven," he said, pointing to the vintage. "It was a really good year."

He handed Zoe the two glasses and took a little white box off the counter. "I cook, but I don't bake," he said as he opened the box and showed her an assortment of little cookies.

They took dessert into the living room. She sat down on the couch, and he sat next to her and took her hand. "I'm glad you found those letters," he said.

Zoe was surprised that he brought up the subject again.

"Why?" she asked.

"Because I think they're a fitting coda to the end of the relationship between the Chapins and Nickersons. It was probably a good thing that the house had to be sold when old Clara died, and now nobody's going to be able to look at that family through some kind of rosy haze of nostalgia. They were ordinary people, no more exempt from greed and dishonesty than the rest of us are."

Zoe nodded, thinking that she herself had certainly been seduced by nostalgia. "I'm guilty of believing in the Chapin mystique," she said. "Or having believed in it, at any rate."

"I can see why. You came here as a kid, and it's natural to look at the people in the big house on the water, who've been here for centuries, as something different from us mere mortals. I think the only reason I never believed in it was that I was steeped in the idea of Nickerson superiority." He gave a little laugh. "That's a kind of reverse nostalgia.

"I'm glad you've got the house now," he went on, looking at her small hand held in his large one. "Its new history starts with you."

He put her palm against his cheek, and she felt just a hint of the stubble coming through. He must have shaved just before she came over.

He reached out and put his hand on the side of her face and pulled her toward him. He looked straight into her eyes for a moment, and then he kissed her.

The touch of his lips was light at first; he brushed hers with his. And then he moved closer and pressed a little harder, and her lips opened so she could taste him. He was salty and sweet, with just a hint of 'seventy-seven port.

He took her glass from her and put both hers and his on the coffee table. And then he kissed her again. She felt his tongue just barely brushing hers, tantalizing and arousing. She felt the strength of his hands on her cheeks, holding her steady. She felt the heat of his body next to hers.

She reached for him, put her arms around his neck, and kissed him deeply. He tasted very, very good.

She got up on her knees and straddled Ethan's lap. She ran her hands through his hair and held his head to her chest. She was wearing a soft, sheer cashmere sweater, and she could feel his breath in the hollow between her breasts.

He reached up under the sweater and cupped her breasts in his hands. He traced with each forefinger the lacy line where flesh met brassiere, and he inhaled deeply, breathing her in.

His hands went around her back, and he had the clasp open on her bra before Zoe had a chance to wonder whether his large fingers would have trouble with the tiny clasp. He lifted her sweater and bra over her head with one motion and then sat back to look at her.

His hands were on her hips and, for a moment, that was all he did—he looked. And then he pulled her to him and took her left nipple—almost her entire left breast—in his mouth. Zoe felt every muscle in her body tighten and warm as she reveled in the sensation of his tongue circling her erect nipple. She felt a longing between her legs, an anticipatory empty space that she needed him to fill.

She pulled back from him and unbuttoned his shirt. She traced the muscles and ridges of his chest, and marveled at how firm he was.

He put his hands under Zoe's ass, leaned forward, and stood up, taking her with him. She wrapped her legs around his waist and her arms around his neck, and he walked her around the couch. Zoe assumed they were headed for the bedroom, but he carried her into the kitchen.

"Are you willing to be"—he considered for a moment—"adventurous?"

Her eyebrows went up. She would have pegged him as pretty straight-up, but it just went to show you never knew.

"What do you have in mind?"

Before he answered, he switched her over to one hip, as though she were a child, so he could free up a hand. With that hand, he took a heavy coat off a hook by the door and laid it on the table they'd just had dinner on. He laid Zoe on the coat.

"I want to combine some sensations in a way that might be new to you," he told her. "It won't hurt you or mark you, and you have my word that I will stop whenever you say so."

Zoe was intrigued, but a little hesitant. As close as she felt to him, she barely knew this man. "Can you give me a hint?" she asked.

He smiled. "If you'll trust me, I'll show you."

Zoe nodded her assent.

He arranged the coat underneath her. "Are you comfortable?" he asked.

She considered. She wasn't comfortable the way she'd be in a bed, but neither was she uncomfortable. Since she wanted to know what he had in mind, she answered in the affirmative.

He undid the clasp on her pants, unzipped them, and eased them, with her panties, out from under her. She lay naked on the satiny lining of his heavy wool coat and wondered what was to come. He touched her, lightly, on her thigh, and looked at her with a combination of lust and tenderness that lit her up.

She closed her eyes and felt his fingertips brush the tops of her thighs and then her belly. He worked his way tantalizingly downward, and she found herself squirming at the anticipation of his touch, but he didn't touch her there. He circled around; he moved in, and then away. He ran his fingers in the crease where her thigh met her body. He traced the top of her pubic hair. But he didn't come any closer.

And then he reached behind him and opened a drawer. He took a book of matches out of it, and took a candlestick down from a high shelf. He took the candle out and lit it. He took Zoe's hand and put the candle in it. "Hold that for just a moment," he said.

He went to the freezer, pulled out an ice-cube tray, and took a cube in his left hand. With his right, he took the candle, which was beginning to drip, back from Zoe.

He leaned over and kissed her between her breasts, and then he put the ice cube just below her navel, and circled it around to make a little cold spot. She shivered at the chill, but somehow the cold of the ice and its contrast to the heat that was coming out of her made her heat up even more.

Ethan then took the candle and held it at an angle over the spot he'd just iced. The wax dripped down the candle, and the hot drop hit her skin with a heat that completely undid the cold.

She gasped. It was almost too hot, but only for a split second. It was one of the strangest sensations she'd ever experienced, and it concentrated her attention on that one spot on her body.

"Is it too hot?" he asked her.

She didn't know quite how to answer. "No, but yes . . ." she said. "It's right, I think." She wasn't at her most articulate.

He iced a spot just over her right thigh. This time she knew what to expect, and she enjoyed the cold sensation, knowing it was a prelude to the heat.

She didn't know how it happened, but the cycle of cold, then heat, and then cold in another spot, heightened her awareness of all her senses. Her skin tingled with anticipation of the ice and the wax, and her whole body was attuned to what was happening to her.

All of this kept her arousal in overdrive. Not once did Ethan touch her cunt, but her cunt was where she felt the effect of all he was doing. The heat and the cold were creating a waterfall within her.

And then he circled her nipple with the ice cube, and she felt her breast try to retreat into itself. Then the wax came, and she was consumed by the sensation. She moaned and reached a hand out for his leg to pull him close. He pulled away. "Not yet," he said in a whisper.

She propped herself up on her elbows. "Then let me do it to you," she said. "It's amazing. I want you to feel it too." She sat up and reached for the candle and the ice cube.

He held them away from her and shook his head. "I know what it feels like, and you can't believe how much pleasure I get out of showing you, out of watching you, out of pleasing you. It's almost like deflowering a virgin." He put a hand on her shoulder and pushed her gently back down.

"Just enjoy," he said. He ran the ice cube around her other nipple, and then let the wax drip. Again, the heat felt like it cut straight through her. He went back to the first nipple, and then did the second again.

She could take it no more. She sat up, and she reached for him. She blew out the candle, took the ice cube, and threw it into the sink.

She put her hands into the waistband of his pants. "You have to fuck me," she said. "I can't stand it."

She unzipped him, and it was clear he was ready for her. He stepped out of his pants, and she stroked the underside of his cock. She turned so her legs were off the side of the table, and she guided him inside her.

They both moaned at once. Her body had been crying out for him this hour and more, and the satisfaction of having him fill her was what she needed.

She pulled him closer into her, but it was as though he couldn't be close enough.

He started to move out and in, but she needed his urgency to match her own.

"Harder," she whispered, and pulled him rhythmically to her.

He did as he was bidden, thrusting himself into her with such force that she felt the table move under her.

And each thrust built on the last, and her peak became higher and higher. She wrapped her legs high around him to try to get him farther in, deeper in, hard against her.

He had made no noise beyond the moan when he came into her,

but she could tell—she could feel—that he was full and he was ready. She tightened her muscles around him, and heard a sharp breath as he responded. Everything was tight, was primed, was stretched to the breaking point.

And then it broke. It broke in an all-consuming torrent that spread outward, and then ricocheted back to the place whence it had come. It overcame her in waves, and she was astonished at its force.

She kept her legs wrapped tight around him, and he put his hands on the table to keep his balance as his knees weakened from an orgasm that was almost as powerful as hers.

They stayed there, letting themselves come down for a moment or two, and then Zoe unwrapped her legs and he withdrew.

"You're staying with me tonight," he said.

She nodded, and he picked her up and carried her into the bedroom.

CHAPTER EIGHTEEN

꧁❖꧂

The next morning found Andrew DuBois again at the door of Lorraine Nickerson's studio, this time with two other police officers in tow. Again, she was with customers, but this time DuBois didn't wait. He flashed his badge, cleared the shop, and turned the OPEN sign to CLOSED.

Lorraine watched in amazement, her hands on her hips. "What's going on?" she asked.

"I have a warrant to search the premises," he said, showing her the paper. He nodded to the other officers, who began their search.

"What's this about?" Lorraine started to get angry.

DuBois pulled the little green shard he'd found in the floorboards out of his pocket.

"Perhaps you should tell me where this really came from."

The color left Lorraine's face, but there was still anger in her tone. "I told you that already. Twice, if I recall."

"You certainly gave me an explanation," said DuBois. "Twice, as you say. But now I want to know what *really* happened."

She glared at him, silent. But scared.

He sat down in the chair by the little table and pointedly looked at his watch.

"Okay, then," he said. "Shall I start?"

No answer.

"This shard"—he held it out to Lorraine—"is either from the original Angie, or from some practice piece you fired before you made the duplicate statue."

He knew. The jig was up. She sat down in the other chair and put her head in her hands. Had she ever imagined anyone would arrive at the truth, she might have had the foresight to have a good story ready, but she had thought herself safe.

"You made a second Angie, did you not?" asked DuBois.

She nodded.

"And you used it to kill Curtis Nickerson."

For a moment she said nothing. He was asking her to confess to murder. But she'd already told him about the duplicate, so the essence of the confession was already made.

She nodded again.

"And somehow you managed to get Zoe Bell's fingerprint on it."

Another nod yes.

"I'm not quite clear on how you did that," said DuBois. "Did you get her to touch it?"

Lorraine sat back in the chair and took a deep breath. Since DuBois knew what had happened, there was no point in withholding the details.

"She handled clay, and I just used it as a mold. I made a fake finger with her print, and used it to put the print on the statue. It didn't come out very well, and I was afraid you wouldn't be able to identify it."

"But why Zoe?"

Lorraine shrugged. "She was convenient; she was easy; she had a plausible motive in that the house would revert to her when Curtis died without a son." She looked at the detective. "I don't have anything against her personally. I rather like her."

It was Andrew's turn to sit back in his chair.

"The one thing I don't really understand is why. Is it a marital grudge that goes back decades?"

"I see you didn't do all your legwork, Detective," Lorraine said, and there was just the faintest hint of triumph in her voice.

He looked at her with genuine curiosity. It was hard for him to believe he'd missed something important.

"You see," she said, "we were still married."

Andrew DuBois was surprised and chagrined. This was something he should indeed have discovered. If Lorraine and Curtis were still legally man and wife, then she was his next of kin. When he died without a will, she would have inherited everything, possibly including the house.

"He never signed the papers," she went on. "He hated the idea of divorce, and I guess he couldn't bring himself to do it. If I'd ever wanted to marry again, I would have had to get him to do it, but one marriage was quite enough for me, and I've never wanted to repeat the experience."

"And, of course, there was the possibility that Nickerson would die and you'd get the house." It was all coming clear to DuBois.

"That's about the size of it," Lorraine said.

"But what about the old Chapin will? Why take the risk when the house might have gone to Zoe?"

She dismissed the idea with a brush of her hand. "I had that will looked at by some of the best legal minds in Boston," she said. "Although nobody could say with absolute certainty that it wouldn't hold up, that was the overwhelming consensus."

She couldn't help telling DuBois the details. If she was going to go down for killing her husband, at least she'd go down for doing it cleverly.

"It was the perfect situation," she said. "The possibility that I wouldn't get the house meant that I didn't have a strong motive to kill him. I was on record as firmly believing the house would go to Zoe. I even had a story about old Clara Chapin pulling me aside when I married Curtis and telling me she'd had it vetted and confirmed its legal authority, and I told it to everyone who'd listen. So even when it came to light that I was still his wife, I had cover."

DuBois could now fill in the blanks. "And you had to do it now, because you somehow got wind of the fact that Nickerson talked to his lawyer about making a will."

She nodded. She didn't see the need to explain her connection to Chad Helmsworth.

"So you made a duplicate of Angie, a duplicate you could plant a fingerprint on."

"It took several tries. I had to smash the rejects, so I guess it's not surprising there's a shard or two lying around." She looked at the two other police officers, who were going through every floorboard and looking into every corner. "I should have been more careful."

But then it was her turn to ask a question. Lorraine had been quite sure that no one would even consider the idea that the smashed statue wasn't the original Angie. "How did you figure it out?"

"It was the bottom of it," DuBois explained. "It was scuffed, but it somehow didn't look old."

Lorraine nodded. She couldn't help but be impressed.

"I used tea to stain it so it wouldn't be bright white, and I marked it up a bit, but there's no way to make unglazed fired clay look old." She shook her head ruefully.

"Once I suspected what you'd done, Ethan Grant and I went through Nickerson's things to see if we could find a photo. I compared the photo to the statue I reconstructed, and there were some subtle differences. It was very close, but it wasn't perfect."

"The rejects were the ones that weren't close enough," she said. "I was working from a photo myself, and it was impossible to make it exact."

Somehow, talking in this matter-of-fact way about the statue and the will and the logistics pushed the horror of what she'd done and the seriousness of the consequences into the background of Lorraine's mind. As long as she and the detective were sitting at that table, talking collegially about how they'd each done what they'd done, the prospect of a trial and of prison could seem remote.

But then Andrew stood up, and the illusion was over. "Lorraine Nickerson, I'm arresting you for the murder of Curtis Nickerson." He took out his handcuffs and read her her rights.

She pointed at the handcuffs. "I'll understand if you need to use those," she said. "But this may be the last time I walk out this door." She gulped, finally beginning to feel the enormity of what she'd done and what was to come. "It's the end of my life, in a way. If you'd let me walk out with my hands free, I'd appreciate it."

He understood. It was a wish he could grant.

They walked out of the studio, and he opened the door to the backseat of the unmarked car. She got in, and he closed it behind her.

Once he delivered Lorraine to the holding cell at the police barracks and finished all the paperwork, Andrew DuBois thought he ought to let Zoe know what had happened. He shut down his computer and was on his way out of the barracks when he turned around and went back to his desk.

He picked up the phone and called Veronica McSweeney.

She answered on the second ring. "You got another smudgy fingerprint for me?" she said by way of greeting.

"No such luck," he said. "But I do have a murderer in custody."

"Tell, tell!"

"It was the ex-wife."

"Now, why didn't either of us take her? It's not like it isn't usually the ex-wife. How'd she manage it?"

"How 'bout I tell you over dinner?"

"I'd like that," said Veronica. "I'd like that a lot."

Andrew arranged the details, and then headed out to Chapin House.

Zoe heard his car pull up, and she felt her gut tighten as she looked out the window and saw who it was. She had just gotten back from

Ethan's an hour before, after having spent the night and breakfasted with him, and had been savoring the glow she still felt. She opened the door as he was walking up the front steps.

"Hello, Detective," she said grimly.

"Hello, Miss Bell."

"After all we've been through, I think we should be on a first-name basis. Please call me Zoe."

"Well, Zoe," he said, "if you'll invite me in, I believe I can give you some news that will put you at ease."

Zoe felt the relief flood through her. There was only one kind of news that would have that effect, and she invited him in with anticipation of it.

"It gives me great pleasure to assure you that you didn't kill Curtis Nickerson."

"I'm very glad to hear it," she said. "But I suspect that the only way you know that is that you've figured out who really did kill him."

"I've made an arrest."

Zoe looked at him, waiting to hear.

"It was Lorraine Nickerson."

"Lorraine!" Zoe was astonished. It hadn't crossed her mind for a moment that it might have been Lorraine.

DuBois sketched out the details for her, and she couldn't help but admire both Lorraine's cunning in coming up with that plan and the detective's cleverness in figuring it out.

And she resented, sorely, being set up. And by someone who purported to be her friend!

"If it's any consolation, she told me it wasn't personal," said DuBois when Zoe expressed her resentment. "She even said she liked you."

"Oh, that's just great. She liked me enough to try to set me up for murder." But Zoe's anger at the attempt was vastly overshadowed by the relief and the sense of closure, now that the crime had been solved. And, of course, she couldn't help but be curious about the old Chapin will.

"Who decides about the Nickerson house?" she asked DuBois. She didn't want to sound greedy—she didn't even want the house, if the alternative was that Ethan would get it—but it was natural that she would be interested.

"That goes to probate court," said DuBois. "My assumption is that it either reverts to being part of the Chapin property, in which case it goes to you, or it goes to Nickerson's next of kin. That would have been his wife, but I believe she forfeits any property that she kills someone to get. Ethan Grant is next in line."

"Do you have any sense of which way it'll go?"

"I'm not a lawyer. I really have no idea."

"Could I forfeit my claim? I mean, I don't know if that's the right word, but could I just say that I want the house to go to Ethan?"

"You'll need to talk to a lawyer about that."

Zoe nodded. "I'll do that." She looked at the detective with real gratitude. "It feels a little awkward to thank a cop for solving a crime, but that's what I want to do."

He laughed. "Now, how could I object to being thanked for something like that?"

"Then I will thank you." She took his hand. "I will thank you with all my heart. If I had this hanging over me, I don't think I could stay in this house. But since you got to the bottom of it, you make my living here possible." Her eyes welled up as she said it.

He was touched by her gratitude.

"This is why I do this job," he said.

∽✴✐

It took Zoe almost a month to straighten out the legal issues. At first, she thought it would be as simple as drawing up a document in which she forfeited any claim she might have on the house, but it occurred to her that Ethan might not take the house under those circumstances, as though it were her largesse rather than his rightful inheritance.

Instead, she found the three best probate lawyers in Boston and paid them for their opinions. Their consensus was the same as the one Lorraine's lawyers had come to: The Chapin will wouldn't stand up in court, and the house would be Ethan's. Only then did Zoe have one of them draw up her forfeiture of her claim.

She spent a lot of time with Ethan over the course of that month, and better acquaintance validated her early impressions of him. She was determined to take their relationship slowly, but she couldn't help but be hopeful about their long-term prospects.

It was after dinner one night, at her house, that she showed him the lawyers' opinions and her forfeiture.

"I want this over and done with," she said in her most businesslike tone. "We can let it sit in probate for months, and the court costs will come out of the estate, or we can end it right now and you can move into the house."

He put the papers on the table and looked at her, thinking. "I'm not sure that's what I want. I'd rather this went through proper channels and my right to it was confirmed by the courts."

She nodded. "I get that. I respect that. And the only reason I'd even suggest doing it this way is that legal opinion is absolutely unanimous. All I'm trying to do is save time and money."

He looked at the opinions again. Zoe could see the conflict on his face.

"Look," she said, "I think I would feel exactly the way you do if our positions were reversed. But you can't let that get in the way of what is clearly the most reasonable, expedient way to deal with this. There's just no question that this is the way it would end up, particularly if I didn't fight it, which, of course, I wouldn't."

He couldn't help but see that she was right.

It was early September when Ethan took formal possession of the Nickerson cottage. On the morning of the day it was officially his, Zoe came over with a housewarming present, a beautiful handmade quilt. They went into the bedroom, and Ethan spread it out on the bed.

"I love it," he said, and kissed her.

"I also have a little bit of news," she said.

"Do tell."

"When I was in town yesterday, I stopped to talk to Tom, Dick, and Bart. Bart said he'd heard about all the landscaping I've done at the house, and he asked me if I'd tackle his house come spring."

Ethan was surprised. "That's a hell of a vote of confidence, coming from old Bart."

"That's what I thought. But I also thought it would be a good way to see whether I'd like to do landscaping for real. For other people. For money."

"It always seemed to me it was a natural choice for you." He reached for her and pulled her to him. "That way, after a long, hard day, with me on the water and you in the dirt, we can unwind with lobster pot pies and a nice bottle of Riesling."

Zoe marveled that even now, two months into their relationship, she thrilled at his slightest touch. The excitement hadn't faded; the force of his draw hadn't ebbed.

"I look forward to that," Zoe said. "But right now, there are more pressing matters, like congratulating you on your house," she added, and ran her fingers through his hair.

"Does this mean you're the welcoming committee?" he asked, with a suggestive look.

"I'm the one-woman welcoming committee. I didn't bring banana bread, but I think I can offer up an alternative." She ran her hands over his chest, feeling its now familiar shape.

"Whatever you're offering, I'm betting it's better than banana bread." He tucked her hair behind her ears and took her face in his hands. "Much, much better."

She took a step back and slowly, deliberately, undressed. When she was fully naked, she hooked her hands in his waistband and looked up at him. "I hope it's even better than brownies."

He smiled as she undressed him as deliberately as she'd undressed herself. Then the two of them stood there, holding each other, naked to the world, feeling the September sun shining through the window.

"Let's see how you look on the new quilt," Zoe said to him, and backed him up to the bed. He lay down obediently, and she admired the combination of his dark brown skin and the variegated deep reds of the quilt.

Zoe sat down on the bed next to him and ran her fingertip along the base of his neck, just above the collarbone.

She ran the flat of her hand down his chest, and took one of his nipples between her fingers. She squeezed ever so slightly, and he closed his eyes and let a little groan escape.

Then he took her hand and sat up. He propped himself against the headboard and pulled Zoe onto his lap, straddling him. He put his hands on her breasts and cradled them, feeling their contours, their firmness, and their weight.

And then he took one in his mouth, circling his tongue around her nipple, sucking just enough so the squeeze reverberated through Zoe's core. She loved the obvious pleasure he took in her body, the way he handled her with relish and enthusiasm, but never with the wrong kind of force.

She slid back so she could feel his erection underneath her. Her juices had begun to flow, and she moved her hips forward and back so she slid up and down his cock. She felt the tip brush her clitoris with each stroke, and her excitement began to mount in earnest.

She felt his cock harden underneath her, and then his strong hands on her thighs, slowing her pace. Only then did she realize that her eyes had been closed, and she opened them to find him smiling at her.

"I can't take too much of that," he said.

"Neither can I," she said, and slid back toward his thighs so they both got a respite.

She rubbed his glistening cock with the back of her hand, enjoying the way it jumped up to meet her.

"You act like that's your own personal plaything," he said to her.

"You mean it's not?" she said, with exaggerated innocence.

"Well, come to think of it, I suppose it is. Carry on."

She did, touching him just enough to keep his desire up, but not enough to put it into high gear.

His desire, the way his body did her bidding, the way he looked at her, kept her desire in line with his, and it wasn't long before she felt an urgent need to have him inside her. She moved on top of him and felt the satisfaction of feeling him slide deep into her.

She leaned forward and put her hands on his chest, his nipples between the thumb and forefinger of each hand. For a moment, she stayed perfectly still. And then she contracted all her muscles, squeezing him tight inside her as she simultaneously squeezed his nipples. Nothing moved except her fingertips and the muscles around him.

He groaned with pleasure.

She released, and then she did it again.

It took some concentration for her to focus on the deep-down muscles she needed access to, but after two or three iterations she got the hang of it. With each contraction, she felt Ethan get harder within her, and she felt herself responding in kind. When her muscles tightened, it sent her arousal spreading outward, from the heat of her cunt to her fingertips.

She quickened, and the rhythm took them both up a notch. Her breathing was getting faster, and his body was moving in time to the pace she set. Every time she tightened around him, they took a step together toward a climax.

And then she knew he was there. She felt the last little bit of enlargement, the rock-hard thrust, the straining of his hips. And that last little movement got her there with him, and she gasped aloud. It was like a dam broke, flooding her.

She collapsed onto Ethan's chest as the waves began to subside, and she felt the tension leave his body too.

They lay there, letting their breathing slow and their temperature cool.

She sat up, moved off him, and sat at the edge of the bed. "I hope that was better than banana bread," she said.

"That wasn't even in the same league as banana bread," he said, reaching out to pat her thigh. "But speaking of banana bread and things in its league, how'd you like to go into town and get some breakfast at the bakeshop?"

"You transition from sex to food pretty easily," she said.

"They're the two most basic human needs, so it makes sense to move on to one as soon as the other is taken care of."

She could see the logic. And she was also hungry. They got dressed and drove into town.

They parked and walked the couple of blocks to the Danmouth Bakeshop. On the way, they passed the general store, with Tom, Dick, and Bart sitting in their accustomed seats.

"So," Bart said to Ethan, "have you heard that Zoe's going to be my gardener?"

"I did hear," he answered. "And I heartily approve."

"And did you hear that Ethan moved in today?" Zoe asked him.

"Oh, yes," said Bart gravely, pointing toward the store's interior. "You know old Hibbard's on top of that." He gestured to the population sign, which still said 813.

"Then why didn't the population go up by one?" she asked.

"Because Lorraine Nickerson pleaded guilty to murdering Curtis, and she got twenty years to life in a prison in Connecticut. It was eight hundred and twelve for about fifteen minutes."

"Oh," said Zoe, who looked up at Ethan. She wasn't sure how to react to this news, and wondered how he would take it.

"Thanks for telling us," he said. "I'm glad to know it's all over."

"It's all over, all right," said Bart. "And I guess that's a good thing. But I have to admit, it's the most exciting thing that's happened in Danmouth in a good long time." He mused for a moment, and then said to Zoe, "Say, how's your ghost? You haven't mentioned him in a long time."

Zoe felt herself redden. She hadn't seen the ghost of Robert Chapin since the day she found the letters, and the memory of him had become distant enough that she was ready to believe she'd imagined him. She hadn't told Ethan about it, and hadn't planned to, but now she was in a corner.

"Haven't seen hide nor hair of him," said Zoe as breezily as she could. She said her good-byes to the three men, and they made their way to the bakeshop.

It was only when they were sitting down over coffee and corn muffins that Ethan asked her what Bart had meant.

"So you've got a ghost?"

Zoe sighed, took a deep breath, and told him the story. She left out some of the most intimate moments, but she told him all the rest. When she was finished, she said, "It seemed very real at the time, but I'm beginning to think it was all a figment of my imagination."

"Does it matter which it is?"

She played with her empty coffee cup. "No, I suppose it doesn't, but all in all, I think I'd prefer not to believe in ghosts. Especially ghosts that lie and manipulate. I mean, he even told me he'd been killed by Curtis Nickerson's father, Paul." She paused. "Your grandfather." She shook her head at the idea that she'd ever believed that, or anything Robert had told her.

Ethan sat back in his chair. He took a long look at Zoe, and then he leaned forward again, forearms on the table. "My grandfather did kill Robert," he said. "He followed him out on the water one day, called him over, and bashed him on the head with an ax handle."

Zoe was astonished. "He did?" And then the more relevant question: "How do you know?"

"He told Curtis, and Curtis told me. My grandfather always said he had seen proof that Robert had jilted Molly, and when you found that letter I figured that's what he was talking about. He took care of Chapin House, and had keys to everything. And once he knew for sure Robert had decided to ditch Molly while she was pregnant, he would have assumed the rest. Either Robert actually pushed her in front of that train, or she killed herself. She knew that terrain and those tracks like she knew her own room, and she wouldn't have fallen by accident."

"He told you he had proof, but he never told you what?"

"Now that I've got a pretty good idea what it was, I understand why. Paul had a real sense of honor. That's what drove him to take revenge on Robert the way he did, and it's what drove him to tell Curtis that Molly had been avenged. He wouldn't exactly have advertised it if he'd read a private letter."

Zoe took this all in. It meant that Robert had been real, and that thought made her a little uncomfortable. She hadn't seen him since she'd banished him, and she hoped she'd never see him again, but if he had really existed, what was to stop him from coming back?

As soon as she thought of the question, she knew the answer. When she'd bought Chapin House, she'd been unmoored, unfocused, unsure, and that had left her psyche open a crack, a crack just wide enough for Robert Chapin to find his way in. He had exploited a weakness.

Now, though, she looked at the flesh-and-blood man sitting across the table from her, and she felt grounded and focused. She was with a fine man who brought out the best in her. Her few months in Danmouth had taught her a lot about people, and trust, and substance. She wasn't quite the same person she'd been when she'd bought the house back in June.

And, somewhat to her surprise, she'd stopped thinking of that big house out by the water as Chapin House. It was her house now.

Printed in the United States
by Baker & Taylor Publisher Services